Webster, Unabridged

Stories

John E. Simpson

These stories are works of fiction. All of the characters, institutions, and events portrayed herein are products of the author's tortured imagination. You may of course know the author, and if so then you may recognize, or think you recognize, certain similarities with the author himself, and he won't argue with you. But he'd discourage you from stretching your own imagination too much on this point.

WEBSTER, UNABRIDGED

Copyright © 2024 by John E. Simpson
All rights reserved.

ISBN: 979-8-88296369-8 (Paperback)

Cover photograph and design by John E. Simpson

First Paperback Edition: 2024

www.johnesimpson.com

Dedication

To Toni, who accompanied Webster and me pretty much everywhere (albeit at some times less willingly than at others) for all the adventures and throughout all the decades during which he kept popping up.

Table of Contents

Introduction 1

The Dig 5

The Shot 29

The Dark 41

The Bug 123

The Card 141

The Job 155

Acknowledgments 167

Introduction

In the mid-1980s, for some reason, I decided I needed to write a short story.

"Some reason": haha. *Right.* The reason*s*, plural, why I so decided would probably yield to five minutes' casual poking-about by a therapist, and in retrospect they're not important. Let's just say I was terribly confused about adulthood, and desperately confused about various theoretically adult-sized holes I'd dug myself into and bridges I'd crossed (and then burned behind me).

But the effect on me of the story I wrote then rippled through the next four decades of my inner and even, to a lesser extent, of my outer life.

That story was called "The Kite." The protagonist, like the author, was confused — unreliable in emergencies, bad at contingency planning, easily distracted by irrelevancies, maniacally afraid of upsetting others, yet quite adept at creating situations which could not help but upset them. This character's name was Pip.[1]

Pip, it seemed, had come upon a kite entangled with its string in some roadside bushes. The kite itself was of no real significance; what mattered was a fading note affixed to the kite's string — one of those common, or once-common, *If you find this* [balloon, kite, etc.] *please contact us at* [address/phone number] notes, identifying it as an artifact of a school or church project: an investigation, as it were, into the vagaries of fate and the winds. How had it gotten here — how had Pip himself, for that matter? And once all, or even *any*, of that was sorted out, what next...?

No: no mystery why that story should have emerged.

---

[1] An editor to whom I submitted the story congratulated me on the name choice. One of his favorite books, it seems, was *Great Expectations*. I, of course, had never read the novel, so had no idea at all that its protagonist's name was Pip. (Duh.)

But I'll tell you one thing, actually *writing* it was damned inconvenient. I had only notebook paper on which to write it in longhand, and only a typewriter on which to "finalize" it...

Within a year or two, having ground out a handful more stories in this laborious, pre-digital way — stories about different characters and situations, playing around with different genres and voices — I finally got my first personal computer. But by then I was bored with everything I'd already written. So I opened up my first word processor, and began a new story: "The Head."[2]

As had "The Kite," this new story featured a one-named protagonist, a *Webster*. (To this day, I still don't know for certain if that's a first or surname. I suspect it's his first name, though; with one very notable exception, no one in these stories ever calls him anything but Webster.) Like Pip, Webster came upon a roadside mystery which so nagged at his mind that he felt uncharacteristically compelled to investigate it.

Furthermore, Webster shared many of Pip's quirks and foibles — psychological tics and hiccups — the conflicting goals of which often left him unable to do much of anything except fret...

I've written elsewhere about how I finally convinced — no, *allowed* — Webster to do something about the various everyday dilemmas he encountered in my stories about him. He remained pretty much the same Webster, but now, it seemed, he *did* stuff, too: odd, dumb stuff, and often *comic* stuff resulting in situations from which he'd then have to extricate himself, and in generally tripping — dumbly, sometimes comically — over his own feet.

Unsurprisingly, I liked (maybe identified with) Webster enough that I kept coming back to him, even with half-formed (or even three-quarters-formed) ideas. I've written five complete stories, plus something like a novella — all of which appear herein — and started but abandoned another half-dozen. (None of those incomplete stories are included.) His story's probably as complete now as it will ever be.

Hence: Webster, unabridged.

---

[2] I later renamed it, as you shall see.

A couple of suggestions as you set forth on this extended narrative:

First, remember that most of these stories first crawled out of my mind's primordial soup in the 1980s and 1990s. Back then, of course, no car or cellular phones were available to pretty much anyone but the uber-rich, and even landline phones were still — especially early on — *wired* ones. (Phone booths were common.) Very little existed of anything like the Internet we've gotten used to. ATMs were a novelty obviously designed to frustrate their users as much as to answer their immediate needs. No "streaming media" lay on this side of the horizon — in fact, even cable TV, at first, took a while to hammer dents in widespread public consciousness. That we might someday experience a pandemic, while not unimaginable, bordered on so unlikely as never to be worried about. (I don't think hand sanitizer was even a thing then, except maybe in hospital ORs.) Politics were something which happened when you entered a curtained booth, alone, and flipped a few levers. Newspapers sometimes came in morning editions and sometimes in evening ones; big-city newspapers might come in both. Even Webster's car in most of these tales is an unlikely relic: a late 1960s-era Ford Galaxie station wagon.

(Aside: I've recently updated one of these early stories, so you may notice it's not quite so outdated.)

In short, not just Webster, but the world he lived in, may now strike you as alien.

Second, and maybe more importantly: you're going to be spending a lot of time in Webster's head. He doesn't narrate any of the stories, but his *manner of thinking* suffuses them. This fact occasionally frustrated readers of the stories as I drafted them and took them through writing workshops. Webster seldom curses, for example: not only his speech but his thoughts are confined almost wholly to the *holy-cow-whoops-jeez-darn-it-wowie* range of "extremely emotional" expression. The situations in which he becomes embroiled may be unlikely, and his responses to them may not make much sense to you… But that's okay. He's just trying — given the battered, misshapen, incomplete contents of his personal psychological toolkit — to get through one moment, to the next, to the one which follows, and eventually out to the other side.

I hope you enjoy the ride with him. I know I myself have… but my own inner Webster counts on that response in no one else's mind.

John E. Simpson

JES
Apex, North Carolina
February 2024

The Dig

> *"The Dig," originally titled "The Head," marks the point where Webster's story arc begins for me. And ditto — for you, the reader — here's where the vague outline of a template was set for what I've come to think of as a "Webster story." Once you've read "The Dig," you pretty much know what to expect from him in the stories which follow. Fingers crossed for both of us (and for Webster!). By the way, I never commuted to a big city like Webster did. But I did travel to one often enough, also via train, and the trip was like this, at least at that time. It's probably better now.*

There was much not to like about public transportation (such as the train now bearing Webster to his job in The City), and Webster indeed liked almost none of it. But what disturbed him above all else was the inability of way too many of his fellow commuters to control their bodily functions. It would drive him *crazy* if he thought about it, which, alas, he often did: a veritable symphony of whooping and hacking and wheezing, sneezing, belching, passing gas; outright bleeding on one another; failing to make it to the lavatory cubicle whose disposal mechanisms never worked anyhow; spitting tobacco, unpalatable mouthfuls of fruit juice, and other unnatural substances onto the floor; upchucking out an open window; even the mere squeaks of bare skin against vinyl and groans of floor and furniture. It made him feel like a corpuscle wandering and lost in some unbearably awful organ of a giant creature about to keel over and die.

It was, in point of fact, really bad. Yet it could get much, much worse: when the main offender was Webster himself.

Take now, for example. The train had made its way to the last leg of its dreary journey, just before slithering like a fat desperate millipede into the tunnel beneath The River and into The City: the slow, ten-minute slog across a marshy industrial wasteland. Abandoned warehouses and factories of mysterious purpose, their chain-link and barbed-wire fenced yards cluttered with thousands of unlabeled metal drums, mountains of rusting cannibalized cars, pools of eerie unnaturally green water, and acres of empty, forgotten truck trailers fitted together like chips in a crumbling mosaic tile. The roads through the marsh (what Webster could see of them) began and seemed bound for nowhere, dirty asphalt ribbons spooling away from the train tracks and disappearing in a distant tan fuzz of marsh grass.

The present bodily mortification started innocently enough — a mere tickle at the back of the throat. But as Webster strove delicately to suppress the tickle, to cover it with a hushed whispering *ahem*, suddenly it exploded into a full-blown coughing fit, a *seizure*. His hands flew instinctively to his mouth, sealing it; the cough, desperate for exit, fled back to the rear lines and then up into his sinuses and out his nose: spraying the back of his hands, suddenly glistening and sticky. Struggling to extract the handkerchief from his left pocket, he succeeded (while continuing to cough) only in wiping his hands off on the inside of the pocket and the lapel of the suit jacket folded neatly across his lap. The man sitting next to him, in the aisle seat, raised his newspaper pointedly and with distaste, oblivious to Webster's spastic muttered "Whoops, sorry!" — punctuated as it was by an outrageous final *Haroonk!* and the splattering of the train window with something that reminded Webster, incongruously, of pineapple preserves. He was smearing at the glass with the handkerchief when he saw, through the window, the head.

It lay face-up on a pile of miscellaneous industrial rubbish and bundled newspapers. The eyes were open, staring (it seemed) at Webster himself. He couldn't make out any of its features, missing even the hair color. Yet it was plainly a head, a man's head, with plainly no body attached to it.

And while he could see no blood in the seconds before it was past, it looked, well, it looked *fresh*.

"Did you see that?" he asked the man next to him, who raised an eyebrow in reply. "A head, you know? Just lying there?"

Startled, the man looked back at his paper. An elderly woman in the seat in front of him turned her head slightly so Webster knew that she'd overheard, but she said nothing.

Webster looked back out into the marsh. The head was gone now, probably fifty yards back. And nothing else, not... well, of course he really didn't know *what* he expected to see. An assassin maybe, wiping the blade of a saber or hacksaw. But there was nothing like that out there, at all. Just empty marshland, trash, seagulls, a nearby warehouse of dogfood-pink brick. No assassins.

The car in which Webster was riding was at the end of the train, a dozen cars back from the locomotive. It suddenly occurred to him that maybe the head had fallen or been thrown from one of the earlier cars. Impulsively he leapt to his feet, lurched across his neighbor — snagging a foot on the man's ankle, the man huffing in exasperation and ostentatiously rattling the newspaper; the suit jacket gripped in Webster's hands whipped overhead, getting tangled somehow in the overhead baggage rack, He fell across the aisle, shoulder-first and arms wildly a-flail, squarely across the laps of two skinheaded adolescents.

He lay there for a second looking up into their faces, which betrayed no passion as they probably considered how best to dismember him. Somehow he managed to right himself, taking care to prop himself up by placing his hands only just *so*, no further contact with those slashed-denim thighs no siree, mumbled "Sorry," and was standing and then running forward up the aisle—

Just as he reached the door to the next car he caught himself, the sudden stop throwing him just off-balance enough to bang the knuckles of one hand painfully on the steel door. He brought the knuckles to his mouth and sucked at them for a second before remembering his last oral interaction with them, and dropped them to his side. His neck and face reddening, swaying at the end of the aisle as the train continued on *chack-aclackalack* away from the head. What the heck did he think he was going to do? Run the whole length of the train if necessary, casting frantic glances down and to either side, hoping-slash-*not*-hoping to come upon a headless torso sitting calmly in its seat, chilly fingers twitching around the folded top of a lunch bag on its lap?

On the other hand he couldn't return to his seat in this car. Everyone present was staring at him, he knew, their quizzical gazes (especially those of the skinheads) augering into his shoulderblades. He could, no, wait, he *couldn't* ride on the teeny platform between the two cars, if he fell, well, God knew what—

So through the door then, momentarily onto the platform in the slow roaring wind and on into the next car. A what-was-it, trainman, conductor, whatever, watching him from the front, leaning against a poster advertising a permanent cure for baldness (*Baldness, a head, I've just seen a head*). Webster slinking red-faced into the first empty seat he could find, behind an elderly man complaining to an elderly woman, in a loud, piercing voice, about the state of the country; the elderly woman (surely the old man's wife; why else would she remain seated in a nearly empty car next to such an irritant?) sat ramrod straight, not turning even to acknowledge her companion's opinions. Not even nodding. Three seats up, a woman with several shopping bags and a canvas briefcase was staring fixedly out the window at the marshland — not, alas, on the same side of the train on which Webster himself had been sitting.

Webster's own gaze followed the woman's. The train was now on a bridge, crossing over a narrow oily waterway twisting between meadows of tall marsh grass and cat's-tails. Seagulls wheeled and dipped in the river breezes; Webster imagined them squawking back and forth to one another in disbelief: "A *head*, a *head*, a *head*...!"

Once, when he was a kid, he'd found half a mouse torso in the street by his parent's house, the other half having been either forcibly removed by predator or cruel children, or driven over by a car and then washed away in a rainstorm. Afraid to disturb the tiny corpse, he'd walked by it for weeks (always at a respectful distance), watching it out of the corner of his eyes as it grew paler and more indistinct from exposure to time and weather.

He imagined the head's progress like that, too, out there in its trash heap: the eyes gradually dimming in the acrid smoke from the burning tires, the fresh wound all around the bottom of the neck cauterizing in the summer sun then gradually withering and eventually dropping away or being eaten by scavengers and bugs, the whole blessed thing at last sinking and blending into the gray of its final resting place.

He sat for a long time in the train after it pulled into the station, until long after the last passenger had disembarked. Finally, squaring his shoulders, he stood and strode from the train, past the cluster of whispering conductors on the platform, strode up the stairs into the vast gray echoing cavern of the station, its domed ceiling far above lost in shadow. Before one of the station's windows he hesitated a moment, looking out at the traffic and the passersby and street vendors. *All those heads.*

Then he shivered, blinked, and went out through the revolving door.

§

Now, Webster wasn't naive. After all, he worked in The City: each day, he witnessed pathological behavior in at least forty per cent of the people he encountered on the street; and each week, he counted himself lucky not to be sickened at least once by some formerly unimaginable physical disfigurement.

So: sensitive, yes. But no, he was not naive. But this *head*, now — this was something different, something that even daily exposure to The City had never prepared him for. Glimpsing it had borne him up to a penthouse of urban grotesquerie about which he'd previously only heard dim, unconfirmed rumors. He felt like a ghoul; he couldn't put the head out of his mind.

And all that day, in the innocuous confines of his office building, he found reasons to be reminded of it.

At first, he just winced, absurdly hypersensitive, at the word "head" however it cropped up in conversation. "...department head," he overheard one person in the elevator; "Heads you win, tails I lose," complained another. "I'm headin' down for coffee," announced a co-worker, and in a heated meeting before lunch one woman exclaimed, "Hey, hey, whoa — let's not lose our heads over this!" His favorite was, "Hey, better quit while you're ahead!"

Eventually he managed to tune out "head" and all its variants. But then he dropped his guard, was wending his way up the narrow corridor between desks in the office, and he happened to glance down. There, resting on a flattened brown-paper bag on an unoccupied desk, lay a partially eaten peach. The person who'd been eating it had gouged a frowny cartoon face into the peach's surface. (Webster imagined the person's taking the first bite, then stopping to answer a lengthy phone call — from a creditor or an ex-spouse or angry customer, someone who'd generate a lot of negative energy — and, picking up the peach, with the phone gripped between shoulder and ear, poking at the fruit's skin with the point of a pencil or nail file.) He started when he saw it, and bumped into the desk; the head — the *peach*, darn it — rolled face-down on the bag.

Later, at the end of the day, he was in the men's room, washing up as usual before leaving work. As usual, he first carefully washed his hands. As usual, he bent over to rinse his face. And as usual, he patted his face dry with a sheet of paper towel, breathing in deeply the familiar musty, wet-paper odor. But as he stood before the mirror, his eyes at first closed then blinking open, he looked at his own face. Tried to imagine his own head placed suddenly, violently elsewhere: saw his eyebrows jump up in surprise and his eyes widen, saw his lips draw back, imagined the face of his assailant burning instantly and unforgettably into his mind just before going blank altogether, like a last frame of film exposed when the camera back pops open.

His friend Jack's nasal voice startled him. "Hey, whoa, Webster — you all right? You look like you seen a ghost."

Webster looked again at his reflection. No, Jack was wrong, he looked like he'd momentarily *become* a ghost: ashen and glassy-eyed, clobbered by a vision of things that rightly belonged to another world. But he just smiled wanly. "Nah, no ghosts. Just — well, tired is all. Looking forward to the trip home, y'know?"

The trip home; oh God. What if the head was still out there? For that matter, what if it was *not* still there? Worse: what if he got the same conductor, the same passengers? the skinheads! He'd have to— no, that was silly, get a grip, he wouldn't have to stay overnight in The City; he'd just have to wait till dark. The important thing after all wasn't whether the head was still out there, but whether he could *see* it.

He rinsed and dried his hands one more time, did not look in the mirror again, and left the building.

§

What was he going to do with his time, maybe an hour, before the train left? A beer, that was it. He didn't even like beer that much, and taverns — especially the dim-lit kind frequented every evening by people who all knew one another by name — positively gave him the willies. After a few blocks' walk he chose a place, just across from the station, where he figured he'd at least know *one* person's name: "Eddie's Dad's Place," the window said. He sat at the end of the bar, beneath the muttering television set; the bartender nodded at him and cocked an eyebrow.

With a mug of draft before him, Webster studied his fellow patrons from the corners of his eyes. One table was occupied by a group of four heavyset guys in business suits and one skinny, weasel-faced character in a purple shirt and tan slacks; Webster noted with distaste that the latter's shirt collar lay flat against his collarbone (Webster *hated* shirt collars that didn't stand up), and furthermore that the guy's voice was as inconsiderately loud as his shirt. "Haw, haw, HAW!" he laughed, and Webster winced.

He drained his beer and semaphored with the empty mug that he was ready for another.

The bartender, whose name tag identified him as Eddie, placed a fresh mug before him and removed the old. Then he reached under the bar and pulled out a TV remote-control device; turning to face the set, he cycled through the channels: news, news, game show, commercial, old movie, news, sitcom re-run, news... He stopped at the last news program, put the remote control away, and began to wipe the bar.

"This name tag?" asked the bartender, unbidden, pausing in his cleanup routine and pointing at his chest. "'Eddie,' right?"

"Uh, yes?"

"I'm not the one in the window though. That Eddie don't work the bar no more. Used to be his name tag, though, see? I give it to the guy who comes on duty after me, he leaves it for the bartender who comes on before me, and it's here waiting for me when I come in. Eddies; all Eddies. See?"

Webster nodded as though he knew that already, or could gauge its significance. Took a sip of the fresh beer. He was trying to figure out whether, let alone how, to nudge the small talk a little further along when Purple Shirt yelled from the corner, "Hey, Eddie! Eddie! Turn the TV up, would ya!"

Eddie obliged, and Webster looked up at the television to see what was so interesting.

Behind the newscaster and off to one side was an inset containing the words "GRISLY FIND," the letters stylized with dripping blood. The announcer was saying, "...torso, missing hands, feet, and head, was discovered on the beach early this morning by an unidentified jogger. A police spokesman said that a large birthmark on the right shoulder has enabled investigators to identify it tentatively as the body of reputed underworld lieutenant Carlo 'Goose' Massa. Massa has not been seen for several days..."

Purple Shirt interrupted the announcer with a braying, "Haw haw haw! About *time* somebody took that asshole! Haw, haw, haw, HAW!" By the time he was through, the news story had concluded and the announcer was saying, "...these messages." Eddie lowered the volume as the first commercial came on.

Carlo "Goose" Massa, was it? Could that have been Massa's head on the trash heap in the marsh? It did seem, he reflected, a little too much like a Hollywood scenario, gangsters didn't *really* do that kind of thing any longer, or well, rather, if they *ever* had. Still...

Without quite planning it, Webster was suddenly standing, beer in hand, by the table in the corner with Purple Shirt and his more businesslike comrades. He said, "Uh, excuse me, hi. I was interested in your reaction to that news story about the mobster..." (*Idiot!* he thought to himself, These *guys are mobsters!*) "... and I was wondering, y'know, could you tell me what Mr. Massa looked — *looks* like? His head, well, his face?"

Purple Shirt threw his head back, mouth histrionically agape. The four other men at the table had not moved their bodies or their heads at all; the two whose faces Webster could see had merely shifted their eyes upward to look at Webster. Their faces were the deeply inexpressive faces of Sicilian Buddhas.

Then one of them grinned, a wide, red-lipped thoroughly artificial grin that reminded Webster of a silent-movie comedian — Fatty Arbuckle? The grinning one said, "Why no, none of us has ever had the pleasure of actually meeting... Mr. Massa." Fatty Arbuckle paused for just a moment and continued, "Why do you ask?"

"Well, see, I ride the train to work and this morning on the way in I thought I saw a head out there in the marsh. A, well, just a head. In a pile of trash. I thought it might have been Mr. Massa's."

Fatty Arbuckle, still grinning, let his eyes flick for just an instant into contact with his colleagues'. Then he looked back at Webster and said, "Well, as I said, none of us knows the gentleman. Besides, those things only happen in movies, you know."

"Yeah," agreed Webster. "That's what I was thinking. Thought I'd ask anyhow, y'know?" Awkward pause. "Well, thanks anyway. Have a nice day."

"And you have a nice day, too, sir," said Fatty Arbuckle, grinning. His grin snapped off as he turned back to the conversation at the table. Purple Shirt continued his pantomime of shock and amazement, watching Webster as he returned to the bar.

Webster sipped at his beer. Maybe he should tell the police. But then he had a mental picture of the morning's conductor, his trainman's cap traded for a policeman's, and he thought that no, he didn't think he would tell the police about this after all.

He drained the mug, and Eddie asked, "Another?"

Webster looked out the window; night had fallen. He turned back to Eddie and said, "No thanks. Headin' home." He smiled inwardly at the locution, and left the bar.

§

The train ride home, as he'd hoped, was uneventful. He sat on the side of the train away from the head, wherever it was out there, and no other passengers on the train reported (if indeed they noticed) anything unusual. His drive home from the station was likewise uneventful, and so was his arrival. No one, apparently, had followed him. Maybe the men in the bar hadn't known Massa after all.

The evening paper, which he browsed while munching on a grilled-cheese sandwich, did mention the discovery of Massa's body, but added little beyond the newscast Webster had seen in the bar. And there was nothing, he noted with relief, about a passenger on a morning train who had seen a head out the window.

He called his friends Bob and Monica, with whom he'd not spoken for a week or so. One way in which the couple shared household duties was by taking turns answering the phone; tonight it was Monica's shift, as it happened.

She and Webster shared the usual desultory conversation about work and TV and current events, then he cleared his throat and said, "Had an interesting experience this morning..."

He narrated for Monica the whole tale; she laughed at all the right spots. "So now what?" she said finally. "What are you going to tell the police?"

"Well, I — no. I don't, well, I guess I just want to stop thinking about it altogether."

Monica huffed in exasperation. "Well, Webster, you do what you want," she said. "But the longer you wait to tell the police about it the harder it'll be for them to, you know, track the killer down. And what are *you* gonna do, you yourself I mean — sit on the opposite side of the train the rest of your life? What are you gonna do *tomorrow*, for that matter? *You have to call the police.* For your own peace of mind."

Webster thought about it, then sighed. "I know. You're right. But it's just, I mean, I didn't even get a good look at it. Suppose it's not a head at all? A mask, maybe, or, well, for all I know if you put a big juice can in the right light maybe from the train it just looks like a head."

"A *juice* can?" she said, clearly unconvinced. "Well, maybe. But I still think you ought to report it."

"So why not a juice can?" Webster grumbled to himself a few minutes later as he stood before the bathroom mirror, brushing his teeth. Well, okay, maybe that was unlikely — but maybe it was something *else* that wasn't a head. A partially inflated basketball. A melon. A stuffed animal, a pillow, a catcher's mitt... Phooey. He'd been annoyed and embarrassed by the certainty that no one would believe he'd seen a head; now he was annoyed and embarrassed that Monica not only believed him, but expected him to *do* something about it. So annoyed and embarrassed, in fact, that he'd taken to arguing the opposite: it wasn't a head, it wasn't even human, but rather something innocent and (most importantly) altogether inanimate...

His sleep that night was troubled by only a single brief nightmare: he was walking across a field toward a figure on the horizon. As he got closer he saw that the figure, turned away from him, was bent over, preoccupied with some task on the ground; the figure was dressed in purple and tan, and just as Webster came near suddenly whirled to face him. It had the grimy, deeply lined face of a monster, a demon, and it needed a shave. In its hands were the remains of a human head, from which a huge bite had been taken. The monster grinned a wide, red grin, and Webster saw scraps of flesh wedged between its fangs. It held out the head to Webster, expectantly.

Webster awoke in a sweat, and knew what he would do in the morning.

§

"No, no, absolutely not — don't worry about it at all," said Webster's boss Larry over the phone. "Just take care of whatever it is. You're a good worker, and we like to help good workers however we can."

Webster had just arranged to take the next couple of days off from work. "Family emergency days," they were called in the employee benefits guide. Webster didn't really have any family to speak of, but he didn't think he was being dishonest — he was his own family, right? In the spirit, say, of IRS forms that let you claim yourself as an exemption. He imagined Jack's putting about the word that he'd seen Webster staring white-faced at his own reflection yesterday afternoon, bolstering the "emergency" claim.

A map, he thought when he got in the car; he'd need a map. He pulled the car over into a shopping center parking lot and riffled through the contents of his glove compartment. The only map there was a map of the whole state; even on the back, in the enlarged view of "metropolitan areas," there just wasn't enough detail. The train line across the marsh wasn't shown at all. Worse, the roads he'd have to drive weren't depicted *convincingly*: the interstate and other highways, true, all appeared in forceful, confident blues and greens; but by the time you got down to what (he presumed) were the roads through the marsh the mapmakers seemed to have lost their nerve. The colors faded to gray; indistinct and tentative, many of these roads were not even identified by name or number.

In a bookstore in the shopping center he found what he needed, a map *book* — a street atlas — blown up to such a scale that streets, even back alleys, appeared not as lines but as narrow, brachiate, intersecting polygons. Highways on this map surged across the web of streets beneath them like swatches of duct tape holding together a jigsaw puzzle. The train line itself was shown, truly, as two rails sweeping from one side of the map to the other, and some poor apprentice draftsman must have gone *blind* drawing all those ties.

Back in the car, back on the road, Webster tried to concentrate on how to get to where he was going — he'd never exited a highway in this area before, and he didn't want to lose his place; he might end up in The City by accident if he wasn't careful.

But a part of his mind kept demanding that he consider not just, uh, the route to the head but the head itself, too — well, no, not really the head *per se*, but how he'd search for it, and what he would do when (*if*) it came to pass that he actually found it.

He thought, for starters, he might sort of weave back and forth across the marsh, exploring the roads that ran beneath the train tracks. Yeah. If he saw a likely spot, he guessed he'd get out, maybe approach the office of the nearest warehouse or factory or whatever, see if they'd let him get up by the tracks.

In his own office, he felt pretty sure, if someone came in claiming to have seen a head on the premises and asking permission to inspect the wastebaskets, Larry would listen intently and with great sincerity to the person's tale. He'd nod finally, having obviously understood immediately how grave this was, how serious. Then he'd call building security for help — not to look for the head, but to remove this weirdo from his office...

Well then okay, maybe Webster would skip the part about getting permission. Maybe he could just — well, he didn't know what he'd do. Maybe end up reporting it to the police after all...

As it happened, he left the freeway where he'd meant to, and was instantly lost. He'd planned for the exit all right, but neglected to consider what he'd do next, what to anticipate, where he'd *be*. On a fast-moving four-lane street now, he was surrounded by tractor trailers roaring like maddened buffalo from traffic light to traffic light, ignorant of sub-compacts cowering in the side streets and waiting desperately for a crevice into which to insert themselves pre-crushing. Webster couldn't see any signs ahead, and could see them to the side only as he swept by, frantically and futilely grabbing at them as the tide bore him along.

The heck with the signs. He had to stop somewhere, anywhere, and get his bearings. He slowed down; the truck ahead of him started to drift away; the truck behind him loomed closer, filling his rearview mirror with the cross-hatched pattern of its radiator grill. The driver of the truck blasted a single, loud note on his air horn as Webster turned right, onto a narrow side street.

There, by the curb, he finally could open his street atlas. Let's see, he was... yes, *here*, and he wanted to get over this way, so he'd have to go, umm... four blocks, turn right, big intersection, through a park...

And so the morning unwound: evaporated, precipitated into the afternoon. He'd gotten out of the industrial urban neighborhood pretty quickly, and over closer to the railroad tracks in the marsh. The roads here were atrocious; from the train they'd always seemed, though dirty, so smooth and well-kept, but in fact they were pockmarked and potholed and in sudden, surprising spots utterly unpaved. Webster had never seen so many truck trailers in one spot in his life, and there were also motorcycle gangs and vacant brick buildings far beyond his experience. Graffiti was everywhere, though he couldn't imagine why a graffiti artist would waste his talent out here where there was no audience to offend. Once, on an impulse, he rolled down the window of his car. Bad mistake: the fumes from burning industrial waste, diesel exhaust, and marsh decay poured into the front seat and across his lap, soaking into everything porous. (When he was a little boy, Webster had owned a toy called "The Clay Factory." You pressed clay into a hopper at the top, turned a crank, and clay came oozing out like primary-colored pasta in the shape of whatever little cutout you'd chosen. The atmosphere here was like that, blobbing into the interior of his car in a gigantic window-shaped mass.)

He got hungry enough at one point to risk a dash from his car to a diner, which he found wedged between the concrete and steel uprights supporting a highway overhead. He sat in a booth by a window, shoveling in a tuna sandwich and coffee and pretending not to listen to the truckers trading jibes at the counter. Occasionally, a deep rumble signaled the passage of a particularly heavy truck on the highway above, and little flakes of rust and ash would sift down through the soupy atmosphere outside and past his window. When he paid his check and left, he noticed that his car was dusted with this industrial snowfall, which blew off as soon as he put the car in gear and drove away from the diner.

Disillusion set in, compounded by post-lunch glucose depression. How could he have been so unobservant when he first saw the head? Why couldn't he have looked for a street sign, or a fence, or a nearby building besides the dogfood-colored one? He'd heard that untrained observers were notoriously unreliable eyewitnesses at crime scenes — describing tall skinny men as fat, and replacing their red hair with black — but Webster had always fancied he'd do better than that. Now look at him; the dogfood-colored building was in fact probably gray, and he'd probably driven past it a dozen times already today.

He was approaching yet another underpass beneath the tracks, maybe the tenth of the day or maybe the same one for the tenth time; rapidly losing whatever vague sense of purpose he'd begun with; ever more easily distracted by the music on his car radio. Through the underpass, he pulled onto the gravel shoulder and shut the car off. He rolled down his window, and while the air in this spot still rolled in a little too assertively, still heavy and toxic, it did feel cool in the shade of the railroad embankment. Webster put his head back, shut his eyes, and fell asleep.

§

When he awoke nearly an hour later, it was to the *waw-waw-waw* of a train booming like a foghorn through his open window. He shook his head, pushed a hand through his hair, and got out of the car. He could see the train, close and getting closer, on its way to The City, and now he could hear not only the whistle but the syncopated *clack* of its wheels. Then it was going by and blowing a little breeze into his upturned face; Webster imagined a passenger on the train looking down at him and thinking with surprise, *There's a man down there*. Then the train was past, already Dopplering into memory, and Webster was alone again.

He looked about him. To the right, across the broken street and coming down to the foot of the embankment, was a rickety wooden stairway. When he crossed the street, he could see that the stairway was overgrown a bit, strange vines clutching at it and maybe threatening to shake it apart the first time it was used. But it *felt* sturdy enough, and Webster began to climb it. The handrail wobbled a bit but the stairs held; he counted fifteen steep steps to the top. Then he was standing between the rails.

Off to his left dwindled the gleaming dime that was the train that had just passed and beyond it, wavering like a mirage, was The City. To his right were only the silvery lines of the rails, converging somewhere over the horizon. Straight ahead, bordered by marsh grass, was a brick warehouse the roseate hue of fresh Ken-L-Ration. And at the foot of the embankment on which he stood was a trash heap, on which lay a human head.

Its eyes were a little mistier now; staring no longer in supplication, the head now seemed resigned to its disembodiment. The lips were drawn back a little in a bitter rictus; flies explored the tightened surface of its skin; and its hair, which Webster could now see was brown, was bedecked with wisps of marsh grass. A crow pecked at the scraps of its neck.

Webster skidded down the cinder embankment, sending the crow off in cawing annoyance. A small animal, mouse or rat, skittered squeaking into the grass. No one else was in sight or indeed shared the same world now: there was only Webster, and the head.

Approaching it, he had a vision of the head's rolling to one side and blinking, then sitting up on the stump of its neck to say to him — what? That it was about time? That thank God someone had come? And then, having been pecked off-balance by the crow, it *did* roll to one side, face down like the peach in Webster's office, and he jumped nearly a foot.

He looked about, a little wildly, for something in which to place the head — a crate or box, maybe, or a plastic bag, surely a trash heap would have at least one plastic bag somewhere nearby? But he could see nothing. The head lay still, its caved-in, decomposing back side now exposed; Webster imagined its voice, muffled by the face-down position, insisting with impatience and perhaps in coarse, Mediterranean tones, "Come on, come on, *do* something!"

A short distance away lay a bundle of newspapers. Webster broke the soggy twine, extracted some papers from the middle of the bundle, and spread them like a tablecloth at the foot of the trash heap. He found a long piece of scrap metal — a sign post, maybe — nearby, and approached the head again, poked at it with the metal bar, and when that had no effect poked at it a little harder. A gang of flies swarmed up. The head rolled then, over and over and down the side of the trash heap, coming to rest, miraculously, in the middle of the opened sheets of newspaper Webster had prepared for it. A picnic centerpiece.

Again staring up at him, cloudy eyed, the head seemed to say, "*And? Now what?*"

He, he'd have to—

Fighting back waves of nausea, he stooped over the head. He reached for the newspapers, closed his eyes, then in alarm that he might accidentally touch the head opened them quickly again. "*Do it*," the head insisted, no doubting the voice this time, and Webster slowly, carefully, folded the edges of the filthy newspapers one, two, over the face, alongside the ears, rolled the head over the papers and then folded down the ends of the paper cylinder, like a butcher wrapping a ham. He gagged a little; just as he folded down the last corner, he thought he heard the head hiss, in triumph and congratulations, "*Yessss!*" Then it was silent, and spoke no more.

Shaking, Webster stood. He didn't know what his next step would be. He surely was not going to ride anywhere with the head in his car, not even in his trunk. But then he remembered: in his trunk, he had a pair of long elastic cords, with hooks at the ends, he'd used them for tying sheets of plywood to the roof of his car, a few months ago...

He picked up the horrid bundle, which was lighter than he thought it would be; carried it under the embankment and across the street; laid it on the hood of his car. From his trunk, he extricated one long cord but couldn't find the other. One, then, would have to do. When he laid the cord across the hood, he jostled the car a little and the head started to roll. He nearly swooned when he caught the head, by reflex, between his knee and the bumper, and the paper (or its contents) crackled a little. He picked up the head again and laid it transversely across the cord. First one end of the cord, then the other — he twined them alternately up and over then back and forth. Almost no slack left in the cord; he'd have to loop the hooks through the grillwork in the front of the car, rather than around the bumper as he'd originally planned. He picked up the head one final time; the elastic, he could feel, was cutting through the newspapers in spots, and there was an instant when something soft and wet and oh so *cold* touched one of his fingers, which he quickly withdrew. To say he was merely revolted would not do justice to the sour, shapeless bubble swelling at the back of his throat, but he managed — somehow — to get the head secured to the grill. It looked like a huge garlic clove, mounted there as though to ward off monsters and ill fortune.

He walked back to the trash heap to see if there was anything else, an obvious or not-so-obvious murder weapon or scrap of clothing or, God help him, a hand or foot. But there was nothing; the trash heap was just a trash heap again. The crow, perched now on a piling some twenty feet out into the marsh, eyed Webster with resentment.

Gingerly, being careful not to smear his hands over more of the surface of his car than necessary, Webster opened the door. He rooted around beneath the car seat and pulled out a paper towel, with which he wiped his hands: palms, fingers, even the backs of hands and wrists, then the fingers again. He almost, out of habit, wiped his face with the towel, but caught himself in time. He hesitated, then shrugged, and threw the wadded-up towel into the marsh.

It was late afternoon now, nearly sundown, and he wanted to be back on familiar roads by nightfall. And so he was, picking up speed as he entered the interstate a little later, the early headlights of passing cars highlighting the flakes of disintegrating newsprint flying back like dandruff over the hood and past the windshield.

§

If Webster had thought about it, he would have gone directly home. There he would have done whatever he was going to do with the head. And then — only then — would he have gone to the A&P supermarket.

But he didn't think about it. During the leisurely drive from interstate to county road, he passed a gleaming chrome tank truck full of milk and, a bit later, a series of three billboards advertising a regional bakery's new line of whole-grain bread in which were imbedded little chunklets of fruit. *THE USUAL*, said the first sign — its artwork picturing gigantic slices of toasted raisin bread. *THE UNUSUAL*, said the second: also raisins, but complemented by slivers of apple. *THE UNUSUALEST*, said the third. How about that, Webster thought. He hadn't even known that kiwi fruit was, what? bakeable?

So what he was thinking about as he exited from the freeway some ten miles from home was not the head, but breakfast. He was just about out of milk. And that raisin-apple stuff, mmm, that would go well with butter, and cinnamon-sugar sprinkled on top. And what the heck, as long as he was going to be in the supermarket...

Aisle 12 — produce. The shopping cart groaning beneath the weight of a solid cube-shaped array of dairy products and a dozen canned items stacked up in neat aluminum towers, a layer of frozen dinners and desserts over the surfaces of whose boxes water was already condensing, and on the top a loaf of raisin-apple whole-grain bread, also a loaf of regular bread in case the fancy stuff didn't work out, four packs of D-cell batteries — not that he was sure he needed them, but you could never have too many batteries — and a twelve-pack of the ultra-luxurious grade of toilet tissue. But there in Aisle 12, suddenly obsessed with the notion of salad, he picked up a cabbage. Hefted it. And underwent a jarring vertiginous near-swoon:

I am in the supermarket, he thought, *selecting a cabbage, and outside* in a public parking lot *I have a human head bungee-corded to the grill of my station wagon...*

He put the cabbage back on its boulderous terrace, where it rolled a notch or two before coming to rest. He looked down at his hands. Wowie, can't put it back on the shelf, he hadn't truly cleaned his hands but merely wiped them on a paper towel... He picked the cabbage up again, balanced it gingerly on the toothpaste, shampoo, drain-unclogging liquid and facial tissue occupying the fold-out rack where a normal person would seat a small child.

Immobilized, he looked at the cabbage again, looked in fact at all the rest of the food in the cart. He couldn't, didn't *dare* eat any of this stuff. But he couldn't put it all back, could he? And leave it for someone else, unsuspecting, to pick up?

But holy cow. *He had a human head mounted on the hood of his car.* He had to get out there, no, wait, he had to stay here and resolve this, but *no*, what about the head...?

In the checkout aisle he kept craning his neck, trying unsuccessfully to see through the windows in the direction of the spot where he'd parked the Galaxie. The man in front of him finally turned, looked directly at Webster, snarled: "Got a problem, man?"

"Huh? Oh, not looking at you," reddening, "my car, trying to see my car, there's a," whoops, almost but not quite, "there's a, uh, there's a problem with my car and I was, was trying to see it, my car that is. Sorry."

The contents of the cart finally piled on the rubber checkout belt, Webster made his way to the cashier. Unfortunately there was a further delay, as the original cashier was replaced — after a two- or three-minute wait — by a trainee, apparently his first night on the job. He'd never used the price-scanner gizmo, judging from the awkward way he kept using two hands to pick everything up and place it down squarely on the ruby-lit glass X, twisting his wrists. And judging from the way he was plucking objects all around the cabbage but avoiding the cabbage itself, he was probably none too comfortable with the scale, either. When he finally did reach for it, Webster's own hands swooped down to intercept the leafy globe.

"You, uh, don't need to weigh it, it costs whatever by the, that is," trying and failing to come up with a synonym, "by the head," the trainee looking quizzically back over his shoulder at his supervisor, who nodded as Webster rushed on, "Here, I'll just put it in the cart..."

Fleeing headlong (haha) from the store, uncharacteristically impatient, almost ramming a cart being pushed by a little girl and drawing from her mother a glance that would have frozen Webster's soul if he'd even noticed it. Trotting as quickly as possible across the parking lot, the shopping cart squeaking menacingly as one of its front wheels skimmed over the asphalt, flailing in useless crazy circles. His car, was it...?

Yes. It was all right. No crowd had gathered. There was no policeman scratching his head, no Channel 7 NewsCopter cameraman zooming in on the face of the driver of the car with the head. Webster went around to the front of the car; the ghastly object wrapped in newspaper was still there. Thank God. He'd never be able to get home fast enough.

Relieved but still a little frantic, oblivious to all but the need to get the car loaded and out of the parking lot, he opened the tailgate and began scooping bags from cart to automobile. So it was that he almost (but not quite) missed the sound of a nearby engine cranking, starting, and lurching forward with a thud and a soggy *crack*, sending the Galaxie a-shudder and Webster's knees nearly collapsing beneath him.

In an instant, the gracious, almost unnaturally well-mannered elderly woman was out of her car and the whole length of the station wagon to Webster's side. "Oh my dear young man," she repeated once, twice, three times, "are you all right, are you sure you're all right?" Wringing her hands as Webster steadied himself, hanging from the overhead tailgate like a drunk from a lamppost.

"Yes, yes, really—"

"Oh but your *car!*" she cried suddenly. "Your lovely car, surely an antique...!" Her voice fading as she ran back to the intersection of the two vehicles' front ends.

Webster staggered after her, bracing himself against the passenger side of his car. Closing his eyes. Steeling himself. Opening his eyes.

The old woman's late-model Oldsmobile had leapt forward with sufficient force that its front bumper had actually jumped Webster's and driven (Webster gasping at the sight) through the grill. What he hoped would be mistaken for automotive fluids were puddling beneath the two cars' osculated chromework.

"Oh dear young man, oh dear," the old woman was saying. "My son, this is his car, and *your* car, oh my, and he hasn't any insurance—"

Webster interrupted her. "Ma'am. Can you — can you back your car up?"

"It's my son's—"

"Yes, your son's car, can you back it up? Not a lot, just a... bit."

Fluttering, agitated, asserting Webster's dearness, youth, and malehood with each step, she resumed the wheel of her — her son's — Oldsmobile. She cranked and started the engine again, put it into reverse. Backed up, the two cars heaving like Jurassic amphibians in the throes of passion, separating—

Wowie. One hook of the elastic cord had gotten snarled somehow on the underside of the Oldsmobile's bumper, leaving the two cars tied together. As Webster watched in mixed horror and fascination, a six-inch pulpy, amorphous mass plopped from the cavity in the station wagon's grill onto the parking lot, rolled a bit, and came to a stop somewhere beneath the other car. The bungee cord thrummed, weirdly, in a single bass note.

"Hey, can I help?" The voice, drawing nearer, of one of the A&P's aproned clerks, out rounding up vagrant shopping carts.

In a panic, Webster fled to the back of the station wagon and around to the driver's side, yanked open the door, started his own engine and threw it into reverse. There was a pause, then an eerie *doong* and a crack as the hook disengaged from the other car's bumper and snapped back up and over the hood of Webster's car. He turned on his headlights (conscious vaguely of a gray ovoid presence in the darkness beneath the elderly woman's car), whipped the steering wheel around and threw the car into drive, and peeled away, the tailgate wide open. As he scooted out onto the street the last thing he saw or heard from the A&P was the clerk, stooping, holding up a round object, calling out to him, "Hey Mister, hey! *You dropped your cabbage!*"

The ride home — through the village, and eventually out onto the dark road where he lived — took fifteen minutes. Window down, tailgate still up, gale whipping through the car. A box of cereal or cube of facial tissue occasionally tumbling out into the blackness behind him. Webster dimly conscious of but not seeing any of it, distracted, reaching for the knob of the AM radio and turning on the all-news-all-the-time station.

"...head," the announcer was concluding. Webster hunching over the wheel and breaking into a sweat. "...discovered earlier today by a sanitation worker in the landfill. Massa's body had come to light over twenty-four hours ago, although his hands and feet have still to be recovered."

Webster sat back in his seat, inflated his cheeks with air; a sigh puffed from between his pursed lips. So then the head, *his* head, wasn't Massa's? He should turn around now and go back to claim it, no wait, he was almost home, but *the head, whose head...?* Wheeling, after an unending instant of indecision, into his driveway.

He fetched his garden hose, coiled on a spindle at the side of the house, and rinsed out the shallow depression in the grill of the Galaxie; got a pair of channel-lock pliers from the garage, used them to remove the traitorous elastic cord and drop it in the garbage can. Remembered the groceries in the rear of the station wagon, rebagged the items that had spilled all over (which was nearly all of them, at least the ones he hadn't lost en route), carried them into his kitchen and put them away.

Thinking all the while of the head, the head that was not Goose Massa's head, lying fifteen minutes away in the parking lot of a suburban supermarket.

He went back outside and fetched the mail and the afternoon newspaper, read none of it but dropped it on the end table by the sofa in his living room. Sat on the sofa, wringing his hands, looking down at them and suddenly recalling what a busy day they'd had; lunged up and away from the sofa and back into the kitchen to scrub them, furiously, with the strongest cleansing product he could find beneath the sink, astringently malodorous abrasive particles lodging beneath his fingernails and stinging the fingertips where he'd clipped the nails too closely. He rinsed them, dried them with paper towel which he immediately placed into a small plastic garbage bag and disposed of in the kitchen trash can. The can's circular lid, hinged at the sides, pivoting once and twice — *whuddawhudda* — before shuddering to a stop. Then he stood for a few moments at the kitchen window, cranked it open, leaned on the sink, looked out into the darkened back yard. There was a pale-blue glow in the night sky at the horizon, just over the treed hills that separated his yard from a view of the village. The supermarket parking lot lights, he imagined...

Back then to the garage to pick up a couple of things. As he opened the garage door the hole in the Galaxie's grill stared at him like the blind eye socket of a cyclops. Accusingly, but also quizzically. *Now what?* the cyclops seemed to be asking.

At the A&P, it took him a couple of minutes to locate the spot where his car had been parked earlier, finally locating it only because of the fragments of chromed plastic glinting like silver nuggets in the mercury-vapor light. No one else was parked in that space now, but the elderly woman's car — her son's car — had been replaced by a matte-red Ford pickup even older than the Galaxie. Beneath and a little behind the pickup's front bumper, a rough indistinct gray lump lying on the asphalt. There was no one behind the wheel of the pickup, which was good, but in the passenger seat was a pale young man smoking a cigarette, which was not. Otherwise, miraculously, no other people visible in the parking lot just then.

Webster sat in the car for a few seconds, staring at the young man in the pickup, who was staring back at Webster. Shoot. He had to get this over with.

The young man finished his cigarette and, as Webster removed the cowhide work gloves, shovel, and garbage bags from the station wagon, lit another. Watching but without apparent real curiosity.

Webster leaned the shovel against the car, where it slithered precariously for a second but then came to rest against the side-view mirror; donned the work gloves; shook the garbage bags open, put one inside another and then put those two inside a third. Shovel and bags clutched in gloved hands, he knelt between the two bumpers.

The head, what was left of it, lay easily within arm's reach but Webster decided to use the shovel. No point in nauseating himself too soon: he still had a couple of long hours to get through. He hooked the blade of the shovel behind the head and dragged it to him, out into the open space between the truck and his car. Started to stand up but a tobacco-scratchy voice behind him said, "Give you a hand with sumpin?", startling the bejeezus out of him so that he lurched forward and stepped *whoops wowie and holy cow* stepped *over* the pulpy thing but felt like he'd pulled a hamstring or what-was-it, the muscle on the inside of his thigh, fell against the hood of his car. Grimaced. Looked back over his shoulder, wishing he could massage the leg but wishing more than anything for the sudden arrival of alien abductors on the prowl for specimens addicted to nicotine.

"Er, no thanks, I'm fine, thanks, for offering I mean. Really."

The young man nodding, but showing neither emotion nor sign of returning to the truck cab.

"Really. I'm fine."

Still no sign of taking a hint. Leaning against the truck fender, looking up into the sky. "Nice night."

Holy cow some people, can't think about it now ignore him... Webster opened up the three nested garbage bags, lay them on the ground, grasped the shovel down by the point where the wooden shaft entered the sheet-metal cylinder at the top of the blade, crouched, held his breath, and *scraaaped* the blade beneath the head, pushed it against the palm of his other hand, balanced it gingerly on the shovel for a split-second until he could deposit it into the innermost bag. Twist-tying the bag shut — his thick-gloved fingers fumbling with the tie — and then twist-tying the second bag and finally the outer one as well. Air had gotten trapped inside all three bags so the parcel was like a balloon, but darned if he was going to try squeezing it out.

As he placed the bags in the rear of the station wagon and removed the gloves, the young man was suddenly at his side. "Shovel," he said, holding it out.

§

An hour later, beneath the dim white light of a crescent moon, Webster had finished burying the bags in an overgrown far corner of his backyard. The gloves, too — plucked with the channel-locks from the rear of the car and deposited in the hole. He tamped down the mound of dirt one final time, then stood on it and bounced up and down a couple of times on the balls of his feet. An audible *ppffff* as it sank an inch or so and then settled, at last, into place. He put the tools away in the garage, washed up again at the kitchen sink, and went to bed.

He didn't sleep, though, not for a while anyhow. He tried to read at first but kept thinking about the burial plot in the backyard, and about its contents. Whose head might it be, or, uh, have been? Where was the rest of the person? How had the head and body come to be separated, how had the head wound up in the marsh by the train tracks and most especially how had it wound up *here*? Well of course he knew how, that last how, but he didn't really *understand* how. Had the head's owner ever driven through this part of the world, perhaps past Webster's house even, and thought to himself, *Nice place, oughtta come back here sometime maybe even to stay*? Was that it — was Webster just acting a part in some weird karmic melodrama?

Sometime over the next few months, before the ground hardened, Webster thought, he might go back out to that section of the yard and plant, um, some bulbs maybe. Irises, day lilies. Something. A memorial plot, since the head's owner probably didn't have a real one anywhere. Sprouting, blooming next spring...

No. No he wouldn't. He'd already disturbed its (and his own) peace too much, he'd just let it lie there. Eventually he'd forget about it; eventually he'd have the sinkhole in the center of the Galaxie's grill taken care of; eventually he'd stop glancing nervously out the window of the morning train; eventually Monica would stop asking him how'd he finally resolved the dilemma; eventually he'd buy another pair of work gloves. Eventually, unseen, the triple layer of dark green polywhatever would disintegrate, the hole et cetera would come to be indistinguishable from the dirt around it, weeds and, who knew, maybe a tree would even take root out there. Yeah, a tree. Webster kind of liked the thought of that: long after Webster himself had left this house for good, even, and a family had moved in. A tree whose leaves hissed in the breeze, while somewhere in its upper branches, an irritable crow pecked obsessively at the bark.

Grinning, but anxiously, he turned out the light, rolled over onto his side, plumped up the pillows, and nestled his head down to sleep.

The Shot

Until now, "The Shot" has always held a unique status in the Webster saga: it's the only one of these tales previously to have seen print, meaning, y'know, print-print: i.e., on paper. I had it in circulation at a couple of literary magazines in 1991-92, and — funny story — it was accepted by two of them within days of each other. The first one was barely a "magazine"; it was printed out of the editor's home, with the issue's cover art hand-drawn by the editor, and as I understood it back then each issue was simply stapled together — one staple, top left corner. So, not an ideal first credit to show off to folks — but, well, what could I do…? When the second acceptance came in, from a university-affiliated magazine, I immediately called the first publication's editor to withdraw my, uh, acceptance of her acceptance. She was FURIOUS. She yelled a couple of unpleasant things over the phone, and slammed down the receiver. I'm pretty sure this is how Webster's own writing career might've kicked off.

Webster didn't get his hair cut all that often, only every three to five weeks or so. But it was an act of vanity that he always looked forward to; it provided his life with an irregular Druidic sort of rhythm, like the intertwining orbital periods of the sun and moon.

The haircut, the act *per se*, did not appeal to him, so much as all its context, the juices in which the act stewed. There were the aromas, for one thing — the complex composite scent of aftershaves and witch hazel and talcum powder, of pomades, of cigars smoked and lingered over years and years ago but still, somehow, clinging stubbornly to the splitting red-vinyl seats, like an old-timer who didn't *wanna* leave just now, thank you very much. Even the simple act of walking to and through the barbershop door calmed Webster's soul: the first sight of the spiraling red-and-white pole as he approached, the backs of the heads of the men sitting like a choir just on the other side of the window, the jingle of the bell suspended on a hook over the door — it felt like, well, like he was approaching some fine and holy altar of manliness.

The barber, no doubt, held the lead role in this sanctified production: he spoke the liturgy, a ceaseless murmured commentary about sports, politics, mechanical breakdowns, and local characters, as though whispering prayers to and seeking intercession from the village deities. *Snip, snip, snip*; "Guess you heard about Ward, huh?"; *snip*; "His kid, I mean, you know, the fat one?"; *snip, snip*; pause to chuckle to himself; *snip*; and so on. It was just talk, mostly. Webster had learned the barber's name from his nametag, but never addressed him by it; such a detail would be, well, almost too secular to interject.

On this particular Saturday, Webster had parked his car where he always parked it, in a small, unattended municipal lot about a half-block away. He walked to the shop's door as always, charmed as always by the magic of the barber pole, silently, ceaselessly unscrewing out of and into nothing at all. He sat in one of the chrome and vinyl seats by the window, drinking in the fragrances, leafing through a months-old back issue of a magazine whose soul was torn between two goals: congratulating local businesses, and casting aspersions on distant ones.

The man just ahead of Webster finally stood up at his chair by the window, and then sat in the big chair; the barber commenced his *snip*ping and his commentary. After a few minutes, glancing up from an article on the blessings of Rotarian membership, Webster saw out of the tops of his eyes that the barber was unpinning the cloth at the back of the man's neck, an act which signified that this haircut would be over in a moment or two.

Webster readied himself. He closed the magazine at just the instant prescribed by convention; he stood up and moved to the barber chair just as the unwritten script called for — not too fast, give the preceding guy a chance to pay his tab, give the barber a chance to sweep up the clippings if he wants to, according to whatever cycle dictated by his barber's psychic metronome... *now*. Webster sat, and the barber clipped the soft paper towel and large maroon sheet around his neck.

"The usual?" the barber murmured.

"Oh, yeah."

Snip, snip. "Guess you already heard about all the excitement out on the highway, huh?" said the barber. *Snip.*

"Something's going on, on the highway? Which one?"

The barber rotated the chair so that Webster faced the window and the row of waiting men, all silently sneaking furtive looks up over their magazines and newspapers, out of the tops of their eyes. Watching for ceremonial cues. The barber gestured with a sweep of his left hand, which held a comb. "The interstate. Just south of town." He rotated the chair again; Webster now faced a wall. *Snip.* "Shootings."

"*Shootings?*"

Snip, snip. Snip. "Uh-*huh*. Some crazy person most likely, or a kid. Maybe a kid." *Snip. Snip. Snip.* "Used a deer rifle," *snip*, "popped holes in a couple tractor trailers, maybe three-four cars, I forget how many." *Snip, snip.* "All of 'em over the last couple days."

"Jeez, no, I didn't know anything about it," Webster murmured. He shook his head a little in disbelief, and the barber steadied it with his fingertips as though quieting a skittish laboratory animal. "I've been out of town for the last few days. A deer rifle, holy cow... Anybody actually get hit?"

"Yep." *Snip.* "Somebody did. Just one guy, though. So far anyhow," *snip*. He swiveled the chair again so Webster now faced the other two barber chairs, both empty and unattended. On the way, his gaze swept over the faces of the five men by the window; five pairs of eyes glanced hurriedly back down to their reading matter.

"He all right? The guy that got hit?"

"Um," *snip*, "yeah..." *Snip. Snip-snip-snip.* "Hit him in the shoulder, I think, collar bone, somewhere like that." For emphasis, the barber tapped Webster's own collarbone with the tips of the scissors. *Snip, snip.* "Went right through, through the seat too, bullet finally stuck in the back seat. Deer rifle," *snip*, "oh yeah, said that already didn't I." He turned the chair so Webster could see his reflection. Webster glanced briefly at his haircut, a little instant longer at his eyes, then finally at the barber's face. They nodded slightly at each other's reflection, ritualistically, first Webster then the barber. The barber hung the scissors on a small hook screwed into the face of the mirror frame, and laid the comb on the counter that ran its length. He picked up a soft-bristled brush and shook talcum powder into it.

"You say they think it's a kid?"

"Hmm? Oh; yeah..." He whisked the brush all around the circumference of Webster's neck, then down the maroon sheet. "Yeah, a kid, probably. They think he was shootin' from a tree or a hill, somewhere up high anyhow, the bullets come *down*, you know?... There you go," he concluded, and unfastened the sheet and the towel. In the reflection in the mirror, Webster saw, behind him, the next customer fold his newspaper and stand up.

§

Over the next several days, Webster learned more about the shootings; they were, after all, Big News for the drowsy little town on whose outskirts he lived.

The portion of the interstate highway where the cars and trucks had all been shot cut through a hill in a long, sweeping curve. To either side were steep, wooded slopes; the median strip here was also heavily wooded; and just at the end of the curve, the interstate straightened out and sped beneath a bridge across which ran a county road, Route 647. The police had no suspects in the case, they told the weekly newspaper's elderly, part-time crime reporter. Oh, they were working on a few theories, but provided no details. There had been no further shootings after the one man was wounded, and the accepted wisdom was that the criminal had quit when he realized this wasn't a game any longer.

That was how everyone referred to the mystery marksman: "the criminal." The populace was alarmed, yes, but also a little titillated: they hadn't had a criminal in their midst for years. "The Death of Our Innocence," the weekly paper lamented in a front-page editorial (although the headline writer lost his nerve and added a question mark). The wounded man became practically a folk hero, even though he didn't even live in this state, just drove through it on his way to and from work. He'd lost a lot of blood, yes, but the bullet wound wasn't as severe an injury as the bruises and lacerations he'd suffered after driving himself off the highway and into a shopping center parking lot: there, weakened, he passed out and with his car still in motion, sideswiped a panel truck which sold hot dogs and soda and finally came to a halt after broadsiding the mayor's car. But he was a hero nonetheless, a "survivor of near-tragedy" — or so proclaimed the paper in a hospital-bedside interview remarkable for its solemnity of tone, as though the man had lived through a nuclear explosion. When he was discharged from the hospital, the mayor presented him with a key to the town and a book of coupons good for purchases at local merchants.

But the wounded man didn't return to the town to use his key or his coupons. And in the absence of further news or breakthroughs in the police investigation, people started to forget about the shootings, even about the criminal. They returned to news about auction prices and local government referenda. The next time Webster got a haircut, the barber told him that he'd had to replace, *snip snip*, his two-year-old water pump that week, thing just *up* and died on him, can you believe it? What was the world coming to, anyhow?

§

One Friday evening some weeks later, as he pulled his car into the garage attached to his house, Webster finally ran over the push-broom on the garage floor. It had fallen away from the wall weeks ago and been lying there on the concrete ever since, like an accusation of disorderliness. But he always forgot about it till he pulled the car in, steering just a little to the left to avoid crushing it under the right front wheel. *Got to pick up that damned broom*, he'd say to himself, then he'd shut off the radio, the lights, maybe the wipers if it was raining, the heater or the defroster, the rear-window defogger, finally the ignition, and he'd reach around to pick up his briefcase off the back seat, walk out to the roadside to check the mail, and — whoosh! just like that — all thought of the push-broom would have flown away. Until tonight, anyhow; until he'd actually gone and done it, drove right over the handle. Split it, of course. This time he made himself walk around the car to the passenger side and pick up the busted implement. He unscrewed the handle with disgust and threw the pieces, *rattle* and *chunk*, into one of the huge molded-plastic trash barrels.

The next morning, Saturday, was misty and chilly; the wet seemed to be burrowing like a live arctic rodent under the rubberized poncho he had donned for his trip to the hardware store. The weatherman on the car radio assured his listeners, just as he and his colleagues had assured them for weeks, that spring was "just around the corner." *Huh*, Webster thought, *must be some long, sweeping corner* — and the image reminded him of the shootings on the interstate.

In the hardware store, his inner tundra rodent still a-shiver, Webster stood before the display of broomsticks. He thought, "Huh. A *display* of broomsticks? How many kinds can there *be*?" There weren't that many, really, but he didn't want to rush into this, you know. Consumerism, right? He picked up one of each size and hefted it, trying to imagine on what basis to evaluate one broomstick against another...

"Can I help you, sir?" asked the store clerk who had materialized at Webster's elbow. He wore an immaculate dark-blue shop apron that had clearly never been any closer to a workshop than it was right now. The clerk's hands, for that matter, were suspiciously soft, pink, and well-manicured.

"Uh, no — just looking for a new broom handle for my push-broom, drove over the old one last night." *Dope; this guy doesn't care about that...*

But the clerk merely nodded sympathetically; he had maybe driven over many broomsticks himself. "You know, you might want to take a look at these over here, much more sturdy... virtually indestructible..."

He led Webster around to the other side of the display rack, sales-pattering the whole time. Here on this side was an array of what seemed to be, well, *designer* broomsticks, fancy high-gloss enamel-painted models — and also the ones to which the clerk now directed Webster's attention. "Aluminum, see? Rugged, light, same standard ASA threading as the wooden ones..."

Webster hefted the broomstick. It was indeed feather-light. "You say this thing's actually stronger than a wooden one?"

"Oh, *absolutely*," and then he was off into a riff of Byzantine techno-babble about "modern alloys" and "coefficients of tensility" and so on, all of which obviously issued forth directly from either a sales brochure or this young man's imagination. Webster ignored him; he firmly clutched one end of the broomstick, then the other, and bracing his thumbs against it for leverage pretended to flex it... What would a consumerist guru like old Ralph Nader want him to do right now?

He bought the aluminum broomstick, of course, embarrassed finally by all the attention showered on him by the clerk, and he hurried from the store. He laid the broomstick across the back seat and started home.

The mist still hung in the air, not quite a *fog*, exactly, more like an indecisive drizzle. Must have been going on all night, big puddles everywhere... He drove slowly through one of these out in the street in front of the barbershop, glancing over at the window as he rode slowly by. The spiral pole was twisting; the barber, waving his hands in illustration of some point for the customer in the chair. Making the Sign of the Comb and Scissors. Webster felt as though he were in an amusement-park ride, gliding by a display of gesturing robots, their feet bolted to the floor. He wondered what the barber was saying to the man in the chair, and then thought again of the shootings. Then he was past the barbershop and waiting at the town's sole traffic light. Off to the right side, a be-drizzled young woman with an umbrella was stabbing with a finger, furiously, at a button on the traffic light pole, a button which was supposed (and obviously failing) to make the light change. A sign fastened to the pole, just above the button, pointed with an arrow down the street to Webster's right; "RTE 647," it said, and Webster turned that way.

He'd been out this way before, of course; not the most direct route home, but he liked to take little unscheduled, experimental drives around town and out on the numbered rural roads where he lived. But he hadn't been out here since the shootings, what were they, five, six weeks ago? And he was suddenly curious. Where out here *would* a marksman have shot from, anyhow?

Snip, went his intermittent windshield wipers. *Snip*. Not so many puddles out this way; the water just drained off the crested pavement and into the ditches on either side. The road was deserted once he got out of town, just vacant fields and forests. A farm or two. *Snip*. His thoughts returned to the hardware store and the little riddle of how to purchase a broomstick. If the threads and length were all the same, was there anything besides weight even to consider? The broomstick's grip, maybe? (*Snip*.) Its finish?

He pulled the car over to the curb just past the interstate overpass, thinking suddenly as he did so: You choose a broomstick if it's *straight*. A little mental tableau took shape, in which he was holding the broomstick in both hands, then lifting it and peering along its length...

Webster got out of the car, taking the broomstick from the back seat. No other traffic out here this morning, and that was good. He zipped up the poncho and tugged its hood up and over the top of his head. He walked to the pavement at the edge of the bridge. Along the top of the waist-high concrete wall here ran a chain-link fence, obviously there to keep kids from throwing stones and other junk down onto passing cars. He looked over the wall. Not much traffic down there, either. A drop of rain fell onto the hood of the poncho: *snip*.

He lifted the broomstick and inserted its threaded end through a gap in the fence, then hunched down to sight along it. Seemed straight enough, all right, what'd he expect? That mystery solved, his mind turned to a fancy in which he himself was a marksman, *the* marksman, the *criminal*, squinting one-eyed down the length of this silvery tube... A car on the highway drove past the end of the broomstick, and he imagined pulling the trigger. *Pop.* His shoulder twitched with the imaginary recoil. Could the drivers see him up here, he wondered? Could he see their faces, for that matter? He angled the broomstick more steeply, so it pointed down at the cars passing more closely beneath him. *Pop.* Yes, that one saw him; the dope stuck his face out from underneath the safety of the sun visor to peer up at Webster through the top of the windshield, a voluntary target: *pop*... A truck drove by. *Pop.* A car, *excellent*, with a sunroof. *Pop, pop.* Another car, this one with a red-and-blue light b— a *light bar*? Oh *shit*—

Webster turned and looked over his shoulder, across the overpass. The state police cruiser had indeed pulled over and braked to a halt, and now was backing at high speed up the shoulder in Webster's direction. *Oh, shit.* Without really thinking, Webster pulled the broomstick from the fence and sprinted towards his car. Thank God there was no exit ramp from the interstate here... He ducked inside the car, tossed the broomstick into the back seat, and slammed the door an instant after hearing what sounded like a real "*Pop!*" behind him. But nothing in the rear-view mirrors...

He drove away from the overpass as fast as he thought safe. Surely the trooper hadn't really seen *him*, Webster, personally, probably not the car either, probably just another unsolvable mystery for them... His car was climbing a hill, fast, when over the hilltop ahead of him, in the other lane, soared a local police car, lights a-flash and siren warbling, speeding in the opposite direction. Okay, just keep your cool, don't do anything to attract his attention, take it easy as you go past him, glance in the rearview mirror— *Damn.* The police car's brake lights came on, then Webster himself shot over the hilltop. Thinking: *He's turning around, you know he's turning around, he saw your car for sure...*

As Webster descended the other side of the hill, his mind racing, he remembered an abandoned or never-started housing development over on the left somewhere, just before the next curve, not much of an entrance, just an asphalt pavement laid down through the woods... *here.* He turned in, left the engine running but shut off the headlights and removed his foot from the brake, and waited. Eyes glued to the rearview mirror. *Snip*, went his wipers, and his pulse answered: *BOOM-ba-boom, BOOM-ba-boom...*

No police car. Was it possible that the cop *hadn't* see him? A distant shriek grew closer, then a sheriff's car whooshed past in the little rectangle framed by the mirror, going toward the bridge over the interstate. But still no police car coming back the other way... *Snip... snip. Boom-ba-boom, boom-ba-boom...*

Now what? What would, say, Bonnie and Clyde do? *Snip.*

He reached behind him and picked up the broomstick from the back seat, and again got out of the car. He peered into the woods which surrounded this would-be driveway. No one about. The silent, slender, gray forms of the trees seemed like a congregation of robed churchgoers, interrupted in mid-service, waiting for him to do something. To speak in tongues, maybe; to witness; to make an offering; why else had he barged in here? He looked down at the broomstick, hefted it in his right hand one final time, reared back and hurled it, like a javelin, into the gloom of the forest. It did not soar gracefully as a javelin, though, but tumbled end over end till the mist swallowed it up. Then he got back into his car, K-turned, and, very gingerly, pulled out of the driveway — no cars coming from either direction, good — and turned right, back onto County Route 647, back toward the interstate highway overpass. *Snip*. Back up, and over, the hill... *Snip*.

Webster could see the flashing lights long before he saw the bridge itself. As he drew near, he saw that there were, hmm, the sheriff's car, a couple of the local police cars, and must be five or six uniformed officers and also a trooper, soaking wet, son-of-a-gun must have scrambled up the hillside from the highway there...

One of the locals waved him over to the shoulder and started to walk over in his direction. Webster knew her. It was, what was her name, Billie? Billie Wingate? *Boom-ba-boom*...

Webster rolled down his window and squinted up at the officer. "Billie. What's all, what's going on here?"

"Hey, Webster. State police officer thinks he might've seen that shooter up here, remember, that guy with the rifle—?"

"No kidding. He shoot somebody else?"

"No, we don't *think* so, anyways. No reports of any shooting yet, he just saw the guy sticking the rifle through the fence here." He gestured over his shoulder.

"Can I, uh, can I get through here, Billie? I'm going into town is all."

"Into town? A little out o' your way for that, aren't you?"

Boom-ba-boom. "Yeah, well, I just like to drive around, different ways now and then, y'know." *Boom-ba-boom*.

Billie hesitated, but just for a second. "Sure, go on through. Stay off the interstate for a while, though, you hear?"

Webster grinned. "Don't worry about *that*, Billie!"

He drove slowly and with great care around the huddled law-enforcement officers, taking special care, as he glanced at the state trooper, to compose his features into something that looked like no more than curiosity at this exotic beast among the local fauna. Then he was away from them, and the overpass was dropping out of sight behind him. Back to the traffic light, turn left. Past the barber shop, *snip snip*, and the hardware store. Right on all the way through town, *snip*, into the next town, to the so-called "home center" there, the hardware (*snip*) super-store.

"Broomsticks?" said the girl at the customer service desk. "Two — no, three aisles down. All the way down the end of the aisle. You need any help?"

"No," Webster replied. "I'll be all right."

Indeed, he knew just what to look for this time. He slid one of the aluminum poles from the rack and hefted it first in one hand, then tossed it, jauntily, to the other. He braced his thumbs against it, pretending to flex it a little. Then he raised it to his shoulder and sighted down its length, pointed down at the other end of the aisle. A stockboy's startled face swam into view down there just as Webster squeezed off the shot: *pop*.

"Didn't hit you, did I?" he chuckled as he walked past the teenager and patted his shoulder.

The boy smiled weakly, a brief adrenaline flush still coloring his face. "No, sir," he quipped, "just grazed my scalp a little."

Webster was still chuckling to himself about that ("Smart kid," he thought) as he drove straight home, no detours this time, paced — *snip, snip* — by the car's wipers, the new broomstick gleaming, sinister, lying prone across the back seat.

The Dark

Oh boy: "The Dark." This is the closest thing to a "novel" which ever (will ever) feature Webster as its protagonist. (A writing workshop participant familiar with the other stories once called this "the Moby Dick of Webster stories," which still makes me laugh.) Like "The Head," it was retitled, but I don't think anyone ever saw (or — haha — remembers) its original title; it was far too faux-literary, and far too polysyllabic. Of all the Webster tales, "The Dark" may be my favorite; from it, I certainly learned more about him (and myself!) than I expected I could.

1

Webster was in a stall in the men's room at work. He had selected the middle one of the three, as always — he'd always leave and come back later if someone else was in there ahead of him — the one with the shelf-like thingum on which he could rest his wrist and elbow and his cup of coffee, the one with the everlasting drip from all the chromework behind the seat, a cozy little island of peace, sanity, and predictability. It lacked only a sampler on the wall.

The local neighborhood freebie newspaper was spread open across his otherwise bare knees. He'd been here for ten, fifteen minutes so far, feigning absorption in the impassioned amateur journalism about zoning outrages and police protection, notices of pets lost and found, reviews and previews of rock concerts by unheard-of bands whose names sounded like failed experiments in semantic eugenics. Not that anyone was going to, well, *check on* him here — like, "Webster? What the heck you doing in there, anyhow?" — but you never knew. Someone might note his absence from his desk; someone else might say, "Oh yeah,

Webster, I saw him go into the bathroom but that was ten minutes ago, you think he's all right?" When the search party arrived and began to question him through the walls of the stall, Webster imagined rattling the newspaper and reassuring them, "Yes, yes! I'm all right! In here, just reading this fascinating investigative piece on the failure of The City's landmark-preservation activities..."

He was, however, only dimly aware of the words on the page, rather attending primarily to the consequences of what his college roommate used to call the "cold fusion" which occurred within twelve hours of eating too much frozen reheated lasagna. (His wife — for Webster was married now — had apologized, last night being the second successive one on which they'd had leftover lasagna. But they'd really had no choice, both of them getting home from work far too late to do anything more like menu planning than to stare dully into the open freezer, willing the wisps of frosty air to coalesce into something at least edible, if not actually nourishing or even appetizing.)

Meanwhile, other men entered and exited the restroom — some of them, for all Webster knew, more than once — but Webster had paid only as much attention to their activities as mandated by his inviolable laws of self-consciousness: clearing his throat, shaking the newspaper pages, peeking through the slit between the stall's painted-metal door and doorframe in order to be sure that no one was peeking *in*.

He'd been alone for a few minutes, but now someone entered the stall next to Webster's; he felt the toilet seat shift beneath himself as the other man, evidently of a large build, sat down upon *his* creaking seat. Webster lifted the corner of the newspaper, crouched a bit, and twisted his head in order to glance down and over at the other man's shoes. They were none of Webster's business — but (he rationalized) how many chances did modern life, conducted out in the open, give us to observe our fellow man without knowing if they were watching us? Right. None. This was it: the lavatory stall.

The man's shoes were brown, scuffed in a way that made it clear that the scuffing had been built into the shoes from the start. Gnarled. "Distressed leather," Webster imagined it was called: *designer* scuffing. That, together with the tan crepe soles, bespoke a literally careless wearer, one who cared exactly zero per cent what people thought of the way he dressed in the business world. (Or, more likely here in The City, someone who cared one hundred per cent about it, desired one hundred per cent that he be noticed, even if in scorn.) What was odder, the shoes were wingtips, a bizarre hodge-podge of classicism and affected ruggedness.

Webster didn't like the shoes at all, and sniffed loudly and rattled the newspaper to signal his disapproval.

Meanwhile he looked down at his own shoes, twisted his ankles about. What would the other man be able to guess about Webster himself from looking at *his* shoes? *Suppose he sees my ankle writhing around here*, he thought, *He might know that I've been looking at—*

That was when the restroom lights went out.

Webster's heart lurched involuntarily, and the man in the next stall said, loudly, "Oh for Christ's sake." Each word, each consonant, pronounced explicitly.

Definitely a fuss-budget, Webster thought. But then the lights did not come on right away, and he forgot about the other man, began to feel restless and — well, oppressed. Why didn't they put restrooms on the outside walls of buildings anymore, where they could at least have light from the windows for emergencies like this? Cripes but it was dark, impenetrably dark, and Webster touched lightly at the metal stall walls to reassure himself that they were still there and not gone, receding, or, more terrifyingly, closer.

Should he get up, or stay? He wasn't done yet, but it felt weirdly indecent to do what he was doing in the dark. A throwback to the Neanderthals, maybe: like a bear, you went in the woods, not in the cave — and you went in daylight. If you were going to make yourself vulnerable, to put your most precious anatomy at the mercy of the natural world, you had to be able to see exactly what dangers might be at hand.

Snake in the toilet, he thought, recalling a series of homeowners' advice newspaper columns on the subject. *With the lights out I'd never know, it would just—*, and at that moment the seat of the toilet shifted and creaked again. His heart thudded uncomfortably once, twice, before he heard the man in the next stall muttering, moving around, rumbling in seismic disgust at the state of the building's electrical system. Preparing to depart, evidently. There was a clink of metal on tile, which echoed louder in the dark than it would have if the lights were on, a miniaturized version of the sledgehammer and stamp at the conclusion of the old "Dragnet" TV show, then a faint *zzzzzzzzzip!*, and the toilet next door flushed. The door of that stall whumped and thudded open and closed, the door to the restroom itself did likewise — a tantalizing instant of gray light from the hallway — and then Webster was alone...

When he was a boy, Webster had had only one recurring dream that he knew of, one that he now recalled although he tried to hold the memory away from him:

Webster, alone. The basement of his parents' house. Nighttime; a single bare low-wattage light bulb glowing from the ceiling. Webster's attention riveted to the small window set up high on the basement wall, through which he can look across the mostly dark street. Galloping across the pavement now toward Webster, passing beneath the yellow light from the streetlamp, a legless apparition, black, the size and general shape of a large dog and *galloping* despite the leglessness, bucking like a hovercraft a foot or so off the ground. Galloping quickly quickly in his direction, yet tormentingly slowly too until *there it was*, hurling itself against the frame of the window of Webster's parents' basement, thumping, growling and snapping, black shiny teeth a-flash like sharpened licorice jellybeans. There for him, for Webster.

The Dark.

Unbidden, unwanted, irresistible: the memory of that dream returned to him now. Exposed — even in the dark — helpless as he was, he huddled over his bare thighs, clasped the newspaper like a blanket around them. He'd been sitting here for so long now that the backs of his thighs and his rump itself were sweating, and they felt clammy, damp to the touch, like the painted cinderblock walls of his parents' basement...

Sometimes when he'd be playing by himself down there in the basement, lost in a fantasy world in which all the plastic soldiers and jeeps were life-size and firing and dodging real bullets and rockets, the old oil furnace behind him would suddenly click on, and little Webster (remembering the dream, startled to find himself *alone, in the basement, what am I doing down here*) would nearly jump out of his skin. Now here in the dark restroom he was immobilized, adhesived in place by a horrible confluence of sticky haunches, ruined digestion, and lurid mental images of reptilian mandibles mere inches away from his convulsing skin, and now here in the restroom, overhead, the ventilation system suddenly whooshed into action. Webster barked out a sharp cry and leapt up, shedding newspaper pages like gingko leaves, scraping a thigh painfully on the wooden shelf and apparently ripping from the back of each thigh some four to six inches of epidermis, lurched forward, rammed his forehead against the coat hook on the inside of the stall door. Something wet dripped onto the back of one of his calves, sweat or worse, he didn't even want to think about it, lunging blindly for the chrome door latch that he knew had to be yes here it was, staggering with his pants and underwear around his ankles into the middle of the darkened restroom floor where he stood, gasping, hands spasmodically opening and closing into fists at his sides.

The door of the men's room swung open, silhouetting a figure there. A masculine voice, twanging with surprise and amusement: "Whoops, sorry!" The figure backed out and the door swung shut again.

Good God. Gotta get a grip here, Webster, I've gotta, have to, have to *get back into the stall, clean up, get out of the middle of the darned floor*— Staggering back now, hands outstretched like a Karloff parody, retracing his path, almost but not quite losing his footing on the sheaves of loose newsprint, back into the flapping mouth of the stall, *leave it unlatched but at least get inside anyhow,* standing shivering, eyes tearing a little, breath coming in great fishlike gulps, and vowing (on the memory of his platoons of dear departed toy plastic soldiers) never never never again, for the rest of his life, to let his wife talk him into so much as *thinking of* the phrase "frozen lasagna."

Slowly, still standing, he regained his wits. He opened and closed his fists one final time. He shut his eyes — shut out the dark — took a breath; counted to ten; released the breath. He faced the rear of the stall, bent at the waist, groped for and found the whatchamacallit, the flush-handle, flushed once, twice, and finally sat down again — hands placed in a mature, adult (albeit white-knuckled) fashion, squarely on his knees: awaiting the return of vision.

When that moment came, Webster had actually screwed up his courage to the point where he was considering re-latching the stall door. The lights came on, the vent fans shut down, and Webster (with a smirk of confidence) reached out and accomplished the latching without further incident.

He surveyed the wreckage. The thigh that had scraped the wooden shelf or armrest or whatever it was, that thigh had actually been *gashed*, on the shelf's corner he guessed, confirming that the stabbing pain in that leg was not a product of imagination. He dabbed at it with some toilet tissue. His forehead throbbed like crazy — at least the hook had missed his eye, something else he didn't even want to think about. Whatever it was he had felt, or thought he felt, on his calf was now gone, absorbed into sock or trousers.

Newspaper pages had gone every which-way, most of them still on the floor of his stall but some out into the middle of the restroom floor and a couple-three-four sheets into the neighboring stalls. Crouching, carefully ascertaining first that those stalls were indeed unoccupied, he stretched out his fingertips, pulled the pages in his direction, gathered them up into a semblance of order. He folded the mangled result carefully, and placed it on the shelf for the stall's next occupant. He stood, cleaned himself with toilet tissue, and flushed once and then again. He bent to raise his shorts and trousers, and saw on the floor a memo-sized leaflet of paper.

It had not been here, he was sure, when he first entered the stall (days, weeks, lifetimes ago). It must have been in that stall there, the one on his left where the guy with the banged-up wingtips had been sitting when the lights went out; it must have been dragged in here beneath the newspaper pages. He picked it up.

It was a note, unsigned, and the memo paper contained no other identifying information, not even a letterhead: no sender, no addressee. The message was handwritten, in a manic cursive script of thick blue felt-tip ink, words floridly capitalized, underscored and double-underscored apparently at random. At several spots in the text the writer — or the recipient? — had pushed a sharp object through the paper, carving out the hearts of o's, dotting i's with a literal vengeance, and on one corner was a smear of what might have been dried blood or fingernail polish or coffee or might have been just plain mud. The note said:

> Please I know you think "this" is right but *NO* "it" isn't. And "it" won't be not for a long time anyhow, you know how I feel but I can't let you do "it." I am so sick of the whole thing I want to scream but *I WON'T SO YOU WON'T* do it! Take a day if you want take two days

even three but keep LOOKING **OVER YOUR SHOULDER** I'm telling you.

§

It was not easy for Webster not to think about the note for the rest of the day — placed, as it was, in his shirt pocket, where it reminded him of itself every time he reached for his fountain pen.

He couldn't believe how many times he used the pen in the course of a single afternoon. Four, he might have estimated. A half-dozen. But jeez, the left side of his chest today was positively tingling from the constant abrasion. (He hoped he wasn't developing a blister there, but it almost felt that way.) And every time he used the pen, feeling the now-folded and -refolded note crinkle softly through the pocket fabric, he thought, *Oh yeah the note, no point, throw it away.*

When he entered the train station on the way home from work, he did come close to discarding it. Half-consciously, automatically, he was reaching up to be sure he hadn't left the pen on his desk at work — *wow, do I reassure myself like this* every *day?* — when he felt the note again and (he was now determined) for the last time. He was moving toward a trash receptacle, note in hand, when there was a sudden voice. Addressing *him*.

"Why thank you sir." A panhandler standing by the trash can, grimy weatherbeaten — *distressed* — fingers outstretched. Looking, and grinning, unmistakably at Webster. "Thank you very much, very kind and generous. Sir."

Webster halted, retracted the hand holding the note, wavered. "No, well, that is, you don't under— I mean..." *Phooey.* He stuffed the note back into the shirt pocket, grabbed a handful of change from his pants pocket, and flung the coins in the beggar's direction.

Although he had plenty of time, he then sprinted to the train, seated himself, panting, staring at his pale translucent reflection in the window. *What a con,* he thought, *great routine, just stand by the trash can and just nail people like that, suck the handouts right in.* The skin of his left breast itching, itching, itching.

2

It was to Webster's credit, he thought, that he did not keep touching the pocket at home that night.

Not that he forgot about it altogether, of course. In fact he could not seem to stop wondering about it at all:

Was it a relic of bitterly failed romance?

Did it have something to do with work? Was the "it" that the note kept referring to a business deal gone wrong, and/or discovered by a more moralistic colleague? Something illegal, a stock transaction?

Or, more fantastically, was it some kind of *political* note? A threat of terrorism? A clash of classes or societies, a vengeance vowed for the betrayal of some idea or its proponents? Should he turn it over to the authorities? Would he? *Could* he?

Its words crawled with possibility, which made Webster's skin itch all the more. Like having a roach take up residence in your clothing. It took all his willpower not to keep pulling it out of his pocket for re-reading, not to *reach* in that direction even, and most emphatically not to try throwing it away, for he was absolutely certain that when he tried to do so, *that* was when his wife would enter the room.

Not that there was anything inherently suspicious about the act of throwing away a piece of paper. But without much thinking about it, Webster knew that he would not be able simply to throw it away. He'd skulk. Listen for the closing of the bathroom door, which would tell him that his wife was momentarily out of commission. He'd break out in a cold sweat. Stand over the kitchen garbage can, looking over his shoulder, shredding the note... and his wife would come into the kitchen.

"What are you up to now?" she'd ask.

Webster would stand there helplessly, mouth moving without sound, fingers twitching, snowflurries of note paper drifting down onto his shoes. Six months later he'd be standing in a Federal courtroom in The City, shackled, as the D.A. and a team of expert torn-note re-assemblers moved relentlessly to link Webster, via the note, with a plot to bomb the Capitol.

"I found the note in the men's room at work," Webster would say in his own defense. "See, we'd had frozen lasagna for two nights in a row—"

Webster's wife would wail aloud from behind the prosecutor's table at that, and the jury — all women — would eye him with resentment at his transparent, and evidently quite ineffectual, attempt to implicate his wife.

No, this was stupid — Webster *himself* could throw it away in the bathroom! Flush it right down the toilet, flush it out of his life!

But the bathroom door was already shut when he got there. He didn't know how long his wife would be in there — if he was lucky and she was not, the cold fusion might be hitting her about now — but he had to risk it.

He raced to the kitchen, nearly running but trying to tiptoe at the same time, he did *not* want his wife to think that he was galloping (*galloping*...) through the house while she was indisposed, blundered into the wall of the doorway into the kitchen, staggered sideways but at least in the direction of the trash can, lifted the lid, reached into his shirt pocket, tore the note in half and then again—

"What in the *world* are you doing now?"

Darn it, no damn *it*. "Nothing. I'm not doing anything. I'm just throwing this, this piece of paper away. See?" Tearing it again, for emphasis. His wife eyeing him the way she did, not looking at the note at all.

"It looks like a note," she said.

Webster's eyelids twitched. How the heck could she tell *that*...? Clutching the scraps still, sort of twisting his head, neck, and shoulders around so he could look at it from her perspective. Yes, the handwriting, frantic bold and blue, plainly visible. *Darn it*.

"It *is* a note. But not, well, it's not a note to *me* or anything, I found it in work today—"

"You took a note that belongs to somebody else?"

"No, I mean yes, I'm trying to tell you, in the restroom today..." His voice trailing off, he couldn't get into the whole thing, *cold fusion holy cow no*, he couldn't even mention *that*, the guy's shoes, the lights—

"Somebody handed you a note in the *men's room*? I'm impressed, sweetie." She was grinning now, and Webster couldn't help it, he broke into a grin himself, blushing, it *was* ridiculous wasn't it, relief coursing through his face, what was he crazy or something, no problem at all, it was stupid really—

"Let me see it."

"Wha—? It's just a weird note is all." Fingers writhing tortuously with the note's dismembered remains, itching to just drop the scraps into the trash, not daring to.

"I know, I believe you, it's just a note you got in the men's room today, I just want to read it is all. If you hung onto it all day it must be pretty interesting, bring it here." Turning and patting the counter by the stove like a loveseat cushion, switching on the fluorescent light mounted on the underside of the cabinet. Patting the counter again. "Here."

Posture collapsed in defeat, Webster brought the scraps of paper to her, his fingers tingling with surprise at his betrayal.

"Hmm...," said his wife as she assembled the jagged quadrants back into a whole. "Get me the tape would you, thanks sweetie."

Webster looked down at the note over her shoulder. Reassembled, it looked like the Frankenstein monster. Unconscious but vaguely threatening. He could almost see its veins pulsing.

"Whoa, she's really unhinged isn't she?"

"'She'?"

"The woman who wrote the note. Girl, whatever."

"How do you know—"

His wife turned, looked over her shoulder at Webster's disconcerted visage. "Oh come on. No way could a guy write a note like this, this intense?" She waved the back of her hand at the note. "No way."

Webster looked down at it, tried to picture its author who, until this moment, had completely lacked identity, including gender. He was uncertain how to proceed with the conversation, he did not know what if anything lay behind his wife's curiosity, and if nothing at all was behind it except more curiosity he did not want to bring on anything more complicated by uttering a poorly thought-out remark.

"She, uh, she looks like she's pretty mad about something, doesn't she?" he finally said.

"Oh yes. Not just the way it looks but her words too. A little unstable if you ask me."

"Unstable?"

"Mm-hmm. A good person to keep at a distance, more than arm's length, kind of dangerous in fact. Look at these holes in the paper, looks like it's been stabbed."

"Yeah, the holes—"

"*You* didn't poke them in the paper, did you?"

"*Me?*"

"So then she did it herself."

It was almost a question. But if so then it was kind of a trick question, and Webster didn't think he should endeavor a reply. But maybe it wasn't a trick question but a rhetorical one. On the other hand, if he said nothing...

"Well," his wife said brightly, finally breaking the silence, "we've certainly got a little mystery on our hands, haven't we?" To Webster's horror, with a magnet she fastened the note to the refrigerator door.

"Maybe over the next few days," she said, "we can come up with some theories to help us solve the mystery, hmm, sweetie?"

3

That his wife might suspect there was something more to the note than the simple (albeit bizarre) truth — which, to be honest, Webster had never really explained — such a possibility was ludicrous. It was not ludicrous because Webster consciously bore any banners of fidelity, but because the prospect of *infidelity* had never occurred to him. He doubted that, given the opportunity and even given incentive, he could ever *decide* on such a course. He had a hard time deciding which lavatory stall to use if his usual one was occupied, for heaven's sake.

So he took his wife's "little mystery" remark at face value. He did, after all, want to know something more about the note — its writer, its audience, the circumstances surrounding its composition. None of it was any of his business; he just wanted, well, just wanted to *know*.

He started with the fat man from the stall next to his, the one with the horrible shoes. But The City was famous — notorious — for its excesses, and fat men abounded. There was no point looking for fat men. He had to look for the shoes.

So that was how he proceeded for the next couple of days, eyes trained on the ground, in the direction of the feet of his fellow escalator and train passengers, watching the feet of men sitting at other tables in the cafeteria, men walking into conference rooms, and — yes — men standing at urinals or sitting in lavatory stalls next to him.

He felt a little like a dog chasing a car. What would he even do if he caught it? Would he approach the wearer of the shoes, tell him, *I have the note you dropped in the bathroom the day the power went off?* Suppose he, Webster, finally saw what he thought were the right shoes, but their wearer was not fat but merely tall? Would a heavy man who was tall make neighboring toilets shift in the same way as a heavy man who was fat?

This was turning out to be a problem not merely of handwriting analysis or psychology but of probability and physics, subjects that in their casual certainty about the way the world worked had always made Webster squirm uncomfortably.

§

"You mean, like, a *pocket protector*, like?"

That was Franny, Webster's boss's secretary, a week after he'd found the note (and failed to lose it). He'd so far come up empty-handed in his quest for the owner of the hideous shoes, as he rather suspected he would, but he still had a related problem. A practical problem, really — how to minimize or maybe even eliminate the damnable chafing sensation beneath his shirt pocket, which had continued unabated although the note itself was long gone, still stuck to the refrigerator at home.

Oh, he'd tried shifting the pen to a different pocket. But he kept thinking he'd lost it somewhere; worse, when he finally remembered (*oh yeah right, it's in the right pants pocket*) and started reaching there for it, his *hip* began to feel rubbed raw. It was a simple practical problem, in short, which was driving him nuts, and Webster had brought the problem to Franny because she seemed to have an unerring instinct for simple practical solutions to simple practical problems. By no means had he anticipated this look of goggle-eyed bemusement on her face, and he reddened.

"No, well I mean yes, something like that only not—"

"Geeky."

"Yes. I guess. More..."

"More cool? Stylish, like?"

"Mmm. Not that, really, I mean not the way it looks, I don't care about that so much, just — well, comfortable. Cushioned."

Franny drummed with the eraser end of a wooden pencil on her desk blotter. Webster remembered reading, or thought he did, that Johnny Carson used to drum like this on his "Tonight Show" desk whenever he felt nervous about something. Webster wondered if Franny might be subconsciously yearning for a commercial interruption.

"Cushioned," Franny said finally. "A *cushioned* pocket protector, like..." She giggled. "A Dr. Scholl's pocket protector!" Laughing, thanking her, mortified, Webster backed away and fled to the corridor.

He left the building at noon, fearful that he might run into Franny or, even worse, that she might from a distance in the cafeteria point him out to her friends. (Giggling women gave Webster the willies.) Besides, he had remembered his friend Jack telling him this past Christmas of a leather-goods gift shop around the corner — just the sort of place, from what he remembered of Jack's description, that might carry something offbeat like a padded-leather pocket protector.

From a chilly April sky poured a torrent of rainwater, forcing Webster, *sans* umbrella or raincoat, to duck from awning to awning, door to door, his route a daisy-chain of plunging nervous parentheses, until arriving at the one he sought.

"Shirts'n'Skins," the place was called. In the murky storefront window were arrayed belts, gloves, Outback-style hats, rawhide vests, sportcoats and long-sleeved shirts whose sleeves and collars were reinforced with *faux*-alligator patches, eel-, doe-, and calfskin wallets, and an astounding assortment of doo-dads and gewgaws: letter-opener sheaths, pocket-comb holders, bookmarks weighted with shot, book covers, snap-on wriststraps and anklets, cigarette holders, golf club covers, refrigerator magnets, zip-up travel kits, bandannas and neckwear, cushions, headrests, pillows, and laser-cut antimacassars, money clips, bedroom slippers, camera straps — leather stamped, tooled, twisted, burned, and tied.

Wild. An entire branch of culture, apparently, that Webster hadn't even imagined existing—

Behind him, a car splashed to a stop in a pothole by the curb, showering passersby and eliciting from them a ferocious medley of shout and curse. One man ran out into the street to the driver's side and began beating on the roof of the offending vehicle, whose owner by way of response blew the horn and gestured in a half-dozen unpleasantly unrepentant ways. Another waterlogged victim joined the first, at curbside, and the car began to rock. A rusty battered pickup truck belly-flopped into another pothole, drenching not only the original combatants but a small crowd who had gathered to take sides and bets, triggering another wave of fury: now, good Lord, businessmen and nannies were joining in, walloping one another with umbrellas turned inside-out and sodden diaper and shopping bags, even ramming one another with strollers. Lest he be caught in the rapidly widening near-riot, Webster ducked through the doorway of Shirts'n'Skins and, breathing hard, carefully pulled the door shut behind him.

The lighting was dim, the air acrid and musty with the perfume of tanning chemicals and neat's-foot oil. From hidden speakers tootled classical trumpet music, muted, muffling the din of civilization in the street and faintly suggesting to Webster — by design, he supposed — the soundtracks of a hundred Western and Great-White-Hunter sagas.

No one else was in the store. No customers; no salespeople that he could see. Maybe they'd all repaired to upper stories in a panic, fleeing the tumult outside. Manning the battlements. Readying the kettles of boiling oil. Webster himself moved away from the front of the store and pretended to be absorbed in the contents of a display case some twenty feet back, well beyond the range of shattering glass.

The display case held sewing paraphernalia. Leather fingertip guards, bandoliers of sewing needles, pinking-shears holsters, some mysterious leather-handled gizmo used for installing zippers or maybe removing them. No pocket protectors.

From outside, a siren taunted *NYAHnyah, NYAHnyah*. Glancing nervously in the direction of the sidewalk and street, Webster moved further toward the rear of the store, his shoes and socks squishing uncomfortably. His shirt soggy, the skin of his left breast itching.

An elderly Asian woman, presumably a sales clerk, poked her head through a set of black curtains against the wall. She looked like the star of one of those old carnival booths, the ones where you pay to throw a pie or water balloon at a clown whose face protrudes from a bull's-eye. "Sir?" she said. "Sir?"

Webster looked over his shoulder. She didn't seem to be speaking to him, exactly, yet there was no one else in the store. He seized the moment, drew back his shoulders, intoned: "Yes. I'm looking for—"

At that moment the door of the store banged open, sending the old woman's head into rapid turtle-like withdrawal back into the folds of the drapes.

"*Jesus fucking Christ!*" bellowed a coarse, husky voice from the front of the store as the door crashed shut again.

Instinctively, Webster ducked behind a wooden pillar. He wanted to peek out, yet dreaded the thought of doing so. Given the temper of the mob outside, the man who possessed a voice like that, giving voice to sensibilities like that, would surely be homicidal and, given the temper of The City in general, almost certainly armed.

"Fucking *nuts* out there!" roared the voice again, and it was followed by what sounded to Webster like the sound of stamping feet and the *shickashickashick* of an umbrella being shaken out. "Yo! Anybody home?"

Webster saw the old woman's forehead venture forth, then an eye, then the other eye. "You," she said, addressing the unseen man at the front of the store. "Ah." She stepped out from behind the curtain and nodded. "You," she repeated.

Furtive, crouching a little, sneaking his fingers around the corner of the pillar for leverage, his spine curled like a tightening spring in order to increase his chances of ducking the expected hail of semi-automatic gunfire, Webster risked a glance. No one in— but wait, yes, there at the end of the counter: not a man after all but a *woman*. And not a big woman at that, but a diminutive five-feet-even, maybe, with—

"Who are you?" she roared, looking right at Webster. "James Fucking *Bond?*" And she threw her head back and laughed.

Now, contrary to expectations, Webster enjoyed a good laugh himself every now and then. But he always caught himself, stopped himself from, well, skittering over the edge into public spectacle. He'd suddenly remember the skein of celery irretrievably lodged between two upper teeth since dinner last night, or he'd suddenly lurch into hyper-awareness of the cup of scalding hot coffee on the table in front of him, and he'd sort of reach out with his breath and suck the laugh back in.

But this woman's deep, back-of-the-throat, open-mouthed laugh was nothing like that. Just like the stereotype, it said, literally, "Haha*HA!*", and although it stopped abruptly it somehow communicated *I have ceased laughing simply because I am done laughing, if I felt like it I could laugh non-stop for the next half-hour.*

"Come on out, I won't bite! Will I, Mrs. Lee?"

The old woman — Mrs. Lee — smiled tightly, humorlessly. "No," she said. "Her. No." She waved her hands, palms down, and shook her head. "No. Not bite, her." A virtual filibuster.

Webster emerged from behind the pillar. The woman customer had already turned her attention from Webster to Mrs. Lee, and Webster lurked by the display of sewing goods, eavesdropping.

Not that he was trying to eavesdrop, but it was hard not to overhear the "conversation," such as it was, between the two women:

"I've got a *prob*lem," said the woman with the deep voice. She hung her umbrella on the edge of the counter, and placed on the glass a cardboard box. "Those shoes I bought here, remember? For my friend?" (*Shoes.* Webster looked up cautiously from the display case; not wanting to appear to be reacting to something overheard, he caught himself, looked around at the unexplored corners of the store. Maybe back there off to the right, behind the hanger racks of leather clothing?)

"No no," Mrs. Lee was saying, and she was pointing firmly at a sign on the wall which said, *Shoes and Underwear Not Returnable.* "No." Shaking her head. A lot tougher than she looked.

So was the other woman: "Yeah, I see that one. What about *that* one?" Stabbing a finger in the direction of a sign next to the shoebox, by the cash register: *Satisfaction 100% Guaranteed.* "So where's the guarantee? Where's my fucking satisfaction? Eh, haha*HA*?" The big laugh again, tinted this time with a pastel shade of victory. She put her fists on her hips, swiveled to face a surprised Webster, caught in the act of insufficiently discreetly observing the little drama: "Eh, Mr. Bond? *Where's my fucking satisfaction?*"

Grinning like an idiot, Webster retreated a couple of paces until bumping into a rack of leather overcoats; the brass chains securing them from shoplifters tinkled and clanked. People like this woman, brash and confident to the point of cocky, simultaneously baffled and excited him. He slipped around behind the rack of overcoats to put some additional distance and physical barriers between her and himself, pretended to be looking at price tags, but continued to look at the woman out of the tops of his eyes.

Short, yes. *Petite*: that was the word. Thick dark hair. Not someone you'd encounter in an elevator and say to yourself (with a quick glance in her direction and an even quicker one away), *Model* — her nose a bit too long, her lips a bit too thin — but not unattractive either. Nice eyes. Hard to tell with the shapeless khaki raincoat she was wearing but looked like nice legs, too, accented by dark stockings with a seam up the back of each leg. His wife had a couple of pairs of stockings like that, pantyhose, whatever, but on his wife they looked kind of, well, awkward. Out of place, like nineteenth-century filigree on a Bauhaus skyscraper. Not on this woman though. And that laugh...

Now she was opening the shoebox, moving past the expository portion of her complaint and into the narrative, now parting the tissue paper, now pulling out the shoes, pulling out *oh my God the* shoes: hideous tan banged-up wingtips. Demonstrating for the pursed-lip Mrs. Lee the details of the imperfections that had not been built into the shoes: a sole that had come separated from the upper, a heel that swiveled from side to side like one of those ridiculous spy phones on "Get Smart."

Mrs. Lee was not convinced, was babbling monosyllabically in self-defense. "Your friend. Too big I tell him. But you. You say no. Say *this* shoe *this* shoe *this* shoe. I sell now you not want. No. No."

"Hey what is this Mrs. Lee? How long I been coming in here? How many people I sent to you? All you know, I sent James Bond here" — gesturing back at Webster, turning her head to look at him, winking — "haha*HA*, yeah, sent James Fucking *Bond* to your store Mrs. Lee, you're going to be famous, *famous* Mrs. Lee, James *Bond* shops here, and now what's this? Now you're going to jerk me around like this?" She flicked a finger at the sign by the cash register, knocking it onto its back. "*Some* fucking guarantee. *Some* fucking satisfaction."

Mrs. Lee stood there, her arms folded. Shaking her head. Picking up the toppled sign, ostentatiously brushing it off, shrugging, setting the sign back up by the register. "No. Sorry but no. Rule."

"Rule, huh." The woman grabbed her umbrella, whirled away from the counter (not failing to knock the sign over again, Webster noted), and before Webster realized what she was doing she crossed the ten yards or so which separated them and was *next to him*, hooking an arm through the crook of amazed Webster's elbow. "Come on, Mr. Bond. Let's go take our fucking business and get our fucking satisfaction someplace else."

Although still overcast it was no longer raining outside, and the automobile-pedestrian riot had calmed, or been quelled by the authorities. They were out the door, up the block — the woman on his elbow, tugging him along, laughing hoarsely the whole way — before Webster realized that the chafing of the skin of his left breast had ceased.

§

Now that they were out from under the olfactory shadow of Shirts'n'Skins — even out here on the still-wet, ozone-reeking street, pressed about by a thousand aromas of roving food vendors' wares, diesel fumes, the body odors and wastes of myriad homeless men and women, sundry anonymous grimes and dusts — out here, Webster became acutely aware that the woman on his arm was wearing, or in any event *radiating*, some striking perfume. She seemed encapsulated in it, as though in an aura, a skinless balloon the boundary of which you couldn't see but could somehow sense as soon as you crossed it.

It was not a perfume (if it *was* perfume) that put Webster in mind of any *flowers* exactly, and it wasn't one of those nouveau-musk scents that were all the rage now, transfiguring dowagers and pre-pubescent virgins into caricatures of a lusty imaginary norm. It didn't sting your nostrils with ersatz cinnamon, and it didn't fill them (and your head) with a trite, explosion-in-the-potpourri-mill cloud.

Rather it was a complex, subtle blend of scent, one tinged with, well, Webster couldn't be sure but he thought it was clover — clover? — yes, and *vanilla—*

The woman suddenly pulled Webster in the direction of a department-store window, out of the flood of sidewalk traffic; then she stopped in her tracks, which (since her wrist and hand were still hooked over Webster's arm) had the effect of swinging him around to face her, propelled by his momentum.

"Thanks for your help back there," she said, withdrawing her hand from his elbow. "Nothing gets to Mrs. Lee like the threat of losing business — probably thinks I'm out here organizing a boycott, eh, haha*ha*?" A far-off cousin of her laughter in the store, her voice still surprisingly deep but without the harsh gun-moll edge.

"Do you — did you — you, I mean, you left those shoes in the store."

"Yeah. Mrs. Lee won't touch them, afraid if she does she'll be legally bound to take them back."

"But don't you want your money?"

"Nope. See, they'll sit on the counter for a few days, drive her crazy, till she gets fed up and pushes them into a garbage pail with a stick. Next time I go in she'll be so relieved she'll practically *give* me a free briefcase, haha*ha*!"

Webster thought that he felt a certain kinship with Mrs. Lee. Out of his league here. If he—

"Anyhow," the woman went on, "as I said, thank you for your help. You have a good afternoon — ha! — Mr. Bond. Good luck on Her Majesty's Secret Service."

"I," Webster managed to get out. But she shook his hand and, grinning, strode off. Not wanting to look at her full in the face (such intimacy between strangers forbidden by The City's ground rules, at least as he understood them), Webster had been just then looking down towards her feet; he saw a flash of dark seam, surrounded by a blur of trouser legs and sneakers and loosely furled umbrellas, and she was gone. The bubble of perfume gone with her.

On his way back to the office, Webster sneaked by Shirts'n'Skins, peeked around the wall and through the window. Mrs. Lee stood behind the counter, staring down at the open box of shoes, the disheveled nest of tissue paper. Wringing her hands.

4

Over the course of the next several days, Webster thought from time to time of the woman in the leather-gifts store.

He thought, first, how odd it was that her personality had changed so subtly yet dramatically in the instant between the time they were standing in the store and then walking up the sidewalk. No "fucking this, fucking that." Not that Webster was a prude, and he understood that something about The City induced violence in nearly everybody, on a scale from the merely verbal and personal on up to full-bore planetary. But people were consistent, tended to... tended to *retain their violences* from one minute to the next.

And it was just plain stupid that he hadn't asked her about the shoes themselves. Was her friend — the one who had split the shoes open — was he the man who had been in the restroom stall next to Webster's? His wife's theory was that the note had been written by a woman; if that was right (which it probably was, his wife was seldom wrong about such things), was *that* woman *this* woman?

He thought he caught a whiff of clover-and-vanilla one morning in the elevator on the way up to his office, and he thought he smelled it one other time in the train on the way home, and although it wasn't possible of course he thought he smelled it one Saturday morning in his car, as he and his wife were pulling out of the garage to go to the supermarket.

(On this last occasion, wincing in anticipation — his wife had been in some kind of unvoiced snit for days now — he actually dared to ask, "What's that smell?" His wife half-turned in the passenger seat and regarded him with one eyebrow raised. "Smell?" she said. *Darn*, Webster thought, *hoped she'd be able to name it for me*. But he said only, "Yeah. Thought I smelled something." *Smelled what? Can't just leave it hanging like that, she'll think I mean* her... "I don't know, guess it was just some kind of flashback or something. I don't smell it now. Anymore, I mean." Shaking her head, his wife looked out the window and muttered something about his senses being too acute for his own good, or for hers.)

The note itself still hung on the refrigerator. Webster didn't know what to do about it, assuming of course that he *should* do something about it (which was not at all certain). For a few days he'd tried to cover it up, push it out of their — his — mind, by shifting shopping lists, newspaper clippings, the crayoned scrawls of his wife's nephew and nieces, yellowing cartoons, and other notes, gradually into place over *the* note, as though it were itself a magnet, drawing to it all the other contents of the refrigerator door, a relentless paper whirlpool. But it hadn't worked. His wife kept shifting the other stuff back.

In short, although the chafing beneath his shirt pocket had stopped, the whole series of incidents and sensations still rubbed at his mind. *Forget about it* (he'd think), *it's not important, get a life. But wait, no, what about...?* (he'd reconsider). The shoes, the perfume, the note, the woman's legs, the note, Mrs. Lee, the woman's thick hair, the note, the men's room, the shoes, the woman's eyes, her voice, her laugh, her legs: back and forth, chafing, ceaselessly chafing.

§

One Friday in early May, the cafeteria at work shut down.

It was one of those inexplicable intermittent upheavals of physical plant (like the power outage in the restroom) that were a part of work and, Webster assumed, life itself in The City. Who knew — ruptured pipes, or maybe asbestos insulation suddenly discovered in the walls; toxic gases hissing from rusted-out pinholes in the coiled tubes behind the industrial-size refrigerators; a vandal's failed attempt to break into the vending machines' change boxes; maybe a cafeteria worker had blown his or her brains out on the job, or the brains of a co-worker, or the brains of a boss, or the brains of everyone within firing distance. Those things just happened, and you learned to deal with them (while never failing to keep an eye on your co-workers).

Whatever the reason, the hand-lettered sign on the cafeteria door gave no clue. It said only: *Closed. Use Caferetiatiria on 14 Floor.*

Webster had never been on the building's fourteenth floor, which was over twenty floors down. Why direct people to such a faraway alternative? Maybe there wasn't a cafeteria on every floor of the building. Maybe the offices on some floors had their own built-in kitchens, obviating the need for a floor-wide lunchroom. Maybe the intervening floors — including their cafeterias — were all ghost towns, vacant and boarded up, tumbleweeds rolling up the aisles between dusty tables and chairs. Maybe the disgruntled cafeteria worker had gone on a twenty-story rampage before running out of ammunition on Floor 15.

Together with a gang of other noontime meal refugees, Webster boarded the elevator with his friend Jack. Jack was on a rant, which was common, about one or another unjust and proportionately immutable office policy. "I mean, I said to him, is this any way to run a business?"

Jack's sharp, nasal voice slapped at the walls of the elevator, and although Webster could not see them he assumed that the eyes of all other passengers (like Webster's own) were shifting uncomfortably in their sockets. Worried that their elevator might be bugged, that silence in the face of Jack's open rebelliousness connoted complicity in it.

By the time it arrived at the fourteenth floor, the elevator was jammed with sweaty, business-suited and -dressed flesh — a tin of potted meat. All of them, as it happened, en route to the cafeteria on the fourteenth floor; when the doors opened there was an enormous *whoosh* as clots of bodies calved off from the main mass and staggered out into the elevator lobby.

They moved in the tide up the hallway toward what Webster hoped would be a gymnasium-sized cafeteria. While ranting, Jack gripped the cuff of Webster's sleeve tightly between thumb and forefinger, an annoying invasive habit of his that Webster hated, but did not feel comfortable pointing out to his friend. (He preferred instead merely to *suggest* his discomfort, sliding his hand into his jacket pocket, shrugging, sort of shaking his arm, *hint hint hint*. To no avail. Jack's fingertips followed Webster's wrist, joined to him like a Siamese twin. And everyone, everyone was looking at them. Wondering which was the ventriloquist.)

"...I said to him," Jack said now, "I said, Ernie listen to me the *floor* is going to drop out from under you one of these days and what're you gonna do then Ernie? What are *we* gonna do?" He shook his head, clearly flabbergasted by Ernie's myopia. With his free hand he held the cafeteria's swinging door open for the twitching, shrugging Webster, who was so far failing to jar himself loose from Jack's Pincers of Death.

Shutting off his attention to Jack, who in any case did not need any more audience than he already had, Webster looked around at the foreign cafeteria. It *was* big, at least twice as big as the one on his and Jack's floor, the far corners shrouded in darkness or maybe just dimmed by the huge volume of air molecules between here and there.

Big though it was, nonetheless it was mobbed; maybe this really was the only available cafeteria in the entire building today. There were a handful of seats which seemed permanently empty — probably the ones in which someone had spilled coffee, or whose legs wobbled dangerously — and others always in the process of being vacated and almost instantly re-occupied, but never more than one or two empty at a table. Noise — an insane cascade of voices laughing and shouting to be heard, trays and dishes and glasses and flatware being dropped, knives and forks scraping plates and spoons going *clink clink clink clink* in coffee cups, salt shakers being knocked over, cans of soda dropping with throaty thuds in the vending machines, cash register drawers sliding open and banging shut, chairs scraping the floor, chairs being rattled into place beneath tables, chairs toppling over, trash cans booming like distant kettle drums... It was like nothing Webster had ever heard; the end of the world would sound like this. Jack rattled on.

Webster picked up a tray, got into line, shrugged, reached for a napkin-wrapped set of flatware. Oblivious, Jack's thumb and forefinger followed along, fastened like a blood-sucking insect to Webster's sleeve. Maybe he should just *pry* it loose, *hold a match to it like you do with ticks, dump ice water on it maybe, no that wouldn't be smart, Jesus no, Jack wears his watch on that side, he's crazy about his watch, obsesses about it, if it got wet Jack would—*

Smack!

The sound, unmistakable, of an open palm connecting suddenly with a face, and it came from behind Webster and to his left — some twenty feet past Jack's puppet-master form — and, except for Jack's armor-piercing voice ("...don't any of these people go to *college* anymore?"), all other sound within a large radius momentarily stopped.

Her.

Dark-seamed stockings going flash flash flash, she was already striding away from her evident target, an enormous young man — *my God, what is he, like six-two, six-three, two-fifty or two-seventy-five easy, she must've had to stand on tiptoe to slap him* — across whose mortified left cheek spidered an even deeper red blotch.

The man called after her, "Mary! Wait!" But he stood rooted to the spot, his glance nervous, darting one at a time to the faces of everyone nearby, all of whom were looking pointedly down at their shoes or up at the ceiling, inspecting their napkins as though winning lottery numbers or IRS regulations requiring all their attention were hidden in their scored and embossed surfaces. All except Jack, of course, who could see nothing but his re-enactment of sputtering disbelieving righteousness before the witless Ernie, and except Webster, with whose eyes the young man's eyes momentarily locked.

Hastily, Webster looked away, in the direction of the almost-gone Mary. *No. Wait. Can't let him see me looking at her, either, the thing to do here is not to look at anyone connected with the little melodrama; on the other hand,* did *he see me looking at her? but I can't look at him to find out...* Staring down not at his own but at the other man's shoes, some kind of mutant half-breed wingtip loafers today, but ai! what was wrong with him, was he crazy, *don't let this terminally-embarrassed gorilla catch you inspecting him at* all*!* Looking up in a panic instead at Jack's raving face, looking at his own wrist suspended in midair, gripped between Jack's fingertips, tugging his wrist a little, Jack still hanging on for a second, Webster now *yanking* the wrist free, slamming his tray down on the stainless-steel tray-slide or whatever it was called, and bolting out of line towards the door, which was still whispering back and forth (back and forth) from Mary's passing.

"...the bottom line, Ernie! The bottom *line*!" sang Jack's voice behind him, then Webster himself was through the door and into the hallway.

The woman — Mary — not in sight. Elevator door closing, but so was the door to the adjacent stairwell. *Too late for the elevator in any case, maybe the stairs...?*

Without stopping to think what in the world (as his wife might ask) he was up to now, Webster ran to the stairwell, threw open the door, was on the landing. The door swung shut behind him. Silence, but for a distant, faint (and growing fainter) tap, tap, tap, and also something else, some other sound, human, animal, *whimpering...*

He leaned over the railing. No one in sight, no tell-tale hand on a lower railing, what was he going to...?, and suddenly he was *calling her.*

"Mary?" His voice cracking. Recovering gracelessly, clearing his throat loudly. "Uh, excuse me, Mary?"

The tapping ceased; the whimpering did not, although it softened, was stifled maybe, embarrassed no doubt, Lord knew Webster himself would have been immobilized with embarrassment if he were in her shoes (*shoes*)—

Something feather-light touched him on the back of the head. He continued looking down the stairwell, trying to decide if he wanted, really wanted to repeat her name a third time, brushed at the back of his head, felt wet there just as a second drop splatted on the back of his hand. Looking up.

There. She was more than a floor, not quite two floors straight up above him. Looking down over the railing at him. Whimpering, no, weeping, a tear going plop onto the stair beside him, another onto his wrist, one onto his forehead.

They stood frozen like that for a long moment. She was gripping the handrail, pressing herself up against the brown-painted steel pipe in such a way that her abdomen pressed flat against the pipe and her black skirt flared over the pipe below the one she was holding onto, not that Webster was, you know, *looking* up her skirt but he couldn't help it really, he couldn't see anything except shadow but he could sure see shadow all right, and he could hear her still softly crying, and he could feel not only the plip plop of tears here and there but also the first incendiary flush of horrification that he was standing here *looking up the skirt of a crying woman—*

He was on the next landing up before he recovered himself. Somewhere down there in the fourteenth-floor cafeteria was Jack, perhaps having latched onto a fresh (more willing) sleeve, but he — and everyone else in that bedlam — still going about the business of the world. The real world. What world had Webster just entered? What was he doing here, on the way *up there?*

"So, Mr. Bond." That voice, deep, husky, totally out of place (like Webster), every other word or so punctuated with a catch of breath. "We, we meet, again." Having moved down the stairs in Webster's direction, she stood now on the landing above him, her arms crossed, hugging herself, her face streaked with water and makeup, blotchy-red. Staring down at him. Her thick hair, her eyes. Her knees trembling visibly, even from here, the hem of her black skirt jittery and a-twitch.

Petrified Webster unable to speak for a moment. Should he explain what he was doing here? (Which, in any case, was *what*?) Should he ask if she was all right? No, that would likely embarrass her, wouldn't it? be a tacit admission that yes, he had witnessed the scene in the cafeteria and therefore suspected that she might be *not* all right? Yet wasn't her very demeanor at the moment evidence of, of, of not-all-rightness...?

The woman — Mary — herself hesitated at first, then with each unspoken question of Webster's seemed to glide soundlessly in his direction, a step at a time. She was still four steps above him when her envelope of clover and vanilla parted, enfolded him again, and the pace of the questions accelerated, mutated into a blurry staccato machine-gun spray of question marks and ellipses, no clear words or meaning, just a telegraphed *question question question question dot dot dot.*

She was on the landing beside him now, again hooking her hand loosely through the crook of his elbow. "Let's, go, go Mr., Bond." The deep voice still catching. "Cafe, cafeteria food, suh, *sucks* anyhow."

§

Down she led him, trip-trap down the whole twenty-eight zigzags of stairs, whimpering-muttering almost without interruption (the word "fuck" and its variants popping quietly here and there, like small-arms gunshots heard through a jungle), pausing only twice — once apparently to catch her breath, swaying backwards with a soft thud against the wall of the landing (forgetting himself, Webster about to ask if she was all right but she leaned her head back a bit to look up at him, raised an erect index finger to her lips and placed the palm of the other hand flat against his chest: *shush*, the gesture said, and *wait*, Webster blushing furiously looking first at her forehead then the crown of her head then simply the blank wall behind her and over her shoulder), and the other time at the ground-floor landing, donning a pair of violet-lensed sunglasses after a brief rummage through her shoulder bag.

But they didn't leave the stairwell there. Mary — now holding him loosely by the hand — did lead him at first towards the exit door. Then she hesitated, seemed to change her mind, and reversed direction, taking them both plunging down another flight of stairs.

"Where are we—"

"Where? What else — wait, don't tell me you've never been down here before? The mall?" She sounded stunned, her deep voice acquiring a sudden whispery breathless edge, but she didn't pause in her forward and downward motion. "Man, you're gonna *love* this, wait till you see it..." The catch in her breath gone, confidence definitely resuming or fully resumed, her hand gripping Webster's now more firmly, insistently. Urgently.

Webster's head was swimming. He had spoken scarcely at all in the several minutes since they'd left the fourteenth floor — in fact uttered no real words until just now, when he hadn't even finished the sentence;

instead, he had merely grunted and *hmm*ed in a way that he meant to imply sympathy but that probably, it now occurred to him, came across as acquiescence. Acquiescence in what, he wasn't sure. The woman flustered him, confused his defenses (normally nearly foolproof, multi-layered, with secondary, tertiary, and quaternary lines of psychological fretwork weaving in and out and through themselves and one another) so that he didn't know if they were registering merely a blizzard of foil scraps or the blips of a real (albeit shapeless) incoming danger. They were going to a mall, she said, but for God's sake Webster *hated* malls, on the other hand he had no idea what a mall in The City would be like, and yet *yikes holy cow, not at all sure I want to find out, what am I doing letting myself be led—*

"...Well, fuck it, right? Haha*HA!*" she said now, concluding her self-absorbed monologue, and with her free hand yanked open the door to Floor Whatever-It-Was. Floor B-for-Basement; Floor Minus-One.

It was like no other mall that Webster had ever been dragged to. The lighting down here was dim — situated, as this mall was, beneath over eight hundred feet of concrete and steel, there was no chance of its receiving any light from the sky, indeed "sky" seemed like an abstraction down here, a bizarre family legend. And unlike in, say, a subway station, the absence of light here seemed willful, not threatening at all. Intended. *Preferred*. What lighting there was, was plain old incandescent.

The walls and storefronts exhibited little of the metallic glitz and razzle-dazzle of a typical mall: many of the walls were actually paneled, in a dark lustrous wood, and all the windows made of some kind of non-reflective matte-surface glass. No chain stores or fast-food restaurants as far as Webster could see, although it was hard to tell for sure because there were no lighted names over the doorways — just simple bronze-like lettering mounted on the walls. It reminded him of one of those old-fashioned private clubs where gentlemen puffed on cigars and drank brandy from snifters served by butlers, not that Webster had ever been inside such a place of course but it was obvious what they must be like inside, just from the one or two or dozen once-overs of their exteriors that he'd given them out of the corner of his eye while pretending to wait for the sign to grant him permission to WALK.

And the weirdest thing was, he saw almost no people at all down here, a fact which Webster pointed out to Mary.

"You kidding me?" she said. "Better — eh, haha*ha*! — better strap on your infrared goggles, Mr. Bond, people *everywhere* down here!"

She gestured broadly with an arm and hand, and now, you know she was right, if he squinted and looked sideways, now he could see them (though how Mary could was a mystery, what with the purple glasses she was still wearing — maybe they weren't sunglasses after all, but, yes, infrared goggles): people alone for the most part, some walking in twos, sitting on a bench here and there in a shadowy corner, passing from the dim light of the central corridor into the dimmer light of the stores. Well-dressed adults all. No crowds. No panhandlers; no mothers or fathers with strollers or chest-borne baby sacks and their writhing contents; no adolescents rollerblading about in unending clamorous hormonal eruption. No *police*.

"Er, is it safe down here?" said Webster, ever mindful of The City's ability to summon screaming horrors from tableaux of luxury and peace.

"Safe? You bet! Only way down here is from the building upstairs and you know what security's like *there*."

This did not strike Webster as a convincing argument, though it was one that he heard before. (Two years ago a bomb had exploded in the seventh-floor office of the trade representative of a Central European republic that had, in preceding months, laid preposterous claim to some one or another portion of the territory actually held by each of its half-dozen neighbors. Everyone welcomed the increased security measures since the bombing — everyone but Webster, who detected in the rugged face of each new guard the lurching erratic crow's-feet of foreign anarchy.)

Nevertheless it did seem quiet down here, amazingly free of trouble. And with the strolling faceless pedestrians, the shop windows that reflected almost nothing of the person standing before them, it seemed not only pacific but *paced*, its rhythm unhurried, unroiled by complication.

Mary was still tugging him along.

"Are we, that is, you, we, you and I, are we going someplace special? Where are you—"

"Ha*ha*! Where am I taking you? To my lair!" She stopped, reached up with both hands, pulled the side of Webster's head close to her mouth. "My fucking *lair*, Mr. Bond!" she whispered. Webster, his mind and sensibilities fogged with clover and vanilla and profound embarrassment, let himself follow.

Her lair was this: this bogus ruined-classical marble restaurant called "Pan's." Something about the apostrophe didn't seem right to Webster; surely supposed to be a plural — a place that served quiches and crepes, a theme park tourist trap kind of place where the waitresses would dress like surreal Heidis and yodel the specialité du jour to you.

But it wasn't. The restaurant was actually presided over by a slender auburn-haired woman named Pan — at least that's what Mary called her, short for "Pandora" she said — who led them through a warren of ever-smaller ever-dimmer dining rooms (the big airy one in front reserved for the hoi polloi, Webster supposed, should any of them by mistake ever find their way here) all the way to one that had to be the uttermost in the restaurant. Surely there could not be one smaller — space here for only four tables, one of which was occupied by another couple who stood to leave the moment that Webster and Mary sat down (she on the banquette against the wall, Webster in the wooden armchair across from her) — nor one more poorly lit: from the teeny flickering flashlight-sized light bulb in the green-shaded table lamp, Webster could barely make out the entries in the menu.

These tables were weird, too. There was something *insufficient* about them. True, they were wider than the normal restaurant table in The City, where everything was cramped for space, but they were also of inordinately shallow breadth, or depth, or whatever the Webster-to-Mary dimension was called. Like leaning on a railing: when he leaned across the table to hear her (for her voice had dropped a notch or two), her face was mere inches from Webster's own. One of his knees brushed one of hers, and he jumped as though pinched. Or electrocuted.

"Well you know, Mr. Bond, I am curious," she said, and removed her sunglasses at last. She was smiling; her teeth were small and even. "How did you know my name? Back up there on the stairs, I mean?"

He didn't know how to respond. If he told her the truth — that he had heard the slapped man call her name — surely it risked embarrassing her, befouling her mood, which now seemed strangely upbeat. She might even start to cry again, and Webster did not want that — not under the watchful eye of the smiling Pan, who sometimes drifted away and sometimes hovered in the archway, just out of earshot.

(It was like being waited on by an untethered helium balloon.) Yet what else could he tell her? Could he lie maybe — tell her that it had come out on their earlier, brief encounter in and outside Shirts'n'Skins? Or how about that he had returned to the store, asked the old Asian woman for her name? No, that would be worse, then he'd have to make up some explanation for why he was curious... But he could hardly say nothing, hardly let her answer the question herself, hardly let her for example think that he'd been, well, *investigating* her or something...

"I'm teasing," she said finally. She sipped at her glass of red wine and licked the rim ("Umm, I just love Beaujolais"), licked her thin lips, and leaned forward, smiling. "I know how you know. You were in the cafeteria, weren't you?"

Webster nodded mutely, sipped at his own wine. He wasn't even sure what kind it was, didn't even remember ordering any. Not Beaujolais. It was pale, pink, pleasantly tart. A *blush* wine.

Mary leaned forward further; a wave of clover and vanilla suffused Webster's head, his soul. "Well," she murmured, "let's just *forget that fucking asshole.*"

She leaned back again, still smiling that incomprehensibly precise smile, and her knee simultaneously slid forward and rested against Webster's. Not pinning it in place, exactly, but on the other side of his knee was the pedestal to which the tabletop was bolted, and he couldn't think how to extricate himself without jostling the little table or being, well, rude. *Is "rude" the word? No: "aloof."* That was more like it. He didn't want to be *aloof*; he'd, he'd run after her in the first place because he felt sorry for her, wanted to see if he could help somehow, but aloofness would hurt and not help her... Yet he didn't really want the knee there, either, yet on the other hand he didn't really want it elsewhere... He cleared his throat and, with as much casualness as he could muster, clinked his wedding band against his water glass.

"My name—"

Mary didn't ignore the clink of the ring — she glanced down at Webster's hand — but she merely interrupted, "No. Shhh. 'Mr. Bond' is good enough for me. For now." She smirked. "If it's good enough for you. You don't know my last name, do you? And I don't know your first. Mr. Bond."

Webster couldn't help smiling a little himself. The spy had never been a hero that Webster could connect with on any level, but he found himself liking the sound of Bond's name attached to his, Webster's, persona. The fiction of it. The *anonymity*.

"Can I ask you—"

"I know. You want to know why I slapped him, don't you?"

"Er, no. That is, *yes*, I mean if you want to talk about it, that's, well, that's okay with me, but no. I wanted to ask you about, about the way, I mean, the way you talk."

"The way I *talk*?" She threw back her head and laughed. Her laughter this time was not sharp and full-throated but musical. Alto, Webster thought: something out of keeping with the huskiness of her speaking voice. "...Oh, Mr. *Bond* — the way I talk...!" One hand clapped histrionically against her forehead as she laughed again, closed her eyes, leaned back against the banquette. She was wearing a creamy silk-type blouse, shirt, whatever, with a flat collar that must have been open a good six inches or so. Blushing, grinning like an idiot, Webster stared at the V where the two sides of the collar intersected.

Mary recovered herself. "What do you mean, how I talk? My voice you mean?"

"Er, well, no, I mean I like your voice, it's a very, umm, very unusual voice, striking actually, I just wondered..." How could he say this? "I mean, at the leather store you kept saying..."

"'Fuck,' you mean? Fucking this, fucking that? What the fuck?" She leaned back in his direction, put her forearms on the narrow table; Webster's hands scurried away, leapt off the cliff into his lap, straightened and re-straightened his napkin. He was still grinning, still blushing, afraid to look up at her but afraid that if he didn't, he might look elsewhere. Might see Pan in the archway, laughing herself. Might see over the cliff at the far edge of the table, into the V. "Great word, 'fuck,' isn't it? Crisp! Delicious!" Her voice snapped like a stalk of celery, then dropped to a deep conspiratorial whisper, her tiny incisors gripping her lower lip, her breath hissing. "*Fffffuuuuu, ck.*" The final consonant a discrete syllable, a clicking thimbleful of significance. "Now you say it."

Webster closed his eyes. Still grinning, red-faced. "*Fuhhhh*," he said, his voice uncharacteristically basso profundo, "*ck.*" Mary giggled, *he* giggled, and a snort of wine shot up into his nasal passages so that he was suddenly coughing as well, both of them giggling, cackling maniacally, when Pan bobbed to their tableside with the salad.

5

Looking back on the lunch during the train ride and half-hour drive home that night, Webster reassured himself, repeatedly, that above all he was glad to have — well, to have distracted Mary, yes that was it; he had turned her day around. Buoyed her. It had been a rather long lunch, but not so long that his co-workers would be alarmed (or check the restrooms for him). Just a couple of glasses of wine, a salad, a burger.

"Adieu, Mr. Bond," Mary had said when she got off the elevator at the seventeenth floor, and added, turning to face him as the door slid shut, "F*ffffff*," just like that, without finishing it; Webster had giggled softly to himself for the remainder of the elevator ride (mercifully shared with no other passengers) to his own floor.

He thought of Mary a couple of times as the afternoon proceeded in its leisurely course to quitting time: thought of her small form moving along the corridors, into and out of offices and conference rooms somewhere far below him, like a car viewed from an airplane; thought of her tears dropping down onto the back of his head in the stairwell; caught himself once — and been overwhelmed with a powerful inexplicable yearning that burned like a bubble of wine at the back of his throat — remembering the pasture behind his grandparents' house in which he'd sometimes lain on his back as a boy, gloriously hidden from view from the house, looking up at the sky, and then he remembered that the crop which had grown there was tall clover. On his way out of the building at the end of the day, the elevator had not stopped at floor seventeen.

But it was no big deal, nothing happened, he said to himself yet again as he turned his car up the street of the development where he and his wife lived. *It was just a lunch. Nothing happened.*

His wife's car was not in the driveway when he pulled in, which was unusual but not cause for alarm. Probably went out to the store for something to eat. Or caught up in the nightmarish commute from her own office, which was in the opposite direction from The City in one of those enormous office-and-research parks that had arisen from former farmland once planted with feed crops, such as clover.

Neither was the case, though. There was a message from his wife on their answering machine:

"Hi sweetie. Awful sorry I'm not home but Mom had a little accident today, nothing serious I don't think, just fell down the front steps and cracked a bone in her hip. I'm at her place now, think I'll stay with her for a few days until she can get up and move around on her own. Give a call if you want. Love you and by the way there's some lasagna in the freezer if you're hungry."

He flipped through the day's mail, which included a slick advertising-and-coupon circular for a pizza chain which he and his wife never patronized because they lived outside the area covered by the chain's delivery guarantee (although well within the area blanketed, as if with grated cheese, by their thrice-weekly junk mail). Folding the pizza ad, refolding it, Webster went to the trash can but then thought better of it. You never knew — maybe he and his wife would be in town one of these days, they could use the coupons then. He unfolded the ad, smoothed it out on the counter, and hung it on the refrigerator door over the note.

Then he took the lasagna from the freezer and zapped it — still didn't have the hang of this new microwave, the tomato sauce in the lasagna's interior still a giblet of chilly red mush — and ate while he read every word of a gift catalog whose copywriters were evidently paid on a scale proportionate to their use of the word "whimsy." Afterwards, he almost did call his wife, but then thought better of that, too, fearing that his mother-in-law would answer the phone. The woman (whose voice on the phone clanged like an avalanche of pots and pans) — with this hip thing, she almost certainly would be overflowing with even more bitterness than usual, and eager to pour all that of it into the ear of her least favorite (her only) son-in-law.

No, he'd call from work tomorrow, when he could beg off talking — or listening — to his mother-in-law on the pretext that the call was on his employer's dime. "Please put your daughter on the phone," he imagined himself saying, his voice firm, although realistically he expected that his wife would have to pry the receiver from her mother's claw long before he managed to get past the first "Uh."

Instead, for two hours he watched situation comedies for the ridiculous plights of whose unfamiliar characters he could not bring himself to feel sympathy, let alone amusement. Then, yawning, a curious hollowness of purpose and a shapelessness of mind billowing within him, he went to the bedroom to press off a shirt for work the next day.

He was tired of white shirts. Well, not tired of them exactly, white shirts were the staple of his work attire; tiring of white shirts would be like tiring of drinking water or something. Maybe one of the pale blue Oxfords, or the pale yellows. Beige? No. He was tired of monochrome, that was it. He had a shirt somewhere here in the closet, he thought, a shirt which was white but with these royal-blue stripes, bolder. Zippier. Somewhere in here...

While hunting the elusive blue-and-white shirt, he came to a length of the closet rod where his wife had obviously taken to hanging clothes of hers that she no longer liked, or that she still liked but were no longer in fashion, or that did not fit her any longer, or that had once no longer fit her but that she had grown back into and simply forgotten she owned. There he found a knit ivory-colored dress that for a time had been her very favorite item of clothing. He removed the dress from the closet, still on its hanger, and sat down heavily on the foot of the bed, the dress draped transversely across his legs.

He remembered the first time his wife had worn this dress, on a date eight or nine years ago — before she was his wife. Some movie they'd driven into The City to see, something high-toned, with sub-titles and an operatic score.

He remembered putting his arm across the back of her seat. He remembered fiddling with this lace-type stuff around her neck and shoulders, this — what was it called? "open weave" maybe? this four- or five-inch-wide band of, well, it was like macramé netting almost. He remembered pushing the tip of a forefinger through one hole, remembered pushing the tip of a middle finger through another hole, remembered pushing a little finger through a hole and remembered finally the agony of pulling the little finger back out through the hole and snagging a partially-torn nail in the material, tearing it, the nail, fully in half. Remembered his not quite strangled yelp that had nearly gotten them evicted from the theater.

But most of all he remembered the sensation of his wife-to-be's skin beneath his fingertips. Each finger, gripped by its little circlet of thread or yarn or jute or whatever this stuff was, had been numbed ever so slightly, just enough to hypersensitize the tip of the finger itself. His wife's skin had twitched almost imperceptibly when he touched it, probably involuntarily, and looking back on it — experimenting with it now, with his own hand on the other side of the fabric — he remembered how uncannily smooth her skin had felt to his tingling fingertips then, and how uncannily warm.

Where had his wife's shoulder gone in the years since then? Had it really ceased to be so smooth and so warm, or for that matter so uncanny? When *was* the last time she had worn this dress, and had he been present with her on that occasion? Had he poked a finger through one of these holes then? Where had his wife gone since then, where was his wife now — not in specific (his mind lunging away from thought of his mother-in-law), but, well, where was his wife *with him*, with Webster?

He stood up, hung the dress back in the closet. He didn't think he'd iron a shirt tonight after all; in fact he just kind of wanted to go to sleep.

Webster dreamt that night a dream that he would not remember in the morning, a dream sufficiently disquieting to bestir him out of its narrative context although not to full consciousness. He remembered only that it had had something to do with his recurring childhood dream of The Dark but different somehow too, something to do with a legless apparition, or disembodied legs. Something like that anyway. And his feet were freezing when he woke up, as though his own legs had been tourniqueted or, yes, cut off; for mid-May, last night had been awfully cold.

6

A day went by, another day, a week. Webster's wife returned from her mother's, was *happy* to be home and with him again, they went out to eat and fell asleep naked in each other's arms — their panting becoming measured, eliding into slumber — for three nights in a row. The cafeteria on his own floor at work was returned to service. Webster did not see Mary at all, and had nearly stopped anticipating the dinging of the elevator between floors sixteen and eighteen, had nearly erased from his mind the urge to press the B1 button every time he left the building.

On the tenth day, as Webster returned to the office from an uncharacteristically carefree lunch — a hot dog in the park — he met, coming *out* of the building, an emergency-response team bearing on a stretcher the grotesquely fractured corpse of an enormous man. The sheet over the body failed to cover one of the man's shoes, an olive-green blucher.

"Yeah yeah, I heard," said Jack when Webster told him about it, upstairs in the office. "Fell down the stairs I heard. Janitor heard a shout, ran into the stairway, guy was, like, *folded* over the railing on the twelfth floor, backwards if you can believe it. Or sideways, something freaky anyhow. Had to fall three, four, five stories to bend him up like that, like *wham wham wham* on every railing all the way down. I'll tell ya they don't give a *fart* for employee safety in this building, that's what I was telling Ernie the other day but you know Ernie, Ernie the big-shot chairman of the big-shot employee satisfaction committee, Ernie the dope, looks at me through those Coke-bottle glasses and starts talking about OSHA, 'That's what OSHA's for' he says to me..."

Gently, Webster disengaged the sleeve of his jacket from Jack's fingertips. For an awkward moment, they seemed to be about to latch onto Webster's own fingers, but with an evasive flutter of digits he managed to escape to his office. He closed the door there, and fell — *wham wham wham* — into an hour of sweaty paralysis.

Had — had *Mary* had anything to do with the man's death? No. It was inconceivable. Wasn't it? The choreography was impossible. How could someone her size have pushed someone of that man's size, pushed him sufficiently hard that he'd fallen over a railing, tumbled down the center of the stairwell, unable to help himself or for that matter unable to take her with him? Yet could the man have fallen himself, or jumped? Such decisive derangement was beyond the scope of even Webster's imagination.

Surely someone would report to the authorities the slapping scene in the cafeteria. Surely they would question Mary, who even if she had nothing at all to do with the man's death would surely remain a prime suspect. Wouldn't she? And then wouldn't her name, her picture show up in the newspaper? Wouldn't Pan, the restaurant owner, recall that a man of Webster's description had had lunch with Mary on a day that the police would trace back to learn was the same day as the cafeteria incident? "Yes," he imagined Pan saying in a voice like Catherine Deneuve's, "yes, *oui*, they had lunch. They laughed. They said the word, how you say, they said that word 'fuck' a lot, no?" Jack would let slip that Webster had simply turned his back and run away from him, had completely ignored the fact that he, Jack, was in mid-paragraph. Their net widening, the police would eventually interrogate Mrs. Lee, of Shirts'n'Skins, who would happily turn over the box of hideous distressed-leather wingtips to be used as Exhibit A. From the witness stand, prompted by the D.A., Mrs. Lee would point first at Mary and then at Webster, and pursing her lips would say, simply, "Them." The crowd in the courtroom would gasp.

No. This is insane. None of that's going to happen, or at least little of it, or at least to such a, haha, ludicrous extreme, and it's not going to happen because... well, because that kind of stuff never happens. Indeed, that kind of stuff had not happened — ever — to anyone at all that he knew, and he was certain of this because he laboriously dredged up from memory, one at a time, the names of everyone that he could think of, everyone that he knew. *No. Never.*

Nonetheless, he slipped out of his office and shut the door behind him to make busybody passersby think he was still inside (panicking for an instant: had he locked it, locked his office key in the office? but whew, no, the doorknob still turned freely), virtually tiptoeing out to the hallway and then to the door to the stairs. He stood on the landing, and then he began to pace back and forth along its short length.

Somewhere down there, Franny had told him when he got back from lunch, the police had stretched yellow plastic ribbon across the railings, blocking off access for ten floors. Somewhere down there a battalion of detectives were going over every step and every landing with... with handheld vacuum cleaners, what were they called: *Dustbusters*, Webster assumed. Dustbusters, yes, and special evidence-gathering cellophane tape. He leaned back against the wall, lifted one foot at a time and carefully inspected the soles of his shoes. Nondescript. Scuffed. Not rippled, not stamped with the manufacturer's distinctive logo. The soles of shoes worn by, oh, probably five hundred or a thousand men in this building. He ran his fingers through his hair, held up to the light the one hair that came loose, examined it meticulously for striking imperfections but couldn't see anything. This was stupid. He put the hair in his jacket pocket.

Then he went at last to the short length of railing that turned to follow the landing before doubling back and down on itself. He gripped the railing and looked down.

It was hard to say for certain, but yes, he believed he could see movement far below him. Specks. Specks of sound, for that matter, faint vocalizations and scratchings and once a deep deep hollow *klonnng* that thrummed up to his ears a moment before he felt it in the palms of his hands, through the pipe. That must have been the sound that the man made, not *wham wham wham* as Jack had said but *klong klong klong*.

Webster's grip tightened on the pipe, and tightly he shut his eyes. *Klong klong klong.* What had the man thought as he fell? What happened in the brain, flooded with adrenaline, in such an extreme circumstance? He felt a droplet of sweat trickle down his forehead, and he realized, too late, that it was *slipping off the end of his nose*, opened his eyes and grabbed for it too late, imagining that somewhere down there was a hard-nosed profane-speaking detective who would suddenly sense Webster's paranoia rattling *dinkadinkadinka* down the stairwell like a pachinko ball, see this drop of perspiration going plop onto a nearby stair and look up *just in time to see wide-eyed Webster—*

Good Lord; he had to get out of here. Yet he couldn't burst out the stairwell door, his co-workers would think he'd come unglued; yet he couldn't run down to the next floor, closer to the police. *Up.* He had to go up — bursting forth, yes, but at least bursting forth among strangers.

But when he did burst forth onto the floor above his own, he did so not in the presence of strangers, but in the presence of Mary — who was reaching for the stairwell door handle from the other side, who grimaced and whispered to herself, "*Shit*," before seeing that it was Webster who had banged her now-flailing hand. Her face lit up. "Mr. Bond!" she said. "My hero! Come to save me again, eh haha*ha*!"

Horrified — *what's she doing on* this *floor, what's she doing speaking to* me, *smiling at me, doesn't she realize that under no circumstances must I be seen with her, what's she doing advancing, holy cow, this way!* — Webster took a step backward through the stairwell door. Mary followed. Another step back, his hands weirdly aflutter, *begone begone begone,* Mary still moving toward him, seeming almost to grow, *uh-oh uh-oh don't want to be here on a stairway landing with her no sir not after what happened to her friend her ex-friend her late friend earlier today*, Webster chanting a litany of false conversational openers:

"Well, or rather, no, yes I mean, here yes, but not to, what are you, er, that is, doing here, your floor, seventeen right? wasn't that, but this is—"

Grinning now, still moving toward him, her tiny white teeth like a mouthful of white sweet peppermint candies, "Oh that," she said, "that wasn't my floor, a friend of mine works there, worked there, *worked* there oh Mr. *Bond*...!" Her expression changing yet again, Webster thinking idiotically of a time-lapse movie of desert clouds, her face suddenly twisted in grief or fear or something unrecognizable but powerful, "Oh Mr. *Bond*," she repeated, and suddenly lunged no *collapsed* forward against him, sending Webster staggering back against the wall.

The stairway, or that part of it surrounding Webster's head, was ripe with the aroma of vanilla and clover; he felt about to swoon himself. His hands hooked beneath the limp and apparently unconscious Mary's armpits — his hands didn't feel, well, exactly decent there, the dual concavity of her armpits suggesting to Webster the convexity of her breasts, inches away, yet he couldn't well he couldn't just *drop* her, she'd slither to the floor, that would be when the SWAT team charged down from the roof, Mary and he slumped together wallowing together in guilt and shame and vanilla and clover... Lurching, he dragged Mary to the flight of stairs leading up, and carefully laid her with her feet on the landing and her head a few steps up.

Something not right about that, he thought; her head was higher than her feet, weren't you supposed to arrange somebody who fainted so the blood would go *to* their head...? He was attempting to accomplish this — one arm wrapped around her back, one arm wrapped around her legs at the knees (*yipe, look at that, some kind of little appliquéd black lace doodads in the stockings today*), grunting, almost got it, careful don't drop her — when Mary's eyes opened.

At once, a smirk stole across her face; she licked from the corner of her mouth a thin trickle of saliva and said, "Well well, and hasn't Her Majesty's Secret Service taught you never to take advantage of a lady?" But she didn't move to correct her now roughly northeast-to-southwest upside-down sprawl across Webster's lap, just lay there. Grinning.

Realizing that his right hand was still gripping her by the back of one leg, Webster blushed furiously, tried to turn her back upright again, succeeded only in bringing her to a sitting position, still in his lap. "You, uh, you fainted," he said needlessly, blushed again, why wouldn't the woman help him for God's sake, tugged at her, the friction of his trouser legs and her black skirt hiking the latter up a sudden six inches, Webster lunging to grab that and pull it back into more seemly position but, gulp, *uh-oh, not pantyhose there after all but a* garter belt, the flash of a black-outlined polygon of pale flesh a mere millimeter away from his tingling fingertips and his hand now flying away as though magnetically repulsed—

Again the impression of boiling clouds: Mary's expression changed once more. Sobered. She sat up, hoisted herself slithering (slithering) from Webster's lap, onto the step beside him, and combed a handful of fingers through her thick hair.

"I think I need to get away for a few days. Can you give me a lift out of the city?"

Webster's mind racing. "I, but I don't, I mean I take the train."

"Fine. I'll take the train with you. Can you give me a lift from the train station wherever you get off? Drop me off, oh fuck I don't know, drop me off at a motel, a mall, somewhere."

It wasn't possible. *No. No way.* Whatever she, this Mary person, whatever she was or wasn't up to or whatever kind of trouble she might or might not be in, *it had nothing to do with Webster.* He hardly even knew her, correction, didn't even know her at all. Not really. And even if he did know her — well, *sort of* know her — well enough to feel sorry for her, well, *sort of* sorry for her, what could he do about it? Without embroiling himself in whatever-it-was? They couldn't be seen getting on the train together. They couldn't be seen getting *off* the train together, and *ai!* could darned sure not be seen getting into Webster's immaculately-maintained twelve-year-old Ford Galaxie station wagon together—

Mary suddenly sagged against his arm. An amorphous sound passed through her lips — soft rag-doll vowel, tattered rag-doll-dress consonants — not a sigh and not quite a whimper but a fluttery heave of breath, a vocalized shudder. Then she did whimper, and clutched at Webster's upper arm with both hands. "Please," she said. "Help me."

"But I can't— What can I—"

"I know, I understand," she said, releasing her grip on Webster's arm, standing on the step immediately above the landing, wobbling a bit and grabbing onto the stair rail. "I shouldn't have even asked you, it's just that... well, I just shouldn't have asked, you don't know me and it wasn't fair to put you on the spot like that. I'm sorry."

Webster himself stood up on the landing, mortified, his thoughts a-tumble. Why, he didn't even know if she had done anything wrong. Not that it was a matter of, of *chivalry* or anything, Mary seemed like someone who could take care of herself without a White Knight's help, but she was a, she was a *human being* wasn't she? Why was *she* apologizing? Shamed, Webster couldn't even bring himself to make eye contact with her, instead staring straight ahead for a second until realizing that he was staring directly at the point between her breasts where the two slopes of the V had met when they were in Pan's restaurant — *no V today, today wearing a kind of black stretchy leotard-type thing, a scoop-neck is it called?, not that casual though, more like business attire* — then hurriedly looking down at her ankles. The black appliqués twitching, as were the ankles themselves. She smoothed her skirt with the palms and fingers of both hands, and then left the hands on her hips. Webster had not noticed her fingers before, but they were long, long and slender, and the nails were like her teeth: tiny and without blemish.

"I could, that is, you know I could *probably* do something," he said, breaking the silence which hung between them like a taut elastic band.

The muscles, tendons, whatever, the *things* in Mary's ankles suddenly flexed, but she did not speak herself.

Webster's mind whirring like an Erector-set motor. An Erector-set motor fitted, ludicrously, not with a wheel but with one of those Erector-set bogus "girders" so that it not only whirred but flailed, off-balance, the stamped sheet-metal strip going *knickaknickaknack* against the inside of his skull. "It would, it won't be real easy though. We don't, I mean that is, *I* don't think it would be a good idea if we—" Thinking suddenly of the train ride, surrounded by dozens of other daily commuters who didn't even know one another but knew *of* one another, one another's stops, one another's preferred end-of-the-day reading matter, a sudden social appendage would stand out like a sore, a downright *mangled* thumb. "We'd have to, well, we'd have to leave work early for one thing."

He risked a look up at Mary's face. The thin corners of her lips were curled up ever so slightly, the lips parted ever so slightly at the center. Just at the very bottom of his field of vision, her long fingers flexed against the black of her skirt.

"And we, that is it would have to be, oh, we'd have to leave by three o'clock, three-fifteen at the latest. I mean the absolute latest, seriously, and no, uh, no side trips or anything, right?" A sudden memory of a phrase his mother used to use. "No dilly-dallying." He giggled, absurdly, and stopped dead, panting, exhausted by the act of crossing a line to decision.

Now Mary stretched out her arms, held his head in her long hands, tilted it back so that he *had* to look at her face. "You have no idea how grateful I am. Really I am. Grateful, you understand me? *Thank you, Mr. Bond,*" the closing hoarse and anxious, and she pulled his face to hers and kissed him in the center of his forehead. "Grateful," she repeated. Kissed him on his right cheek (brush fires erupting spontaneously every few feet in his mind), and then turned his head and kissed him on the left cheek, "so grateful," and then with a sudden surge of vanilla and clover and some kind of mysterious imperceptible shift of the alignment of their faces she was kissing him on the mouth.

Webster had forgotten such kisses: kisses that bespoke emotions swirling outside the bell-shaped curve of everyday life, kisses which hinted at the existence of experiences not necessarily, no, well, not *better than* but simply *other than* those of the "norm." Experiences that real people never really lived through but that showed up in books and on movie screens. He had, oh sure, he had experienced such kisses before, after all he and his wife before she was his wife had had their share of passion of course—

From somewhere above or below came the creak and slam of a stairway door, and Webster, in a spastic paroxysm of fear and confusion, pulled his face from Mary's. "Look," he said, listening with one hundred per cent of his concentration for the *triptrap* of approaching footsteps, studiously ignoring the way that Mary's thin lips were flexing in and out, their corners twitching, "we have to — well listen, here's a plan..."

7

It was, rather, just *sort of* a plan. He must have been crazy. No. He must have been panic-stricken. But he'd formulated it on the spot, and spilled it to her, and then fled the stairway without even getting Mary's phone number so if he wanted, if he *needed* to get in touch with her there was no way he could.

Which was a problem, because an important component of the plan was that he would call his house and leave a message on the answering machine, explaining to his wife that he would be home late because something (something vague, but at the same time something *definite and unavoidable*) had come up at work. So on and so forth. No cause for alarm. Do not call out the gendarmes. All of that was a problem because when he called his home number, the phone rang, and rang, and rang, but the answering machine did not pick up.

Not that he really expected to be late, like *really* late; he and Mary were, after all, leaving The City on the three-twenty-eight train. But he had to cover himself in case things, well, in case things went awry.

And now this, sheesh: the plan to cover himself had itself gone awry... Well, no help for it. He'd just have to get home on time.

But his mind wouldn't let the matter rest there. There were so many chances for things — things in the *real* plan — to go awry:

He and Mary would meet in the train station at a safe distance (he had explained to the grinning Mary), somehow signaling to each other across the waiting room. They would move separately, at another safe distance, in the direction of Track #4, from which all the trains on Webster's route home departed. They would get off separately, Webster would go to his station wagon and Mary would walk to an intersection a couple of blocks away, where Webster would pick her up. They would drive to a mall, where Mary could pick up a couple of changes of clothes, and then they would drive to some chain hotel where Mary could stay and, er, collect her thoughts for a couple of days. After that, she could get a cab back to The City. Or something.

Yet it could fall apart at any one of a dozen points, delaying his arrival home until God knew what hour of the evening. The three-twenty-eight train might not leave until four o'clock, or even later, or it might even be delayed so long — Webster knew what mass transit was like around here, always shuddering, heaving, threatening to collapse or *actually* collapsing under the weight of the expectations and needs of a million riders — might even be delayed so long that the transit company would scrap it altogether, merging its passengers with those of the first real rush-hour departure, at four-fifteen.

Or suppose Mary, or Webster himself, were somehow delayed in even getting to the station in The City. Suppose they missed each other's signal. Suppose one of them — probably decisive Mary — got on the train and one didn't. Suppose Webster finally, at seven or so, gave up waiting for her to show up at the station, and got to his own little suburban stop to find Mary waiting patiently for *him*.

Actually, now that he thought about it as he got on the elevator to leave, actually there were a thousand more places where the "plan" could go awry than there were places where it could *work*. He must truly have been whacked out on panic, out of his mind. For *life was always like that* — always, without possible exception, the way things actually happened was only one out of an infinity of possibilities. The best you could ever hope for was to limit their number to a lesser infinity.

Infinity. Yes. He had to cover himself for an infinity of things going wrong. He had to somehow make up some story to tell his wife in case he didn't breeze in the door until like four a.m. or something. Or he had to cover himself in advance, like with an answering machine message. But the answering machine had fouled that part of the plan, even though Webster had called it six more times, hoping irrationally that whatever power failure or lightning strike had knocked it out of commission would be magically nullified by another of equal magnitude but opposite polarity...

On the other hand maybe there was hope. Maybe nothing else would go desperately awry. So far so good, after all: Mary was sitting by herself on one of the train station's fake wood-look steel benches (wood-look, an attempt to put passengers in mind of The City's revered romantic past; steel, an acknowledgment of its self-consuming present). Wearing a lightweight denim jacket over the black top, one leg draped casually over the other, the casualness belied by the nervous *jigglejiggle* of the leg and ankle on top. On the bench across from her was a guy in an outfit that looked something like a zoot suit, wearing shades and a scarlet baseball cap, pretending to read a newspaper but actually looking, and looking hard, over the tops of the sunglasses and the top of his paper at Mary's knees. *Jigglejiggle.*

The zoot-suit guy standing up—

Heading off another in the infinity of unforeseen possible outcomes, Webster walked swiftly to the bench on which Mary was sitting, and sat down beside her. A cloud of vanilla and clover swept up and over him, drew him in as though *he* were the one needing protection.

Mary looked startled but pleased to see him at first, then the corners of her mouth curled simultaneously up and down. Rueful. She touched his leg with a long fingertip. "Mr. Bond. Change your mind?"

Meaning what? "Well, yes, I mean *no*, haven't changed my mind about the general idea, but yes, about staying separate, *too* separate — too many things, uh, things that can throw us off-schedule." Mary palpably relaxing; Webster glaring — attempting to glare — at the would-be jitterbug or whatever he fancied himself to be, now sitting again in the bench across from this one; no idea if it was working or not, the guy had his shades pushed up on his nose so you couldn't tell whether he was watching. Webster continuing, his voice lowered, "Plus I had to talk to you, a glitch, couldn't get through to my answering machine."

Mary put her entire hand on his leg now, and though Webster couldn't be sure he thought he felt a bit more pressure from it than could be accounted for by gravity alone. She leaned toward him, lowered her own voice, and asked, "What are you going to do?"

Vanilla and clover; clover and vanilla; her hand there, and then not there: *shush*, and *wait*. Something stirred at the V where his trouser legs met, but he willed it away and stood up, looking at his watch. They had a bit less than fifteen minutes.

"Uh, come on with me. I'll have to, to try one more time." He pushed a hand through his hair. "Get your ticket yet?"

Mary stood up (grinning, nodding her head) and patted the slit of a pocket in her skirt.

They were at the pay phone before Webster realized how crazy this was, this last-minute attempt to salvage the answering-machine component of the master plan. Suppose by some miracle the machine picked up this time; then what? Could he seriously leave a message on it that said, for example, *Hi, something's come up, big contract suddenly about to fall through, gotta work late and you know how it is?* While behind, overhead, and all around him boomed an unmistakable nasal-mechanical voice

John E. Simpson

declaring gates, tracks, times of departure? *Was he crazy?*

"No, forget it," he said, swinging an arm around Mary to reverse her direction. "I can't do it from here, too much, too much noise. Let's just get on the train, I can, I don't know — call from a store or restaurant. Something. Let's just get on the train."

They moved across the waiting room in the direction of Track #4. At this time of day, not the mob scene that Webster was used to at his normal departure time, the usual surging sea of bodies with its powerful sucking undertow always threatening to drag you in the direction of a gate, a track, a destination in which you had no interest. *Wow, oughtta try to leave work this early every day—*

Mary slipped a wrist and hand around his elbow. Muttering again, as she had been when they were descending the stairs en route to Pan's on that other occasion: "Oh man, what the *fuck* am I going to do, I don't even know why I should be worried, I didn't have anything to do with that asshole..." Webster, dark forgotten corners of his mind suddenly glittering and jagged, fascinated in spite of himself but also distracted by the clicking of Mary's heels and by the presence of her wrist on his arm, but *hmm, not actually saying anything of substance, is she, just thinking out loud*, Webster understood that, not that he ever actually thought, you know, *out loud*, but he understood the disjointed way that a mind in panic functioned... Now they were moving down an escalator, Mary holding on more tightly, her words trailing off to inaudibility in the growing roar of voices and the echoes of locomotives passing gas in the vast concrete subterranean chamber where the boarding tracks were located, the bodies of other passengers now more numerous, a bit more crushing as they funneled toward the train, Mary's left hip vibrating against Webster's thigh with the movement of the escalator, the air down here warm and dank and redolent (as always) of corruption and danger but also simultaneously of roasting chestnuts and soft pretzels, of coffee and cigarettes and perspiration and a foreign but really quite refreshing hint of vanilla seasoning and clover context, and now nearing and boarding the train itself and finally now sitting in a three-wide seat all the way at the rear of a car. Mary first, by the window. Webster in the seat on the aisle. The seat in the middle conspicuously empty, Webster pointedly staring straight ahead and ignoring the question marks that Mary was shooting in his direction (caroming from his oblivious skull, ricocheting around the inside of the car).

The middle seat empty, that is, until Webster suddenly felt a presence alongside him, in the aisle. "That seat taken?" Mr. Zoot Suit, from the train station. His hands in the pockets of that ridiculous jacket, with something — coins, or keys, or coins and keys together — something a-jingle. *Tinktinktink* like an infinity of possibilities.

"Hmm?" Webster looking up at the man's broad-grinning countenance (feeling, beside him, Mary looking up as well), looking back and down, feigning surprise at the void there, "Whoops! Uh, *haha*, yes it is!" Sliding to his right, leaving the aisle seat open.

Zoot Suit nodded, still grinning. "Thought it might be," he said, and with a tug at the bill of the baseball cap, rather than sitting down next to Webster he moved towards the front of the car. He took a seat in the first row of seats which faced backwards, on the same side as the seats that Webster and Mary occupied. Ten rows in front of them. Inscrutable behind the shades, his face turned straight ahead. Looking, Webster assumed, directly at Webster.

"Mmm. That's better anyhow," Mary said, leaning against his upper arm.

That arm felt weirdly leaden where it was. It would be the most natural thing in the world, but at the same time the most unnatural, to just lift it up and drape it across Mary's shoulders, indeed it almost felt as if she were, uh, well, of course this couldn't be possible but it almost felt as if she were *nuzzling* the arm... Webster looked down and to his right; Mary's legs were held tightly together, angled slightly in his direction. Her skirt was in place, thank God, but "in place" for a skirt like this one was a good two inches above the knees. He squeezed his own knees together, his hands clasped in his lap (white-knuckled, the left prohibiting the rebellious and/or merely adventurous right from sailing off into further uncharted waters) and prayed for salvation.

Salvation arrived in the form of an elderly white-haired gentleman in a three-piece suit, *literally* a gentleman of courtly manners and endearingly out-of-date vocabulary and syntax. "Good afternoon, sir," he said to Webster, removing his fedora and adding, "Madam," for Mary's benefit. "May I accompany you in your passage out of the metropolis?" Without waiting for a reply, he sat in the empty seat to Webster's left and launched into a melancholic account of how he had suffered since his Victoria had departed this our vale of sorrows.

"You young people," he said, and sighed. "It does refresh my soul and makes my heart sing, to see such as yourselves. How well I remember the first time my Victoria — Vicky, I called her, sometimes Vix — the first time she and I rode the rails in search of adventure..."

Mary seemed to snuggle closer to Webster, if closer were possible, and the whole situation might have become not less dangerous but explosively moreso, if Webster had not noticed and focused his mind on the faint reek of urine and the damp expanse of trouser fabric at the top of the old guy's legs.

"Shangri-La!" the old man rhapsodized, apparently unaware of what for Webster would have been an immobilizing puddle of humiliation. "The call of the wild, the quest for the exotic, ah the human spirit ever in search of a, of a mythical land flowing with milk and honey, ever just beyond the next horizon...!" His hands waved in the air and his body shifted, Webster not sure but he thought he might have heard a little *skkkkkk* as the old man's soggy trousers momentarily disengaged from the vinyl of the seat cushion.

"My Victoria, alas, she drinks of milk and honey no more." Suddenly the old man was shuddering and, Webster realized, crying. "Ah Vicky...!" Mary leaned across Webster and patted the old man's knee with her right hand; evidently mistaking it for a gesture of sympathy, the old man patted Mary's hand in return, too overcome with remembered grief to say more. "Mistaking," because Webster suspected that he knew the real reason behind Mary's gesture: it was so that she could, while leaning across Webster's legs, grip one of Webster's own thighs with her *left* hand, and place her elbow just *so*—

Holy cow, was this train never going to pull out of the station? Webster untangled his hands from his lap (Mary's breasts moving against his knuckles), examined the face of his watch as though an explanation for (and not merely confirmation of) the delay might be engraved upon it. Sheesh. Fifteen minutes late already. Meanwhile he had no idea what to do with his hands, he couldn't possibly force them back between his legs and the now-horizontal Mary, but to simply lower them would mean putting them on Mary's back, but to raise them higher might attract the attention of other passengers — Zoot Suit still grinning at him although he couldn't possibly have any idea what was going on back here — or, worse, the attention of a conductor, as though he were signaling for help or something... He lowered his hands to a fraction of an inch above Mary's back, floating there as though trying to levitate her. Mary unaware or uncaring of the old man's urinary problem, still patting the knee, her body pressed against Webster's thighs.

A moment before the train really did begin to move, another fifteen minutes later, the old guy (now recovered from his sorrow, in response to the ministrations of Mary's hand) excused himself and stood up to go into the car's restroom-cubicle.

What a relief, thought Webster, the muscles of his upper arms were beginning to atrophy, his lap in turmoil — the site of an erection so prominent that he dared not move for fear that it might announce its presence to Mary, *yikes God only knows what she'd make of that.* She sat up at last (with a rapid knowing flicker of a glance towards Webster's lap), Webster's hands momentarily in contact with her back, musculature rippling through the fabric of the stretch top and the denim jacket. The train lurched forward. Webster's hands rebounding and springing together back into his lap, his thoughts desperate.

"Was that, uh, I mean, was that your friend that, you know, today, this afternoon, lunchtime...?"

Clutching at straws but with the desired effect: Mary suddenly sitting bolt upright, no more than a fraction of an inch from Webster but at least now that far away. Ostensibly looking out the window, which as the train passed through the underground tube had become an onyx mirror.

"My friend, eh haha*ha!*" she barked. Nearby passengers' heads swiveling nearly imperceptibly. "Yeah, that was my fucking friend. Ex-friend. Fucking *late* friend, ha*ha!*"

Webster not really wanting to know more, in fact wanting to know as little as possible, yet needing to preserve this fragile attention for matters other than the contents of his lap, blundering on: "Did you, I mean, that is, do they, uh, have any idea what happened? On the stairs I mean?"

Mary turned away from the window, cheeks flushed, her smile blinding. "But of course, Mr. Bond, don't you remember? You offered to protect me there!"

Grinning nervously himself, remembering the kiss, "Uh no, I mean yes, I did, sort of, but what I mean is what, not what happened between you and me, *is* happening, happened, you know what I mean, I mean what happened, did your friend, uh, fall?" *Klongklongklong.*

She snorted. "Oh yeah. He *fell* all right."

"Did you, uh, were you—"

"He fell down five stories, guess you heard that right? You hear about his pants, too?" His *pants*? "Eh haha*ha*!" Nearby heads definitely turning to listen in now. "Yeah Mr. Bond, ha! — *his fucking pants were open!*"

The last declaration not muted at all. Webster panic-stricken as nearly everyone in the car, including the trainman, turned to look at them. Zoot Suit laughing outright, removing his shades to wipe at his eyes, which were small and porcine.

Jeez and wowie holy cow. The man's pants were open. What did that mean? Just, like, unzipped? Down around his ankles, draping the olive-green bluchers? How could Jack have failed to report that? Did Jack even know about it? How did Mary herself know about it for that matter — *is it just, uh, like a well a grapevine kind of thing she'd picked up, or was she indeed there—*

Just then, as the train exited from the tube into daylight, the old man staggered out of the restroom, distracting the attention of the other passengers for a moment. He wove up the aisle, not thank God sitting back down next to Webster again but even better thank God walking up the aisle and collapsing into the seat directly across from Zoot Suit, the fedora blocking the latter's view. Webster could hear the old man's voice from all the way back here, complimenting Zoot Suit on his retrograde wardrobe and recalling for his edification the manner in which he himself had been garbed when he had first gone to call upon and court the still-departed Victoria.

"That, uh, that guy up there," said Webster as Zoot Suit shifted his head to peer around the old man's bobbing knobby dome.

"The old-timer? He's a riot isn't he, cute though in a way—"

"No no no, uh-uh. The, uh, the guy in the..." *The what? Can't say "zoot suit," that's what some out-of-touch rube might call it, probably some famous glitzy contemporary high-fashion ersatz-European name, "stiletto jacket and matching faux trousers" or some such...* "Guy in the glasses. Shades. Baseball cap. Kind of suspicious-looking—"

"Oh, the guy in the zoot suit? He's cute." Mary sat up straight, looked ahead, and waved to Zoot Suit, who grinned and touched the bill of the cap again. The train passed over some anomaly of the rails, the tracking or whatever, a succession of ripples in the steel or discontinuity in the gravel of the roadbed, and the wheels rumbled for a few seconds just as Mary slumped back down in her seat and, leaning towards Webster, dropped her voice even lower than its low norm and rumbled into his ear, "Of course, I think *you're* cute too, Mr. Bond." She placed her right hand upon the almost-successfully deflated erection; her thumb and fingers seemed to hug it. "The cutest." The train dipped and lurched suddenly, forcing her hand down, or Webster up, or both, into even more excruciating contact.

Webster was horrified at the betrayal of his body not merely by his body itself but by his *routine*. He must have ridden over these tracks, discontinuities and all, uh, ten thousand times (maniacally doing the calculation: *say two hundred fifty work days a year at two trips a day, that's five hundred trips a year*, and then he'd been working in The City for, uh, sixteen and a half years, *no ten thousand was too high, make it eight thousand and change*), and this ride had *never* affected him this way. *Holy cow did this kind of thing go on all the time*, and Webster not even know it? He stole a glance across the aisle at a middle-aged man in steel-rimmed glasses and a gray pin-striped suit (the jacket neatly folded and placed in the overhead luggage rack), who was reading or pretending to read a newspaper. Webster glanced down at the man's lap, which was being tapped, lightly, by the V of the newspaper's crease. There didn't seem to be anything going on down there at the moment as far as Webster could tell anyhow but good Lord, did other men *have erections* all around him all the time?

The man turned the newspaper page and, with a glance of his own at Webster's lap (where Mary's hand still lay, resisting the tugging of Webster's own hands), looked up and smiled at Webster. The smile seemed steel-rimmed, too. Burnished. He turned back to the paper.

"Look," Webster said. Mary was playing some kind of damnable game at the moment — her arm would suddenly give way, and when Webster's tugging hands were thrown off-balance she'd put her hand back on his lap, and the on-again/off-again pressure there was nearly sending the lower half of his body into convulsions. He didn't want to hurt her (didn't know if he *could* for that matter, such a prospect would require entirely too much directed thought and action) but this had to stop. "Listen. I don't, I mean, you can't do this."

"*Mmm.* Can't I, Mr. Bond? Can't I? Please?"

"*No,*" he insisted, and with a sudden unaccustomed surge of energy — diverted maybe from the writhing nuclear stockpile in his groin — he picked up her hand and placed it in her own lap. "No. Jeez, come on, I'm trying to do you a favor, I can't let you do, uh, this. That."

"A favor, Mr. Bond?" Mary was still smiling as she looked down at her lap, where one of Webster's hands clasped hers. "Yum, I love favors. Is it my turn now?"

Like game birds startled into flight by a whiff of hound, each of Webster's hands bolted into the opposite armpit. Hugging himself. Chortling, Mary laid her head against his upper arm again, and seemed to subside into sleep.

The cloudy-bright May sky had darkened to a gray the color of the other guy's pinstripe suit, and soon fat raindrops were plashing up against the windows as the train, elevated, crossed over a now-suburban landscape. The dark gray was now dark purple. The train stopped at the first outlying station — Webster and Mary would be getting off at the third one on this nominally express train — lost a handful of passengers, picked up a handful more, pulled away. And as the purple decrescendoed to black, as thunder boomed distant and suddenly nearer, as they began slowly to cross a bridge over what passed for a rush-houred Main Street in some small town whose name Webster did not know because it did not have a train station and so was not identified twice every day on his usual round trip, as the clouds unzipped and an avalanche of water fell upon the train's roof and windows, so then the train's lights went out and it shuddered to a stop, Mary and Webster situated just this side of the double yellow stripe below them on Main Street. From somewhere at once in the front of the train and beneath Webster's feet came an enormous mechanical sigh, like the last heaving breath of the Loch Ness Monster.

Mary stirred against his shoulder but as far as Webster could tell in the flicker of lightning and the crazy everywhere-at-once blurry zigzagging illumination from the car and truck headlights below, she did not awaken (assuming she was indeed asleep, *not at all a sure thing but who cares*, at least she was no longer visibly, alarmingly conscious).

Slipping a hand from within its enfolding armpit, he checked his watch in the runny light. *Four-fifteen, no, -sixteen. Seventeen, absolute latest.* He thought they were still okay for time as long as the darned train got *moving* soon and they didn't sit here for a half-hour, not that he had any clear idea exactly how long whatever-they-were-going-to-do would take but he was beginning to sense that it would not be anything like trouble-free, no God forbid it should go according to plan—

Plan. Holy *cow* he still had to do something about his wife, she'd get home about six or six-thirty, he himself might be home by then (he pictured himself when she walked in: he'd be sitting at the dining room table, reading the mail and whistling something one hundred per cent innocent, the theme from "Leave It to Beaver" or something, and then he pictured his wife suddenly sniffing the air and asking, "What's that smell?", his whistle suddenly expiring as he tore a page from the catalog in his hands). Yet maybe he wouldn't. He could get home he figured as late as seven-thirty and his wife would without questions accept a tale whose credibility hinged upon the fragility of public transit — it wouldn't really be a "tale," though, this *was* costing him much more time than he had to spare wasn't it? — but suppose it wasn't until nine? His wife would accept that he'd been delayed that long by a combination of forces both natural and man-made but would she accept that he had somehow, mysteriously and uncharacteristically placid and even-keeled, not called to let her know about it? He could claim that the answering machine was kaput — *truth!* — but on the other hand suppose she got home at six and reset it then how could he claim that it was out of whack the entire evening, that he had tried calling every fifteen minutes et cetera—

"Ladies and gentlemen," announced the voice of a trainman in the front of the car, stilling a muffled hubbub of passengers' nervous laughter and conversation. "Sorry about the delay, we think it'll be taken care of in a few minutes and then we'll be on our way—"

Another voice interrupted. The old fellow. "Excuse me, my good man, should we perhaps address the needs of women and children?"

Another voice chimed in, also at the front of the car. Nasal; mock-plaintive. Zoot Suit maybe or maybe some kid: "Nearer my God to Thee...!" Giggles.

Another few minutes, Webster repeated to himself. Calling out in the direction of the trainman's voice, "Excuse me. Sir? Any idea, will it be, like five minutes or more like a half-hour?"

The voice answering everyone and no one. "Please, everyone, just stay seated and in a *few minutes*, no more, we'll be moving again. Okay? Okay!"

§

But whatever the source of the problem — a tree down on the tracks, a flood, some anomalous failure of machinery or human nerve — its resolution took more than the trainman's promised few minutes. They were stranded there in the nightmarish flickering darkness for another three-quarters of an hour.

Webster obediently sat, twitching, the whole time. Certain he could feel the hum of his electric watch through the skin of his wrist. Braced for the inevitable crash as another and more on-time express plowed into the rear of this one (trying without success to remember how many cars were behind the one in which they were seated), or as the tracks over Main Street caved in. Once, a train flew by on the adjacent track, in the opposite direction, and the *boom* and the *whoosh* nearly stopped his heart.

Mary likewise did not stir or even speak for the most part, except once when she excused herself to go to the women's room, at the front of the car. She was gone for six-and-a-half minutes, re-appearing just when Webster was screwing up his courage to contemplate going after her. Wordlessly, she sat back down in her seat by the window and resumed her near-cowering posture, clutching Webster's arm, head against his shoulder.

But finally — after the storm itself had passed and daylight was stepping tentatively into the sky again — finally the lights came back on and the train began to roll forward. Webster craned his neck to look down at Main Street as he and Mary glided across the now-submerged yellow line; unaware of the disaster epic unfolding over their heads, kids were frolicking in the pond of stormwater down there.

The remainder of the trip to his own stop passed blessedly without incident, which was a blessing because Webster was in a panic that he might lose the thread of the enormous nest of dependent clauses in his head: *if this happened then the other thing needed to be considered, and if it did not happen therefore the following was true and so the world was just slightly different in this respect, which would require the following adjustment to the course of action...* He wished desperately that he had stayed hidden behind the column in Shirts'n'Skins, or that he had gone out for lunch that day that the cafeteria in work had shut down (well, all right, he corrected himself, he *had* gone out to lunch — at Pan's — but that wasn't what he really meant, he meant *alone*, or with the fanatically adhesive Jack), or that he had stayed in his office this afternoon (huddled in the kneehole of his desk, the door bolted, the shades drawn, waiting for the FBI to burst in), and he wished desperately that since he had clearly done none of those things, wished he'd had the sharpness of will necessary to just say to Mary, *Look, this really is insane, I'll drop you off at a mall or a hotel or an airport or bus station, here's fifty dollars cash, here's my ATM card, good luck, sayonara,* and then with hands plunged deep into the pockets of his trench coat he'd stroll off into the foggy darkness — his shoulders slumped beneath the sad weight of the recognition of some things that could never be and a multitude of other things that always had to be — while Mary stood there whimpering, her small body heaving with stifled sobs.

But that was stupid, and what was stupid about it only *began* with the fact that Webster had never owned a trench coat. Its stupidity had only marginally to do with the fact that Mary would not stand there weeping, that she would far more likely pummel him with tiny fists as she repeated, over and over, her husky voice grinding away at the sharp edges of his self-respect in deep rasping iterative strokes of accusation, "Fuck *you*, Mr. Bond! Fuck *you*, just fuck you fuck you *fuck you!*"

No. What was stupid about it was Webster's growing sense that he was (as the expression went) caught up in something larger than himself — borne along on a sudden surging tide of events and personalities and sensations over which he had little or no control. He could only oscillate rapidly back and forth over this sea's surface like a nervous waterbug, as it took him wherever it took him.

As they pulled away from the stop which preceded his own, looking down at Mary, at the black breve of her collar in stark contrast to the ivory of her collarbone, he thought of his wife's dress in his closet — the one with the macramé-style collar. He thought of his wife, at this moment (checking his watch for the seventy-first time in the last twenty minutes) maybe still at her desk in work; he thought of her talking on the phone to one of the seemingly hundreds of sales reps she dealt with each day, thought of her listening to the rep's tale of helpless ineffectuality in the face of competition, thought of the characteristic way her eyebrows would converge when she came to a sudden decision and instructed the sales rep to fall back to Plan C or Plan D. He thought of her hanging up the phone and leaning back in her desk chair, and he thought of her longing to get home and kick off her shoes the way she did, stockinged toes flexing in the carpet pile.

He looked down at the apparently catnapping Mary, tried to peer through her dark hair through her skull into her brain her mind her soul, but all he could see there was a dark chaos, a tangled-up tumble of odd notions and impulses shooting every whichway, unpredictable, and while he recognized a certain similarity to his own thoughts at the moment, hers were, well, *messier*. Frayed. While his were...

Thinking again of his wife's feet hugging the carpet, he looked down at Mary's legs, which were slightly parted and shifting as she maybe dreamt of flight. One of the appliqués, an ebon butterfly, twitched. He remembered when she had passed out on the stairway, slouched there helplessly on the stairway while the skirt had ridden up to expose — almost beneath Webster's fingers — the black garter belt. When she had first moved in the direction of consciousness then, her legs had opened and then sharply closed and opened again. Like scissors, Webster now thought. *Snip.*

Something stirred again in his lap and he pressed his own legs together, shivering with a sudden confluence of fright and pleasure. Mary stirred against his arm, murmured, "Mmmm." Opened her eyes and tilted her head back, grinned incongruously at him. Looked out the window and back at Webster. "The fuck *are* we?" she asked dreamily, grinning.

As though anticipating the question, the PA system crackled to life and blared the name of Webster's own station. He grinned back down at Mary, said simply, "We're, uh, there." Mentally flailing his arms, pinwheeling, slapping fecklessly at the encroaching ever-deepening blackness whose enormous fingers were reaching through the walls for him, for Webster, and simultaneously reaching toward them with his own fingers, with his entire arms, grinning, embracing the darkness, grinning, sucking up every last molecule of the aroma of vanilla and clover until there was no more to suck up, grinning, terrified, sated but not satisfied, swallowing and being swallowed up, lurching, lunging, plunging, never and always, here and there, light and dark, the train shuddering to a halt by the platform, Webster standing and then leaning over to take Mary by the hand and lead her to his car. His face grinning, a petrified rictus of terror.

8

The first thing Webster noticed when they got out onto the platform and the train crawled away was something that he wasn't sure that he noticed and wasn't sure that he wanted to notice, which was actually not a tangible *something* but its fleeting disappearance: a flash of crimson about head-high, around a corner of the glass-block-and-concrete wall of the stairwell enclosure which led down to the parking-lot level. Zoot Suit's cap? Had Zoot Suit disembarked here, too?

Still linked to him, hand over his elbow, Mary was waxing lyrical on the myriad beauties of suburbia versus The City. "This is *lovely* here," she was saying, "is this where you live? Look at the trees! I bet everybody out here is really friendly and they stop to help you change flat tires and stuff, don't they, oh Mr. Bond I think I spend too much time in The City, I forget there are places like this..."

No, Webster explained as they arrived at the top of the stairwell and he peered down into the dank grayness lined with faded posters advertising the continued availability of choice seats for musical comedies that had closed months ago, *no, don't live* here, *exactly, we've still got another half-hour drive more or less to get to the development where I live*... With his attention actually focused ninety per cent on confirming the fact or fantasy of Zoot Suit's departure and, crazily, *another* ninety per cent on retaining his grip of the complex logical structure supporting his current version of the Master Plan, he did not notice the first-person plural which had slipped into his reply. Mary's grip on his arm tightened.

Zoot Suit was nowhere in sight, however, which was a relief because now Webster needed to free up the first ninety per cent of his consciousness in order to locate his car.

Over the years — in fact, ever since he'd been taking the train to work — he'd parked in the same spot in one of the reserved sections: out by the chain-link fence, two spaces to the left of the wooden utility pole, the space over which hung the *Reserved Parking Only Violators Will Be Towed* sign.

Last week, though, the local agency responsible for maintaining this station had embarked on an unannounced renovation project; the work had so far yielded no visible signs of actual change in the area except for a slick veneer of mud and a cheap wood-and-wire barricade starting at the utility pole and extending the three spaces to the left. As a result, the three regular tenants of those spaces had been forced to roam the lot first thing every morning, bumping latecomers from their spots so that they could go on to bump someone else, and so on, a chain reaction of chaotic dislocation that at the end of the day always had a half-dozen or so people standing around on the sidewalk, scratching their heads, shading their eyes and wishing that they could, like movie-serial cowboys, simply whistle for their missing steeds.

Aha. There it was. He remembered now.

This morning, on a sudden inspiration, he'd pulled up alongside his blocked regular space and actually gotten out of the car, without parking it, to look west across the lot. Yes. Perfect: just as he'd imagined. The parking-lot engineer (or whatever he or she was called) had designed the lot symmetrically; another wooden utility pole stood directly opposite this one, and two spaces to the right — affixed to the chain-link fence, over yes! an empty spot! — was another *Reserved Parking Only* sign.

Forgetting Plan D, or was it E?, according to which he would get in his car and pick Mary up at a nearby street corner, Webster led her to the station wagon. Under the windshield wiper was a small piece of thick stiff tan paper. Webster groaning in dread. Yep: reserved parking in the East Lot and that in the West Lot were two separate jurisdictions or whatever. Fiefdoms. Duchies. Fifty dollars.

"I am sorry, Mr. Bond," Mary said. "But here, look." She took the ticket from Webster and an instant before he realized what she was up to and long before he could grab it back, shredded it and cast it into the light breeze. "There," she continued, slapping her hands together. "Bye-bye ticket. Fuck you, Mr. Meter Maid."

Gaping at the manila snowfall fluttering down onto his car, Webster was horrified. Was she crazy? No way could he find a cubicle inside his head into which to stuff a new paranoia, especially one the magnitude of something like this: defiance of legally-constituted authorities et cetera et cetera, *fifty dollars plus seventy-five dollars in punitive damages and God knows what else—*

"I, uh, I really, that is, wish you hadn't done that."

She stared at him as though he were the crazy one. "You kidding me? What's the problem? The ticket blew off in that thunderstorm, right? And got caught, who knows, got caught in a lawn mower, one of those nylon string-whackers or whatever they're called. Don't worry about it."

"But, uh—"

"I know, I know. They'll catch up to you eventually. But in the meantime save your fifty bucks, put it — eh haha*ha*! — put it in an interest-bearing account or something if you're worried about it, by the time they find you you could be a rich man, Mr. Bond, *rich*!"

She was grinning at him and, inexplicably, Webster found a grin spreading across his own face. She was right. Why didn't he ever think of things like that, why'd he always have to be so *nervous* about everything, so... so... *anal-retentive* (blushing inwardly at the very thought)? In fact he knew exactly the account he could put the money into, the "emergency money" savings account he and his wife had set up, *what's the account number, four-eight-nine-something?* In fact he could stop on the way home and transfer—

His wife. Good grief.

Panicking but suppressing it, he opened the passenger-side front door for Mary, stood there like a humble royal footman while she got in but not so humble that he failed to notice the distinctly three-stage manner in which she sat in the seat. First one leg, then a leisurely languorous pause, then the other; black of appliqué butterfly; white of thigh; black of something else. Looking up at him — the grin softer now and also shyer but slyer, a smile — the whole time. *Snip.*

No. His wife. He had to stay focused. The plan.

§

"I, uh, we, I mean *I* had to change the plan around. A little."

This was Webster, as the Galaxie toodled down the interstate at precisely the speed limit, pickups eighteen-wheelers motorcycles buses commuter vans blasting past them like an artillery barrage. Webster, trying to fill with answers the void of unspoken questions that he sensed lay between Mary and him.

Not that much else could lie there; Mary was practically sitting in his lap, jammed up alongside him on the bench seat. "Ummm," she said. "Surprises. If there's anything I like better than favors, it's surprises."

"Come on, I'm trying to be serious."

"You're not succeeding very well, Mr. Bond." She traced with a fingernail the right inseam of his trousers and the car lurched to the right, onto the shoulder, as though the inside of its own thigh were being tickled.

"Mary! Wait, I mean no, not *wait*, you know what I mean, *don't*, you shouldn't do anything like that to someone driving a car!"

Heart pounding, Webster looked back over his shoulder for a break in the traffic that would enable him to get back onto the roadway. It was a long time coming; a visitor from another planet, observing the scene from above, might conclude that the slow-moving Galaxie was some kind of wounded or sick or dying animal, maybe wounded *and* sick *and* dying, shrugged off by its herdmates and left for the jackals to pick over.

"Listen," said Webster as he closed his eyes and swerved leftward into a minuscule breach, hoping Mary was not hearing the enraged klaxon of the tractor-trailer whose chrome grill filled his rear-view mirror, "my wife, it's after five o'clock, she'll be home soon, we have to stop at my house."

Mary's eyebrows levitated mischievously. "That right? Are we going to surprise *her*?"

Yikes I hope not, Webster thought. "Now, uh, just listen. There aren't any hotels, motels, whatever, right nearby for me to drop you off at. Closest one is about another half-hour past where I, where *my wife and I* that is, where *we* live. I have to stop at the house, leave her a note. In case we get hung up."

"'Hung up'?" Internal quotation marks audible. She snuggled closer, though that seemed scarcely possible, and giggled. "Thought you were just gonna push me out the fucking door as we drove past the hotel. This *is* a change in plans, Mr. Bond." Suddenly she braced her feet on the transmission hump in the center of the floor, threw her left arm around Webster's shoulders, elongated her legs and body so that her mouth was by his right ear. "Remember this? *Fffffffffff*," she hissed.

The free one per cent of Webster's mind was still giggling about that, the inside of the earlobe still tingling from the fricative of breath and cloud of moisture with which she had sprayed it, when they at last exited from the highway onto County Route 647 (Spur). The winding undulant blacktop that would take them through town — past the hardware superstore, past the grocery store and past the barbershop where Webster got his hair cut every month, give or take a week — through town, and onto County Route 519: the road to the development where Webster and his wife lived.

§

"This is, uh, it."

The car was in the driveway, its engine still running. Webster had finally succeeded in convincing Mary that if she wasn't going to scrunch down in the seat so she wouldn't be visible to the more meddlesome neighbors in the development — she had offered to lie across the seat, her head in his lap, but Webster had vetoed that without even his customary hesitation, just a loud "*No!*" that surprised them both — she could at least sit discreetly at the far end of the seat.

"Gee, it's cute. Fucking *cute*."

"Umm. Yes. It is. Listen, you stay out here and I'll leave the note and be right back out. Stay, right?"

But she didn't stay. As Webster's door swung open with a moan of ferrous distress (*gotta oil that thing one of these days, hmm, the oil can's right here in the garage, could probably do it right now— no,* darn *it, no time!*), so did Mary's own door, and she was out of the car and over by the garage entrance that flanked the overhead door, standing pertly and (he could almost believe) innocently, her hands clasped before her like a flower girl's.

Webster slammed his door. "Come *on*, Mary, you can't—"

"Yes I can. Have to. You know. Powder. The fucking nose, right?"

"*Sssssshhh!*" Holy cow, suppose the neighbors could read lips? "All right," unlocking the door, admitting her, "just, uh, just get inside, the houses aren't that close together here but God knows what they can see."

He hurried her through the garage, to the door that opened into the kitchen. "That way," he directed her, "up the hall. Down the end."

"Let me guess. Little room, right? Has a sink, tub, toilet?"

Waving his hands — *yesyes, just go, go, go, yikes almost six already, wife could walk in here anytime in the next fifteen minutes to half-an-hour* — he turned his back on her, and after a frantic rummaging through the kitchen junk drawer finally came up with a grimy sheet of notebook paper, folded and flattened and stuck inside the phone book's front cover. He took the paper into the dining room, sat in the ladderback chair at the head of the table, and took out his pen.

There was a phone number written in Webster's meticulous script on the top of the sheet — 555-1212 — followed by a colon and the word, "INFORMATION." Good God. Had he at some time actually written that down? He was about to cross it out before proceeding to pour the entire contents of the vast logical structure from his head into the body of the note, then thought better of it — *never knew, might need the number in an emergency or something and not be able to recall it, on the tip of the tongue and so forth and so on* — so instead he merely circled it and wrote alongside, "Ignore this number. Doesn't have anything to do with anything. It was at the top of this sheet of paper and couldn't find any other paper and didn't want to cross it out because it might be important."

He read over what he had written. *Dope*, he thought, and crossed out all but the first sentence. There. That would do.

Now on to the important part. But first: "Mary? Everything okay in there?"

No reply. Maybe she didn't hear him. A brief lurid image composed itself in his mind, Mary slumped over the side of the tub, a hypodermic syringe stuck in her forearm ("911," he added at the top of the sheet, "EMERGENCIES"). Maybe he should go back there and — no. *Take care of this first.*

Although he'd been worrying at the precise phrasing for what seemed like his entire life, the note to his wife was much harder to write than he'd anticipated. A *lot* of crevasses among logical alternatives to be filled with explanation. Not only did he need to lay out the central thesis — that on a sudden impulse, he and Jack had decided to take the afternoon off, they were going to play a round of golf, stopped off here at the house to pick up clothes to change into and then went over to the course (not sure how close the nearest one was but trusting that his wife would not know, either), and then, boys being boys et cetera et cetera, they'd be going to eat someplace, he didn't know where, so don't bother trying to call or God forbid visit the restaurant in search of them, then maybe have a few beers someplace else before he got back on the interstate and drove Jack back to the train station — he also needed to make sure that it all *made sense*.

He had to explain about the answering machine. He had to explain that he had tried to call several times, and he had to explain that leaving a note like this was probably a sounder, more rational way to explain the whole thing. He had to justify his acting impulsively, surely the least credible stone in the whole foundation, by explaining that he had been talking at lunch today with a company shrink (adding a little smile symbol next to the slang, hoping his wife would find it amusing as well and, ideally, be sufficiently diverted not to wonder why he would have been eating with a psychologist) who had said to him, *Listen, you've got to relax a little, have a fling* — no, cross that out — *go out with the guys sometime.* "Let your hair down," the shrink had said. (*Would a shrink say that? Even over an informal lunch?* He crossed it out. "Do something to release your pent-up hostility," crossing out the last word too and adding, "tensions." Studying the result; re-studying it. Better. Not really *okay*, but better.) He had to point out that because he had never done anything like this in his adult life he had no way of predicting when he'd be breezing in the door. Jack might have to get home early. Or maybe they'd change their minds and not play golf after all, maybe they'd just eat. Or go to a mall. No, he reminded himself, he hated malls and his wife knew it, he'd never in a thousand years go to a mall to relax. Crossing out the last alternative and just leaving it at that.

"Love you," he wrote, and signed his name.

There.

It wasn't the prettiest missive he'd ever seen, with barely a square inch left unscored by second-thought insertions and big black-ink gashes. No time to work on æsthetics though, it would have to do, surely his wife would recognize in the note's mangled appearance the workings of a defenseless mind knocked off-center and reeling by spontaneity.

There. He placed the note under a candlestick, moved the candlestick a bit to one side so that it didn't obscure the phone numbers at the top, and stood up.

Mary's voice, deep, called to him from the kitchen. "Mr. Bond? Could you help me with something?"

He glanced at his watch as he moved to the doorway between dining room and kitchen. *Ohmigod, six-twenty.* This better not be something that would delay them any longer—

Mary was standing in the kitchen, naked except for the stockings and garter belt and ludicrous purple sunglasses, lounging as though drowsily with her back against the refrigerator. Her lips glistened in the lowering sunlight which pierced through a break in the cloud cover and stole through the kitchen window; her nipples were almost shockingly red against pale white breasts. Her denim jacket, black top, and black miniskirt were folded neatly and placed on the kitchen counter.

Webster, thunderstruck, literally screeched to a halt — the soles of his shoes doing a little one-two squeakie on the linoleum. "Jesus, Mary, Jesus, Jesus *Christ*—"

She smiled. "Can you help me?" The voice suddenly little-girlish. Pause, clearly savoring the drama. "I couldn't find the toilet paper."

Beside himself with psychological turmoil, Webster rushed to her, grabbed her by one arm. "What, what in the name of God—"

He yanked on the arm, and Mary moved in his direction. As she did so, the skin of her back pulled with it, like a plaster, the pizza advertisement that Webster had hung there eons ago. The magnet clattered to the floor. The note — *the note* — fluttered away from the door as well, and landed (after a crazy back-and-forth falling-autumn-leaf dance in mid-air) on the floor. Squarely between them. Face up.

Mary's eyes, hidden behind the sunglasses, evidently followed the note's passage. She stopped, and stiffened, and her head tilted back a little to look up at Webster.

They stood like that — the man in the rumpled business suit and loosened tie, the woman in scarcely anything at all, immobilized, the film snagged in the projector and threatening to burst into flames — for surely a full ten seconds. Then a voice from the garage, dimly at first but growing nearer: "Sweetie? Why is your car sitting out in the driveway with the engine running? And what's that smell?"

Holy mother of God, Webster thought, scooping up Mary's clothes, the pizza ad, the note — *the note* — with the very first syllable from his wife's mouth, the motion unconscious, a blur, hustling the still stiff Mary out of the kitchen, into the hallway, across the living room to the front door, pushing her out the door with the bundle of miscellany now in her arms, not his, hissing at her, "Get dressed and for God's sake keep your head down, get in the car, *the back seat*, got it? I'll be out in a few minutes," *holy cow please oh please let the neighbors all be out in their back yards watering their lawns, facing Mecca or whatever just please oh please not facing this house*, shutting the front door with a click just as the back door clicked open, unseen, in the kitchen.

"Sweetie?" came his wife's voice again. "Yoo-hoo?" A rattle as she kicked into the magnet on the floor.

"I'm in here," Webster called, gulping for air, frantically pushing his heart and other internal organs back down into his torso where they belonged. "In here."

By the time — indeed no more than a couple minutes — that he'd kissed his wife, waved her in the direction of the dining-room table, babbled something about *Gotta run, Jack's waiting at the course for me*, dashed into the bedroom and grabbed a pair of jeans and stiff, never-worn golf shoes, and fled out the back door to the car, he was so distracted by terror and anxiety that he scarcely noticed the taxicab parked on the street a few houses down. *That's odd*, came the fleeting thought, *never see taxicabs out here, certainly not parked on the street instead of in a driveway*. But then he was in the driver's seat, backing the station wagon onto the side lawn and around his wife's car, and hurtling from the development, barely conscious of the passenger recumbent and mercifully unseen on the back seat despite the presence of her hand and fingers, tickling like deranged gnats at the back of his neck.

9

For twenty minutes they rode around aimlessly but in the vague direction of the nearest mall, where Mary could pick up whatever she needed for her overnight stay. Mary quiet except for an occasional soft chuckle.

Webster himself? His head boiled with noise, and hence the

aimlessness: the shouts and alarms of neurons long-dormant now suddenly a-pop, the clank and groan of mental gears pistons flywheels and camshafts lurching about in directions and at rates of speed they'd never been programmed for, and a general *rhubarb rhubarb rhubarb* undercurrent of disquiet. Put out by Mary's little surprise, he was, but clouding his irritation was a mist of, well, excitement... Yet, he thought: *Come on.* Excited? How could he be *excited*? He was too old to be excited. Shoot, now that he thought about it, he was too old to have embarked on an adventure like this in the first place, driving around with a naked woman, well, a *nearly* naked woman (quick covert glance into the rearview mirror, correction, whew: a *formerly* nearly naked woman) in the back seat of a twelve-year-old Galaxie station wagon (while his wife, he imagined with a twinge, was still staring out the window at the manic cloud of dust raised by his departure). On the other hand maybe he was too young not to seize the opportunity for such an adventure. And yet wasn't he too old to be knocked for such a loop by all this? Shouldn't his mind be made up about, well, about almost *everything* by now? Shouldn't *nothing* surprise or disorient him?

He realized with a start that it was dark, and switched on his headlights just as the Galaxie turned off the main drag into the mall parking lot.

"You go on," he said to Mary (carefully maintaining at least six inches of distance between them) as they entered the mall. "There's an ATM somewhere in here, I think, and you can, well, I guess, you can charge stuff. I'm just going to sit down at the whatsit, the food court. Have some coffee. Come back to earth—"

"Oh? Have you been off someplace else, Mr. Bond?" Chuckling.

But Webster, still mostly lost in thought, would not take the bait; after they agreed to meet back here at the entrance in a half-hour, he then wandered off towards the center of the enormous structure.

As malls went, this one did have one virtue: non-orthogonality. It was roughly star-shaped — like one of those Old West sheriff's stars, with a six-theater movie complex bulging at one of the points and so-called "anchor" stores at the other four. The architects had even gone so far as to taper the corridors away from the central three-story atrium, exaggerating perspective so that those wings of the building looked, from the atrium, even longer than they were.

There in the center, Webster sat with a cardboard cup of coffee at an unevenly-balanced table of ridiculously wrought iron and glass. Looking up at the glass pentagon set into the ceiling. Dark now, of course, at least when viewed from inside. He imagined being outside, in an airplane or helicopter far overhead. Looking down. Seeing himself sitting here looking up, a business-suited little pinpoint in the center of a cloudlet of steam from the coffee cup, illumined in artificial light. Imagined with a jolt of panic the lights going out. *Did* the lights ever go out in these places? Good God. Having thought the thought, he could not for several minutes rid himself of it. He saw darkness pushing at the surface of the bubble of light, heard the bubble's creaks and groans, saw the bubble bursting, light flying off, obliterated, darkness pouring in to fill the vacuum. (*One hundred per cent the speed of light*, he thought, twisting in his chair, recalling his entrapment in the men's room at work and the consequent memory of his recurring childhood nightmare: *the speed of dark*.) Suddenly, no one else in the whole crowded mall would be at all visible. Gone, as effectively as if they'd been physically erased.

That was the panic-making thing about "alone in the dark," it occurred to him: that no one else was visible; not so much the *dark* as the *alone*. He'd made a desperate life's work of being sufficiently "acceptable" never to be alone — inoffensive, mild-mannered to the point of anonymity, absolutely determined never to make anyone else uncomfortable even though the effort kept Webster himself writhing in distress, vanishing into the woodwork so that no one else would. Life, meantime, proceeded without and all around him; crowds of people swirled about his hesitating ruminant form, parting like a torrent when they collided with him and reforming again on the other side. Occasionally someone stopped, attention snagged by the perplexity sticking everywhere out of Webster's persona: stopped, scratched his or her head, and eventually moved on. That one of those someones had ever been sufficiently snagged to marry him probably came as much of a surprise to that someone — his wife — as it now did to Webster himself. So yeah, he thought now: ironically, despite all his best (or his worst) efforts, he had *always* been alone, probably would forever (panic a-bubble) *remain* alone... And yet there was this woman, this Mary, something about her that both acknowledged his aloneness and (while toying with it) said that it did not matter; and yet she was wrong too, see, because the darkness, the massive loneliness, still crowded in...

He suddenly realized his mouth was hanging open, slack-jawed. What was wrong with him? He snapped it shut, bit the inside of his cheek, wincing, hands flying involuntarily to his face. Suddenly catching himself, hands reversing their direction. Looking furtively around to see who might have witnessed this ballet of neurosis. People at nearby tables looking pointedly in other directions or engaged in conversations whose camouflage of irrelevance did not fool him. Standing, he poured the remainder of the coffee into his mouth, scalding the wound on the inside of his cheek, *whoops*, more coffee left than he'd thought, much too much to swallow and *ooooo* it was hot, gad he couldn't possibly even begin to swallow it when it was this hot, *Couldn't you rupture your esophagus or something?* Uncrumpling the cup, spitting the viscous, steaming mouthful back into it. Depositing the cup in a trash can. Fleeing the food court.

Not altogether to his surprise, Mary had not yet returned to the mall entrance although the agreed-upon half-hour had expired several minutes ago. Or maybe she'd been here already and when Webster himself, lost in woolgathering, had not appeared, maybe she'd gone on to loiter — where? not on the sidewalk outside; not standing outside any of the oddball miscellany of retailers and mall services in this little out-of-the-way corner (travel agency, vacuum-cleaner sales and repair, fundamentalist Christian bookstore, mall information and stroller rental, pipe-and-tobacco store).

He stood before a kiosk on which the floor plans of the mall's three stories were depicted in yellow, blue, and green, one color per story. Representations of the escalators and elevators running between floors were animated, shimmering from one color to the other as they made their way up or down; somewhere, in one of these asymmetrical little polygons of retail space (the shapes forced upon them by the architects' avoidance of rectangles) or on one of these iridescent ribbons, somewhere at this moment was a little dot which represented Mary. A dot moving, he hoped — quick glance at his watch — in the direction of You Are Here. Looking up again, into the yawning maw of the mall before him. Failing again to catch a glimpse of her. Pacing. Then, worried that someone would mistake his pacing for, uh, well, like for *stalking* or something, like he was casing the joint, easing over again to the window of the Christian bookstore.

The selection of reading material arrayed therein was an odd stew of the benign and the ominous, of the promise of not only joys but also terrors unimaginable. The world was a beautiful place, it seemed, yet shuddered on the threshold of some kind of mysterious retributive crash. *SonShine!* sang one of the titles; *Thirteen Sins That Weigh on Your Shoulders*, gloomed another. Webster looked up at his reflection. Nothing on *his* shoulders. Drawing them back. Vision suddenly clarifying, focus settling on a person on the inside of the window looking out at *him*, a kindly-looking young woman — a deaconess, he decided, if there were such things — who was smiling as though welcoming him to the eucharist. Horrified, he looked quickly away and moved on to the tobacco store.

Mary not here either, but its display window reminded him an awful lot of the window of Shirts'n'Skins, and hence of her. No riot on the street behind him, thank God, but brown everywhere. Humidors. (Or was it thermidors?) Cigars and the wooden caskets in which you kept them. Lighters. Those little doodads, what were they, pipe tampers. Swiss Army knives—

As though echoing the bright red of the knives' housings, a sudden reflected-crimson flicker in the window drew his gaze up, then back over his shoulder. Yes. There, now already twenty or maybe even fifty feet away. A crimson baseball cap. Now gone.

He took off in that direction. Couldn't imagine what he proposed to do even if it *were* Zoot Suit. It could be mere coincidence; *lots* of people whom Webster had never met lived in this area, and many of them commuted to and from The City just as Webster did, and if, say, Zoot Suit were one of them then it stood to reason that Webster had never encountered him on the train because it was, after all, an earlier train that they had taken out of The City this afternoon (even if it hadn't arrived at all earlier). But Webster couldn't let it rest; there was something, well, annoying about Zoot Suit — like he was cocky or something, smug maybe — and the annoyingness translated into suspiciousness. Too transparently interested in Mary, he'd seemed, not that Webster himself was, uh, *interested in* her exactly, but he was... he was *responsible* for her. He was— But darn. No Zoot Suit to be found. Maybe it hadn't been Zoot Suit after all. Just some kid. How many crimson baseball caps must there be in the mall at the moment? Dozens, Webster bet. *Dozens.*

So no, no Zoot Suit. (True, he also saw none of the putative dozens of other crimson baseball caps. But that was beside the point.) But he did encounter Mary, much to his relief, on her way to the mall entrance. In her arms, paper-handled shopping bags from two department stores. Breezy and casual, as though time were not of the essence.

"Okay, Mr. Bond, let's get the show on the fucking road, eh-haha*ha!*"

Webster took one of the shopping bags for her as they headed out to the parking lot. "Sheesh, I thought you'd never show up. You, uh, you have any kind of place in particular you want to stay at?"

Grinning. "No. Do you?"

Blushing, the remembered vision of her pink nipples suddenly fresh. "Cut it out, Mary. I mean, like, do you want a fairly cheap place? A national chain, I don't know, you have some kind of travel discount or something?"

"Restaurant. A place with a restaurant. And God, a liquor license, if I don't have a fucking drink soon I'm gonna explode. Or *im*plode. Some damned plode or another, ha!"

Restaurant, holy cow, she's right. It was after eight o'clock and neither of them had eaten anything at all yet. "There's a Hilton not too far from here, that, that okay? or if that's too up-scale—"

"Hilton. Right. Fine. To the Hilton, tally-ho!" Sitting again in the front seat, again the subtle one-two-three seating action. Webster swallowing, hard. Wondering anew.

§

At the Hilton, Mary insisted on leaving her packages in the car, on the back-seat floor; she didn't want to "lug them all around the fucking restaurant. And surely you don't want to check in right away, do you, Mr. Bond? Are you in such a hurry?"

"Yes, I mean *no*, maybe it would be better if, you know, if *you* checked in first."

"Come on, relax. I won't bite you. I am famished though." She reached across the car seat, patted his stomach. "I bet you're plenty hungry, too, hmm?"

There was some kind of airline-pilots' convention at the Hilton this week, and the restaurant, while not full, was occupied mostly by men in dark uniforms and white shirts. Webster felt vaguely nervous surrounded by so much quasi-officialdom, which seemed to suggest the possibility of imminent arrest, but Mary claimed to be excited by it and kept looking eagerly about, her cheeks flushed. She was seated on a banquette along the wall, as she had been at Pan's, and Webster was in a chair at one side of the table; as she crossed and uncrossed and recrossed her legs, one of them kept making contact with one of his, at first seemingly by accident but then, with increasing frequency, plainly by intention, until at last hers settled firmly into place alongside his. He didn't know what to do, how to react — either to the pressure of her leg or to the once-again swelling presence in his lap. Not that he was into the habit of *enumerating* his erections, but this was what, the third, fourth time today? Wasn't that if not exactly remarkable at least a little unusual?

Later, Webster would not be able to recall much of what they had talked about over dinner. They probably talked about their jobs, about where they went to college. Or rather Mary probably did.

Oh, he would remember talking about the note — *the note* — which he had again glimpsed on the back seat of the car just after Mary had put her packages on the floor back there, just before she shut the door and the light went out. "That, uh, that note," he began, but Mary interrupted him. "Ha!" she said, "I saw that, she must've been plenty mad Mr. Bond, man, you must not be as meek as you come across. A real dark side, huh." Webster, confused and embarrassed, had dropped the subject until he could figure out some way to crowbar her remark into the mainstream context of everything else he had thought about the note since finding it.

But for the most part, he remembered only ducking his head furtively whenever their waiter approached. Dimly remembered being conscious of Mary's settling into an awareness more fully of him and less fully of the airline pilots, her attention elsewhere diminishing a drop at a time as each of the other tables was vacated. He certainly ordered at least four too many glasses of red wine with the meal, and then an after-dinner liqueur and then another before responsibly (as he thought) calling for an Irish coffee and then a second one of those, too. Watching, dimly fascinated at first, then embarrassed at the fascination, then fascinated all over again at the way that the sharp tip of Mary's tongue disposed of the whipped cream deposited around her lips by her own Irish coffee, and then both mortified and excited by a sudden vision — he could in truth feel it, her thin lips would flex beneath his tongue — of licking that whipped cream himself. Amazed that it was not Mary but he himself who leaned over and whispered, giggling: "Remember? F*ffffffffffff*." And out-and-out thunderstruck when she giggled in reply but then fell silent — thunderstruck not by the giggle nor, exactly, by the silence, but rather by the look, or what *seemed* to be the look, or what he *thought* seemed to be the look, that passed from her to him at that moment.

The back-and-forth dialogue that would remain most firmly fixed in his mind later took place when he gathered what was left of his wits, wrapped around himself the remaining scraps of adult responsibility, and said, "Well. I, uh, are you ready?"

Mary licked her lips, dabbed at them with the corner of her napkin (which was crimson, reminding Webster of something but his mind staggered away from whatever it was), and then her eyes shining she nodded and replied, "Yes. I'm more than ready."

She checked in at the front desk while Webster paid the restaurant tab and lurked about the periphery of the lobby, feigning great interest in the identity of the potted plants and lithographed artworks (and speculating dizzily about their provenance, as if he knew anything at all about such matters).

"Guess I need, need to get my things outta your car," she said as she once again looped her wrist over Webster's forearm. Her speech was slurring slightly, her carriage unsteady, as they walked to the revolving door. Her scent was if anything stronger, clover and vanilla flooding not just his olfactory but *all* his senses: he could see waves of it coming off her, he thought, an ivory and brown and soft green aura into which he wanted to plunge his face, and he could hear it rustling against the surface of his earlobes, and he could feel its velvet beneath his fingertips (even as his hand slid limply, not quite casually, down her back and up under the denim jacket, the curve of the black stretchy leotard-type thing tantalizing). Above all he could *taste* it, the soft tang of her vanilla, the light sugar of her clover, and despite the fullness of the meal they had just eaten Webster felt an unfamiliar hunger coursing like a racehorse through him.

She leaned against him the whole way across the parking lot. Silent.

He thought he could hear her breathing — realized, while thinking what a bizarre thing to realize, that he *wanted* to hear her breathing, and when they got to the car he impulsively swung her around to face him, moving fast in her direction so she was backed up against the fender, bending his head down so he *could* hear her breathing but she misunderstood and reached up for him, tendrils of vanilla and clover looping up and around him, pulling his face to hers, yes she *tasted* of vanilla and clover too, *wow*, Webster didn't know that he had ever been so hungry, his erection pressed up against her, her cocoon of vanilla and clover literally holding him in place—

"Fuckin' *bitch*!"

Wha— Whirling. Jolted with adrenaline. Wha—?

Zoot Suit. Crimson baseball cap, ludicrous shades still in place. No longer grinning; no longer tugging amiably at the bill of the cap. Jacket with squared-off shoulders and lapels and pleats now seeming not stylish at all but a riot of planar cacophony. Deranged obscenities tumbling from his mouth in their direction. But his most attention-getting feature the bulge in his jacket pocket, the jacket pocket in which his right hand was placed, the bulge larger than his hand alone could possibly be and larger by far than its now rapidly-dwindling counterpart in Webster's trousers.

"*Bitch*," said Zoot Suit. "Fuckin' *cunt*. Look at you. You fuckin' disgust me you know that?"

Mary was wobbling, still clutching at Webster's arm for support, but otherwise immobile. "The fuck?" she said. "The fuck you talkin' about? Don' even *know* you."

Mary Mary shut the heck up don't antagonize this goon, Webster's mind scrambling blundering from thought to thought, question to question—

"And *you* you moron," Zoot Suit said with a sneer in Webster's surprised direction. "Mr. Fuckin' Suburbia. Stupid dickhead. Don't you know what she is?"

What she—?

"I'll tell you what she is. Fuckin' bitch. Whore. Fuckin'... fuckin'..." He paused, took a deep breath, seemed to draw into himself all the unattached hostility anywhere at all within a radius of miles. "...Fuckin' *woman*," he concluded, ridiculously, as though it nailed everything firmly in place. But Zoot Suit wasn't operating in clarification mode, and in fact at that moment began apparently to disintegrate, his body trembling all over and a tear rolling out from beneath one lens of the sunglasses. "Fucking *woman*. I said to, to him, usedta, usedta watch you, tried to tell, tell, but he wouldn't, wouldn't fuckin' believe me, well fuh-fuh-fuck him too," sobbing, choking between phrases, *Jesus Mary and Joseph what was going on...?*

Suddenly Mary stiffened, and lashed out with her free hand in the man's direction. "*You!*" she cried. "Fuckin' nuh, fuckin' *nut!*" she yelled. "Don' even *know* you," she repeated, "know *about* you though, fuckin' creep, it was you wasn't it, get away get away, back under the rock—"

Zoot Suit did back away a little at that but then, still weeping, stood his ground. "Maybe I will," he said, "and maybe, maybe I'll put you under a rock first..."

Shutting his eyes, shutting his ears and not even trying to comprehend, Webster tried to block out the surreal, blustery-machismo interplay between the two of them. What could he do, before this got really ugly, well, ugli*er?*

Think (he kept thinking). *Remember all those cop movies and TV shows. How would whatsizname handle this, or whatstheirnames, those two crazy kids on that show, what was it, the fat little sheriff or mayor or whatever he was, Boss Hogg, no wait, wrong show, the two other guys... Starsky and Hutch? Yeah. What would Starsky and Hutch do here? Or Burt Reynolds?* Opening his eyes, looking wildly about the parking lot. *Yeah, Burt Reynolds. Clint Eastwood. Or...* His frantic gaze falling upon a Jaguar parked on the far side of the Galaxie. *James Bond, Webster, how would* James Bond *handle it? He'd... he'd wrench the door open, knock Zoot Suit off his feet, then he'd, uh, he'd leap over the car door (stopping only for an instant to press his lips against Mary's and adjust his cufflinks) and he'd*—

But shoot. It was no use. Zoot Suit wasn't standing anywhere near the Galaxie's door. And Webster wasn't Starsky or Hutch, let alone both of them together. He wasn't Burt Reynolds or Clint Eastwood. He wasn't even Boss Hogg. And Lord knows he wasn't James Bond, except maybe in Mary's (and his own) fantasies.

"Listen," he said, interrupting them and addressing himself to Zoot Suit. "I, uh, I don't have any idea what's going on here but obviously it's between, well, between the two of you. If it's all the same to you I think I'll give Mary here the, uh, the things, her packages and then I'll, uh, I'll be on my way."

Zoot Suit's mouth dropped open a brief but gratifyingly silent inch. "'Mary'? That her name? Ha, fuckin' Mary is right, some fuckin' Virgin all right!"

"Hey fuck *you* fucker!" she yelled, and they were at it again, slugging at each other verbally and with great (but apparently not greatly satisfying) gusto.

Mary seemed not to have noticed that Webster had just offered to abandon her to this patent sociopath's mercy. Just as well, Webster thought as he slipped his key into the door lock; let them both be distracted. Reaching inside, unlocking the back door, opening the back door and leaning waaaay across the seat and picking up the shopping bags, tugging them back outside the car and while Zoot Suit and Mary continued to shout at each other, threatening at any moment to lunge across the narrow space separating them, Webster upending the bags onto the surface of the parking lot, *yipe she must have spent a fortune in the lingerie department*, Mary yelling "Hey!", black and off-white and red lacy things slithering-skittering everywhere at their feet, Zoot Suit jumping back and away as Mary dove for all the undergarments and as Webster hurled the tire iron which he had retrieved from beneath the front seat straight through the windshield of the neighboring Jaguar which, *yes!*, yowlyowlyowled in misery and shock when its alarm went off, Zoot Suit clapping one hand and arm over his head and high-tailing it halfway across the parking lot but blinded by the glasses and residual tears, ramming painfully into the corner of a mini-van, bent double and then tackled — as lights blinked on all over the wall of the Hilton — by a gaunt, gray-haired figure suddenly rushing out of the shadows. Mary, on long slender-fingered hands and delicious knees at Webster's feet, shouting repeatedly, "What the fuck was that, what the fuck's going *on*, what the *fuck*...?"

10

An hour later, Webster and Mary were right back where they'd just come from: the Hilton restaurant. Quite a bit soberer, for sure. A complimentary, mostly-empty coffeepot on the table in front of them.

Sitting side-by-side on the banquette, across from the now-vacant seat which until a few moments ago had been occupied by one Lieutenant Alf Gilly, of The City's plainclothes-police detective squad: he of the gaunt, gray-haired frame, and he formerly of the rumpled disgustingly reekingly damp three-piece suit on the train from The City: the dear departed altogether fictitious Victoria's erstwhile swain.

("Ha, yeah, that *was* pretty disgusting," Gilly had conceded — in his real voice, casual and not at all old-fashioned — "but it worked. Couldn't get him to pay attention to me no matter how I tried!" For his part, Webster could simply not imagine, and did not want to ask, whether the urine stain was a standard bit of plainclothes business, or something the lieutenant had been inspired to try on his own. Was it some kind of animal urine, or ammonia compound, or had he, well, had he actually *wet* himself—? Mentally bounding away, the notion too horrible to ponder.)

Mary, chuckling softly and shaking her head, clicking the table with her fingernails, had not spoken a word since answering the cop's final questions. Her silence was beginning to oppress Webster a little.

"Some, uh, some story," he finally ventured.

She thought a moment more; then, sidling up closer to him, her hip against his, dropping a hand onto his leg and patting it, she agreed, softly, "Yes. Some fucking story all right."

The pivotal figure in the whole melodrama, according to the Gilly version, had not been Zoot Suit and had not been Mary, certainly neither Webster nor Gilly himself, but Mary's late friend, the former occupier of Webster's neighboring lavatory stall, the wearer of eccentric footwear.

"Weird shoes, right," Gilly had confirmed when Webster volunteered the latter detail (keeping the former to himself). "That's our guy. Wasn't the only thing off-center about him, either." He looked at Webster, then with more interest at Mary. "Swung both ways."

Yes, Mary had confirmed: she knew it. Mr. Shoes had finally told her the night before the slapping incident in the cafeteria. She hadn't volunteered the information when the police interrogated her this afternoon (Webster glancing down at his watch, correction: yesterday afternoon) because it didn't have anything to do with her or for that matter with anything else, did it? What the fuck, *she* didn't kill him, who cared what had happened to their relationship? But according to Gilly the slapping hadn't been the end of it, except maybe in Mary's mind; Mr. Shoes had been vacillating for weeks already, and now, after the scene in the cafeteria, had finally attempted to break off for good his relationship with his other lover: Zoot Suit.

"So there they are in the stairwell," said Gilly, "the two of them. In flagrante, you might say, in delicto even, with your friend's pants around his ankles and the other guy on hands and knees."

Webster could picture it, all right, although it was a scene from a movie he never imagined he'd come to see (let alone participate in, even in what was literally a walk-on role): Mr. Shoes, even while leaning back against the railing in an ecstasy, trembling, insisting *No no, I told you, I can't* do *this any more, I'm sorry but no, stop*, and Zoot Suit, frustrated not only by the moment's turn of events but also, maybe, by his life's in general, driven over the edge but determined not to go alone, suddenly lunging forward and butting Mr. Shoes backward and head over olive-green-blucher heels. *Klongklongklong.* What was it the note had said — the Zoot Suit-to-Mr. Shoes note, as it turned out, the one still lying on the back seat of Webster's station wagon? "I am so sick of the whole thing I want to scream... keep LOOKING **OVER YOUR SHOULDER**." And so Mr. Shoes had, as Webster saw the scene: head-first and looking back for a final instant over his shoulder, broken once and then repeatedly by the freak ricochet from railing to railing. *Klong.*

Whatever Zoot Suit intended to do with them, Mary — and Webster himself — had not been in any real danger as it turned out; he had not been "packing a rod" (as Webster put it, hesitatingly at first but then rushing in, the phrase causing Gilly to burst into an excruciation of laughter) but nervously squeezing a hollow pink-rubber ball, which he apparently used to exercise his hands. "Don't even ask," the cop had said, rolling his eyes, when Webster sought clarification.

But now Gilly was gone, and the restaurant manager and staff were making a grand show of removing the coffeepot and cups and silverware, the tablecloth, the chair in which the cop had been sitting; soon, Webster imagined, he and Mary would themselves be carted off and placed in the dishwasher overnight.

Mary, too, evidently sensing another change in the evening's direction, standing up. Running the palms of her hands down over the fabric of the mini-skirt, ostensibly just smoothing it but incidentally managing to draw Webster's attention to it, and to her hands. "Yes, some story, Mr. Bond."

Catching himself staring at the skirt, her long fingers, jumping, Webster looked guiltily up but not directly at her face — which he imagined to be brushed lightly with amusement — but to one side, off over her shoulder. Clearing his throat and standing. "Uh. Uh, well, now I, uh, I'll see you to your room and then I'll be. Uh. Leaving."

"Fair enough." Her voice just exactly like he imagined her expression. "Got to make a stop first on the way up though, powder the et cetera one more time."

Webster following her in silence from the restaurant, thinking to himself, *Jesus can't believe what time it is*, adding to that *Suppose I had a flat on the way home, car broke down, I could get home even later couldn't I?*, flipping back and forth in his mind the two concepts "credible" and "merely possible," like a ping-pong ball transmuting in mid-flight into a badminton birdie. Waiting outside the women's restroom, trying hard not to look as though he even existed, not that there was anyone else up and about at this hour, not even housekeeping staff, but you never knew when some stranger might come wheeling around a corner and down the hallway in your direction only come to find out it wasn't a stranger after all but Jack, say, or holy cow his wife, "What on earth are you *up to*?" as though Webster had any idea at all, *Just, uh, I needed to stop off at the Hilton for...* for what? But then Mary swinging through the restroom door, fresh nimbus of vanilla and clover preceding her and enveloping him.

In the elevator on the way up to her floor, the sixth. Mary beside him, holding onto his arm. Not looking up at him exactly, as far as he could tell out the corner of his eye — he himself pretending merely to be observing the incrementation of LED floor numbers over the doors — but definitely looking *up*, the underside of her chin, her throat exposed.

"Appreciate everything you did for me today and tonight, Mr. Bond."

"Well, I didn't, I mean I'm not, it was just—"

Interrupting him without saying a word, just snuggling up again. Webster suddenly bizarrely conscious of the skin of his thigh (still tingling and pink-scarred a little from that painful scrape of the shelf in the lavatory stall millennia ago) separated from the skin of hers by two thin layers of fabric. And well of course the stockings, the black stockings, the butterfly-appliqué thingies closest to the knees a bit ragged from the stresses they'd suffered against the asphalt out there in the parking lot, the stockings were there too though now not merely provocative but endearing, the stockings of a life-battered waif, and maybe was that the doohickeys, the clips or whatever? the things holding the stockings to the garter belt? was that what he felt against his upper thigh, pressing through his trousers themselves and on through the pocket...? "6," said the LED. The doors slipping open soundlessly, Mary's vanilla and clover envelope drawing him with her through the doors and up the hall—

No, he corrected himself as they passed through the door of her room, *no I am not being drawn by her, I am doing this because this is what I want to be doing*.

He wanted to be standing, as he was, just inside the room's mysteriously somehow-closed and somehow-latched door when Mary excused herself for yet another visit to yet another bathroom, wanted to be standing there still when she emerged a seeming split-second later — still fully dressed, she was, and not (as he might have expected, although on the other hand wasn't that just a stereotype?...) merely in stockings and garter belt. He wanted to be silent, most especially not stammering, when she said to him, her amazing voice hoarse, "What do you look like without a tie, anyhow?" and then reached up and loosened it, slipped it from his collar, and went on to add, "...without a jacket?" and removed that, too, Webster all a-tremble, head and senses clouded with vanilla-and-clover haze, "...without a shirt, Mr. Bond?" and off came his shirt in her hands. Wanted to be putting his own hands around behind her, as indeed he was; wanted to be feeling the hard curves of her shoulder blades, to be reaching up, hooking his fingers over the rim of the black stretch jersey, wanted to be pulling it down (as he bent to bury his face in her vanilla-and-clover hair, the vanilla-and-clover intersection of her neck and shoulder) and off her shoulders, his fingernails lightly raking the skin of her back, wanted to be feeling the denim of her jacket slipping from her arms with a barely-perceptible clover-and-vanilla shrug, slipping from her arms and over his knuckles, cascading to the floor on top of his feet (which had mysteriously somehow lost their shoes and socks) and hers (*no shoes either and my God her feet, her feet are well they're* pretty *they're* exquisite...). He wanted to be reaching down further then, the jersey around her waist, his hands now beneath the waist of the black skirt, and wanted to be grabbing her hard from behind, wanted to be hoisting her in a miraculously easy leverage of hands and wrists, hoisting her up hard against him, the lovely stockings and especially the lovely legs and ankles and feet inside the stockings hooking around behind him, wanted to glimpse as they staggered like a top-heavy monster past the open bathroom door the evidence of her split-second visit — the black panties draped casually over the edge of the sink, like a sudden salty taste on the tip of the tongue — and wanted above all to feel this: the sensation of falling, toppling, not *klong* at all but mere *whoompf* onto the bed, not even bothering to strip down the bedspread, wanted to be putting his mouth on every exposed surface and when that had all been staked out wanted to be exposing more, wanted to be feeling the perfect fit of each of her thighs in the curve of his palms, again wanted to hear her breath in his ear, her breath coming harder now, and faster, or was it just that he was somehow, well, *hearing* harder and faster? could you do that?, putting his mouth on one of her earlobes and feeling a small shock, *Cool to the touch, the lobe is smooth and cool*, his wife's were never but then shoving that thought deep back down below the surface and sucking harder at the earlobe, moving to the other side, *wowie, that one cool too*, they were lovely, even better than her feet, he *loved* her earlobes, he couldn't stop licking at them (except once or twice or maybe it was three times when he moved down to her breasts)— And he suddenly, incongruously realized: it was not vanilla and clover he had been smelling all these weeks, but, well, the scent of *desire*. Was that possible? could you want something, even a simple *concept*, could you want it so desperately that you could smell it? and if that was possible, could what you smelled smell so, so... sweet? so complex? so much apart from anything else that you had ever smelled or tasted that you made up something else that you thought it smelled like instead? maybe the sense of smell—

But then came the dissolution, and he did not finish the thought.

A half-hour later. Done dressing, Webster standing alongside the bed, Mary dozing, despite her assurance (just before they'd both temporarily lost consciousness) that she'd be awake when he left. Should he wake her or just, well, *leave*? What would a gentleman do? (*Was* he a gentleman?) He couldn't imagine shaking or even softly jostling her by the shoulders, couldn't — could no longer, now that he had set his mouth so hungrily on them — imagine leaning down next to one of her earlobes and whispering, "I'm going now," was afraid to touch her again for fear that he'd then touch her again, and then, well, *again*, couldn't even imagine clearing his throat loudly enough to get her subconscious attention.

Finally, his hands knotted, he sat on the edge of the bed.

"Mmmm," Mary said, her voice even huskier than usual. Throatier. "Mm. Leaving, Mr. Bond?"

He nodded. "Uh-huh. You want me to shut off the, uh, the bathroom light?"

"Sure, fucking boogeyman's gone now, you took care of him remember?" — teeth of her grin gleaming up at Webster — "so sure, turn it out, I'll be all right. And you know, I kind of prefer it like this anyway, being alone in the dark."

The hair bristling at the back of Webster's neck, up and down his arms.

"...and thanks again for stopping so I could pick up some, heh, some clothes. And for the meal. And for rescuing me, eh haha*ha*. And for, well, you know." Her fingertips brushed his arm and came up to brush along his neck.

No idea how to handle a conversation like this, though he must have known sometime, years ago, mustn't he? "Uh, okay and, uh, I guess I should say thank you too." Blushing furiously, invisibly in the dark. "I mean for the, uh, the company."

Laughing. "I know what you mean, Mr. Bond."

What was he supposed to do next? Hug her? He didn't want to get anything started just when it (whatever *it* was) seemed to be winding down. He stood. "Well." Swallowed. "Guess I'll, uh, see you?" Not meaning to raise the pitch of his voice there to imply the question mark, repeating "...see you" in a flat monotone, no interrogative at all, not waiting for an answer, not sure that there was one or if there was that it would be forthcoming and not sure, if it was forthcoming, whether he wanted to hear it, impulsively he bent at the waist as though executing a sweeping bow and kissed her on the cheek.

"Mmm," she said again, and with her arms around the back of his neck repeated, "Mmm. Yes. 'Bye Mr. Bond."

Then he was away from the bed, then he was at the door, and then he was in the hallway, the elevator, scurrying past the front desk (eyes lowered, thinking, *Don't worry Mr. Desk Clerk, not skipping out, room's paid for, she's fine yes fine I just need to be somewhere else*), again through the revolving door, at last behind the wheel of the Galaxie. Starting the ignition, turning on the headlights, looking up at the wall of again-darkened windows a final time. Reflected moonlight glinting. Which one of them was Mary's room? That one? That one? Engine giving the characteristic little reminder (like a gentle un-Jack-like tug on the sleeve) — a brief small-scale racing of the throttle — that it was ready to go now. Pulling out of the parking lot, turning onto the interstate.

The radio was all staticky on the usual all-news station, a fusillade of crumpling cellophane. Darn. One of these days he'd have to upgrade this old AM thing to an FM... Distractedly knobbing the tuner. *Boy it's dark this time of morning,* suddenly thinking *Morning, whoops didn't even talk about the morning, what's she going to do, able to get back into The City okay?*, just as suddenly realizing what a ridiculous question that was: of course she could...

He drove slowly, carefully; despite the night's earlier frenzy and later coffee he had, after all, had an awful lot to drink, on top of which his eyes were still jagged with burrs of near-sleep. Setting the radio to the first clear station he landed on, a country-western station — he normally never listened to the stuff but it felt somehow right, at this time, to be twined-about by jangling guitar chords and voices yodeling in heartbreak. Mary's scent everywhere, *all* of her scent, the vanilla and the clover and all the rest of it, everywhere, he could not *not* sense it: in his hair, in his chin and brow, pressed into the backs of his hands and wrists, rubbed like liniment into his pores; indeed, while he wasn't literally inhaling it anymore, now he seemed to be *ex*haling it. Scent of desire.

He rolled down his window. The morning cold came roaring in at him and he hung his head out the window and into the wind; it roared around and over and into the pores of his face and scalp, blurring his vision and scrubbing scrubbing his skin but leaving untouched the scent at his core. A thousand questions glittered down at him from the sky, one question per star, only the least consequential of which were sure to be forthcoming from the Jaguar owner's insurance company but for the most part unanswerable questions about what he was — well, *thought* he was — and what he wanted (or, well, all right: *thought* he wanted) to be, and what he had done and would have to do now, what he *could* do now and what he would never be able to do again. Lined up behind a tractor trailer which was mysteriously obeying the speed limit, on a wild impulse Webster reached forward and shut off the Galaxie's headlights.

Bobbing like a cork, borne on desire, face to the wind. Heart racing, alone in the dark.

The Bug

Although, as I said, I probably appreciate (emotionally and intellectually) "The Dark" most of all Webster's stories, I've got to say that "The Bug" was a heck of a lot more fun to write. Furthermore, it came close, or at least sorta kinda close-ish, to publication in a Big Name periodical; the editor who rejected it described it as "very funny" and "very wise" but, of course, also wanted it to be (in unspecified ways) tightened. I was quite excited by the praise, and the near-miss, but quite embarrassed that someone thought I hadn't already tightened it up so much, in my estimation, that it vibrated like a piano wire. Indeed, that was the last time I submitted a Webster story to anyone without an invitation. Funny to re-read this story now, post-2020: how differently we all feel about respiratory ailments; how differently the medical systems themselves work. Life staggers on, eh?

Some nameless, aggressive ailment had started prowling the hallways and cubicles at work on Monday, its rheumy-eyed victims wheezing and sneezing, spraying one another with the watery detritus of respiration, lobbing the bug back and forth like a soggy medicine ball.

The company executives seemed immune to the bug's effects, insulated as they were by hermetic elevator access to the floor they occupied. Everyone else got it, though. First to go were the secretaries, who were most frequently talked to and hence rained upon by everyone else; then the housekeeping staff, who picked it up on their hands and fingers while ministering to restroom fixtures, desks, and floors; finally the middle managers, who rarely ventured forth from their offices except to meet with one another — by which time the bug, with no potential victims left uattacked out in the open, had moved on to the conference rooms, and waited silently for fresh meat to come to *it*.

Webster picked up the disease sometime on Tuesday. In retrospect, he thought it might have come from a communal coffee mug he'd found on the counter between the office's aged Mr. Coffee machine and the now-empty institutional-size carton of Kleenex. Distracted by the eerie unwonted silence of the coffee room, he'd neglected to wash the mug out more than twice before using it. Normally he was a fanatic about that, even at home — let alone at work, where God only knew who might have used it last and for what purpose.

By the end of that day, his handkerchief was soggy and limp, his nose incandescent; his hands trembled like newborn puppies. But the bug had first declared its presence at around lunchtime in the form of a dull throbbing ache to either side of his nose, inside his sinuses. It felt as if his face were bulging upwards, and his cheeks stretching to merge with his eye sockets. Or so he told Dr. Morse when he stopped at his clinic on the way home early from work.

"Mm-*hmm*," said Dr. Morse, noncommittal as usual, echoing Webster's words as though they'd really registered. "Merge, you say? With the sockets?" He put the mirrored disk of his stethoscope on Webster's chest and said, "Cough," which Webster did. Then he removed the stethoscope from his ears and sat back in the dainty typist's chair from which he conducted all examinations, his hands in his lap. Held loosely in one hand, the stethoscope's vermillion rubber tubes writhed spasmodically, like an earthworm run over by a bicycle tire. Webster's gut churned in sympathy.

Dr. Morse regarded Webster solemnly for a moment. The news, Webster was certain, was not good. Then what? He lived alone — who would take care of him during his decline? Who would pay his bills, fix his meals, change his bedclothes, wash his underwear, and at the last summon 911 to apply those huge electroshock suction cups, futilely, to his chest...?

Suddenly Dr. Morse was seized by a sneezing spell whose onset so startled him that he jumped to his feet. He sneezed three times (weird yelping sneezes they were, *Arp! Arp! Arp!* like the neurotic vocalizations of a toy dog) — not into the tissue he'd yanked from a box on the exam room's counter, but into the hand holding the stethoscope. Wheezing and sniffing, he mopped at himself with the tissue. "Sorry," he said, "excuse me. I was going to say, it's just something going around. A bug. Nothing to worry about." He recommended that Webster stay home from work for a few days, get bed rest. And fluids, lots of fluids. *Flush those poisons out*, he said, *arp*ped again, and patted Webster on the shoulder.

§

Webster seldom took sick. Nor did he otherwise usually stay at home, indoors, for days at a time. So he wasn't prepared for it now. He'd need to prepare, he thought as he walked to his car from Dr. Morse's office. Stock up on fluids; food, too. Maybe soup and Saltines? His mother had always fed him soup and Saltines and something called "flat Coke" when he was sick. Unfailingly, the regimen's monotonous grue had sent him, heaving, to the toilet. *Flush the poisons out*, his mother always said.

He stopped for his sick-food at the only convenience store in town, a 7-11 owned and operated by a Native American couple.

All Webster knew about the Indians came from his neighbor, Mrs. Fanson: The Local Enquirer. "*The 7-11!*" she'd yelled to him across the road once, months ago, when they'd walked out to check their mailboxes at the same time. She paused while a tractor trailer roared past, and megaphoned her mouth with cupped hands. "*Did you hear?* Indians! *I don't know what tribe but they're Indians all right! Yes!* Indians! *From Oklahoma!*"

Mrs. Fanson's willingness to share such data tended to be inversely proportional to its truth. Still, this did explain the countertop display: from a little wire rack beside the Slurpee dispenser, the couple sold decorative swatches of cowhide hand-tooled with an assortment of primitive objects and mystical geometric designs — pyramids, herds of antelope pincushioned with the shafts of stylized arrows and spears, radiant eyeballs. "EVERY ONE UNQIUE!!!" said a hand-lettered masking-tape label on the rack, through which showed the words TV GUIDE.

"Oh no. Don't let that hand-tooling fool you," Mrs. Fanson had confided to him on another occasion, having run across the road and collared him on the front lawn before he could escape into his house. "It looks very exotic but why, you could do it yourself." Her eyebrows twitched. "They used a plain old *soldering iron*! Bought it at a Sears in Tulsa, they say. A soldering iron, you believe that?"

§

At home, Webster put the Caffeine-Free diet Coke in the refrigerator and (while water for his Cup-a-Soup heated in the kettle) changed into pajamas, bathrobe, and slippers. He rummaged through the steamer trunk in which he stored seldom-used linens, extracting from it the red-white-and-green afghan he'd bought at a neighboring church's annual Christmas bazaar, years ago. Musty, yes, fragrant with the perfume of neglect, but it would do. He draped it over himself as he sat with his feet up on the coffee table, mug of instant soup and plate of Saltines and glass of soda on the end table beside him. He picked up the satellite TV remote control, turned on the set, ate a cracker, and clicked the channel-guide button.

Nothing in the complex program-listing grid seemed the least bit interesting, and he exited to the main screen. Maybe his eyes, burning with fever, would latch onto something visual which had not appealed to his brain when presented in the dull black-and-white text of the on-screen schedule. This satellite receiver/DVR had the strange habit of tuning itself to apparently random networks overnight, possibly in response to atmospheric conditions or instructions beamed down from Satellite-TV Central Headquarters; when the channel guide cleared now, he saw that it had selected some sort of real-estate promotional channel: washed-out low-res photographs of split levels, condos, and ugly vacant lots, accompanied not by voiceover sales pitches but by muted Latin dance tunes, cha-cha and mambo, a tango for apparent variety. He blew his nose into the paper towel he was using as a napkin, scattering crumbs. Then he took a sip of soup and a sip of soda. He ate a cracker, clicked the remote's channel-up button, gulped down another spoonful of soup.

A twenty-four-hour channel of Scandinavian-language music videos was next. Unlike the real estate channel, he bet, this one probably got lots of viewers, all day and all night. But Webster himself had never been able to identify — let alone identify *with* — any messages presumably being communicated by music-video dancers' writhing hormones, the deadpan irony of VJs, the vocalists' dreamy soft-focus slo-mo closeups as they seemed to brood about Satanism, body-piercing, sex with one another and animals, and all the reasons the pains and terrors of youth lacerated the soul more savagely than those of adulthood. He swallowed some soup and ate another cracker, leaving its crumbs in his mouth as he drank an ounce of diet Coke and swished it around, and again pressed channel-up.

An all-day weather channel was next, followed by all-news-all-the-time. Situation comedy re-runs, police-drama re-runs, home shopping networks, preachers of sundry creeds and credibilities, twenty-four-hour auto racing, twenty-four-hour standup comedy, and twenty-four-hour cartoons, legislative sessions, and Japanese celebrity news...

At last, his mug of soup and glass of diet Coke empty, his clogged head threatening eruption, he settled on a channel specializing in broadcasts of old and foreign movies, swung his feet up on the sofa, and pulled the Christmas afghan up to his chin.

This movie was both old and foreign, a strange, grainy black-and-white romantic musical comedy made somewhere in Europe in the early 1930s, its stars' lips inexpertly dubbed into English in British accents of unlikely breeding and tone. Not until the movie was nearly over did he realize he had seen it before. The guy, oh yeah, right: he got the girl and the two of them jazz-danced away down a winding cobblestoned Autobahn eerily empty of traffic, vanishing into the orb of the setting sun and their presumably blissful future. Unforgettable, now that he remembered it.

He blinked groggily, looked at his watch. Nearly eleven o'clock. *Plenty of bed rest*, Morse had said. Webster sat up and pointed the remote control at the television, meaning to shut it off but pressing by mistake the channel-up button.

"—in Idaho this week," a gray-suited announcer was saying as he aimed his own tiny remote-control at a map of the United States and zoomed in on the eastern portion of that state, the plaster cast into which Montana pressed its craggy western face.

The rectangle in which the map was set was bordered by a thick frame of solid black. At the top of this frame, lettered in a dull caterpillar-green, appeared the phrase NORMALIZED MORTALITY RATE. The announcer's hand passed in circles over Idaho Falls and Pocatello as though blessing them. They evidently needed some kind of sacrament: laying siege to both cities, all the way out to their farthest suburbs, were a pair of ashen ovals, at each of their centers a smaller charcoal-gray blob. Twin cigarette burns in the map's flesh. Checking the grays against the black-to-white scale conveniently provided below the title, Webster saw that these sections of Idaho were currently experiencing a Normalized Mortality Rate — whatever that was — in the range of six to eight percent.

The announcer, smiling back over his shoulder at the camera, still waving his hands over the map, was now explaining something about "the correlation between the urban violent-crime rate and the overall normalized mortality rate." Webster wasn't really listening, though; he was trying to figure out just what he had stumbled upon.

He pressed the remote's channel-guide button again. The grid informed him that it was now 11:06 pm and that he had tuned to channel 1463. Webster didn't even know channel numbers went that high. And this row of the grid contained no individual cells for specific programs, just a solid blue bar labeled *TDC*. So then this TDC — whatever it might be — must go on all day.

But what *was* it?

No sooner had he asked himself that question than the announcer answered it for him. Still smiling, he put his remote control into a side pocket of his suit jacket and patted the pocket flap down over it. "In a few minutes we'll take a look at the national morbidity picture here on The Dead Channel. But first, these messages." His image and that of Idaho's Normalized Mortality Rate dissolved, replaced by a station-identification panel — bordered in black, with a soft-focus photo of lilies in the lower right corner — which confirmed (in an elegant shadowed script which created the effect of having been embossed upon Webster's screen) that this was, indeed, The Dead Channel.

It showed ads, even. One limned in lyrical but non-specific terms the mission and philosophy of something called the National Society of Bereavement Professionals; one detailed the "grace and sophistication" of a line of sympathy cards and thank-you-for-your-sympathy stationery manufactured by a subsidiary of a huge multi-national company not generally noted for its depth of human feeling; and finally one proclaimed the terminal virtues of the DeForrest Memorial Works, right up the road from Webster's house. DeForrest, it seemed, currently featured a two-for-one sale: "Purchase one of our 'Asphodel' series headstones and the second is yours with our compliments! One purchase per household *please*."

After the commercials, as the smiling announcer had promised, a different national map appeared, depicting the MORBIDITY INDEX. A different announcer now manned the helm, too, this one not as slick and well-practiced as his predecessor; he wore not a suit but a camel-colored sportcoat and dark green slacks. The sportcoat was not buttoned, and from its open portal protruded a stout belly. This announcer had thinning gray hair and a bristly gray mustache, and he seemed not particularly comfortable on-camera — as though only doing this temporarily, to bring in some extra bucks, or perhaps filling in for a vacationing nephew. A title which flashed on the screen for a few seconds identified him as Jack Llongo.

"Okay," said Llongo, "look, here's the morbidity thing." He winced, perhaps receiving some kind of off-camera prompting, and corrected himself, "Index, right, the morbidity *index* I mean."

The Dead Channel, Webster was still thinking. Maybe the undertakers' association, the bereavement counselors or whatever they were called, maybe they'd dreamt up this Dead-Channel thing to get around the taboos, the cultural obstacles to selling their services the way other industries did...

Jack Llongo continued to grope his way through the Morbidity Index's complexities. The map was drawn and re-drawn like one of those time-lapse computer-enhanced satellite radar views of storm fronts, with luminous green and yellow waves of disease washing over the nation from left to right. Llongo rapped the Great Lakes with the knuckle of his right index finger. "Chicago, see, and Detroit. Here's Cleveland. All the way over here to Buffalo, which is... here, no, *here*. That old morbidity index is climbing, flu and colds, those diseases are really *coming at you*, heh heh, tough suckers—" He winced again. "Anyhow, let's check out one of the biggest trouble spots right now."

And when Llongo pointed at the map with his remote-control, it zoomed in, thrillingly, on Webster's own little corner of the universe:

There was The City, laved and re-laved by green and yellow foam as the map cycled through again and again. In the lower left corner of the map sat Webster's own little suburb, a pinpoint which time-lapsed from beige to yellow to green like a mood ring sensing Webster's return home a few hours ago.

"Up here," Llongo was saying, "like the map shows, up here you're getting clobbered. My advice to you folks? Stay indoors, get bed rest, drink plenty of fluids, and heh heh, yeah, watch where you sneeze and keep your hands off the doorknobs—"

Llongo and his Morbidity Index map disappeared, abruptly replaced by a solid green screen with black-lettered data. A piano sonata provided the soundtrack. REGIONAL CONDITIONS, said the title: mortality totals; mortality subtotals by age group; causes of death today, month-to-date totals, percentage of various causes of death compared to a year ago today. DISPOSITION OF THE DECEASED, one set of statistics was labeled, a table illustrating raw numbers and percentages of in-ground burials, mausoleum interments, cremations, burials at sea (currently zero), and "Other."

Webster returned from the kitchen with fresh soup and soda. Now The Dead Channel was plugging its own schedule: medical programs, gavel-to-gavel coverage of a Senate probe into "the bereavement industry," and a weekly "Dead Channel FilmFest" (which this Saturday would feature "that uproarious slapstick comedy of bereavement starring Rod Steiger and Jonathan Winters, *The Loved One*").

Webster looked at his watch again. Now almost 11:30. Darn. Too late to call anybody; he dearly wanted to discuss this thing, this "dead channel"—

"... and coming up at 11:30 on The Dead Channel," said a woman's voice, "it's the popular 'The Dead Channel Live.'" A talk and call-in show of some kind, hosted by someone named Rita de Jesus; tonight's featured guest was a popular psychologist and advice columnist, a woman who would with Rita de Jesus's help explore "first death," whatever *that* meant.

Webster blew his nose into the paper towel, swallowed the last of his soup and reached for the final cracker. What was wrong with him? Why was he watching this stuff? He was again about to turn the TV off to go to bed, when "The Dead Channel Live's" subdued theme music and title came up over the image of Rita de Jesus and her guest, sipping coffee or tea and chatting in silence on a set which reminded Webster of the ill-lit parlor of a Victorian bed-and-breakfast in which he had once spent a night of claustrophobia: dark, heavy drapes; stained-glass lamps; coarse upholstery and carpeting; and on every surface, no matter how frequently dusted and polished, a filmy patina of antiquity and gloom.

Throughout Rita de Jesus's opening remarks on the evening's topic — which was "how people cope with their first exposure to death" — she smiled. The smile did not communicate irony exactly, nor imply at all that she was, well, *amused*. It was rather a faint suggestion of a smile, a *mortician's smile*, a smile which murmured to you that yes yes it understood, a smile which took you by the elbow and led you to a chair where you could grieve in private. Webster was so fascinated by Rita de Jesus's mouth that for a moment he lost track of what she was saying.

And her dress...! It was a loose-fitting thing, emerald green, with an outsized neckline which drooped a bit, the dim shadows on her collarbone hinting at the presence of her breasts, and Webster felt a remote stirring inside his pajama bottoms which he had not felt in the many months since the cataclysmic affair which had polished off both his marriage and then the affair itself. His ex-wife had owned a dress like that. Not that cut, but the same color. Or no, wait, it had been his ex-girlfriend's dress, hadn't it? Er, no— well, *one* of them had owned such a dress, anyhow. And seeing this one now, draped on Rita de Jesus's slender frame, rustling against her shoulders when she leaned forward to pick up her cup, slipping around her knees when she sat back in the overstuffed sofa, well, it was making him a little nuts...

Jesus, he thought, sneezing, laughing, and shaking his head to clear it. With effort, he focused again on what Rita de Jesus and the psychologist were saying.

They were soliciting phone-ins for tonight's show; a 900-number flashed at the bottom of the screen. Each call, said the fine print, would cost $1.75 per minute. "What we want," said Rita de Jesus, tugging a little at the back of her dress's collar so it hiked up but then slid immediately back down again, "are calls from any of you who have ever come face-to-face with death, and are willing to talk about that experience. No stories about funerals or wakes, please. We'd like to hear from viewers who were actually present either when the deceased passed away, or shortly thereafter. How did you *feel* when you saw the deceased? What did you think? And what did you do next? We'll take the first callers after this brief message from our sponsors."

Webster pressed the mute button on his remote-control. More bizarre commercials — florists, a different manufacturer of stationery, The Dead Channel promoting sales of its calendar for the coming year. The calendar, said the text on the screen, cost "only $19.95"; daily little blurbs provided the year and circumstances of "over five hundred Great Deaths in History." What was that, four cents a blurb? Webster congratulated himself for shutting off the sound.

But, snuffling, he was also staring out of the corner of his eye at the old first-generation-wireless telephone handset. It sat on the end table, where he had moved the empty soup mug and the nearly-empty glass. He thought he might have a story for Rita de Jesus, although he didn't know if he'd actually have the courage to pick up the phone and punch the number in.

And he had to get that bed rest.

On the other hand, there was the possibility of hearing Rita de Jesus's voice and the hint of her half-smile in his ear, speaking to *him*, murmuring consolation and sympathy, and the restlessness in his pajamas clearly lobbied in favor of this possibility.

Yet what were the chances he'd even get through? Weird though it was, this program almost certainly had thousands of regular viewers, probably a hundred of whom had lunged for their own phones the instant the 900-number had lit up on the screen. No way. Forget it. He'd never get through.

While he dithered, still, about shutting the television off, the commercial break ended; on the screen once again, again superimposed with "The Dead Channel Live's" title and logo, floated Rita de Jesus's haunting face. She still had that smile, Webster saw while pressing the mute button again, this time to turn the sound back on, but she had somehow imperceptibly altered it. It now seemed a smile donned in order to cover up some awful disappointment. Something about her eyes, he thought, her eyes which were a mournful brown. Webster put the remote-control down on the end table, next to the phone, and blew his nose. His ears popped.

"... and please," Rita de Jesus was saying as Webster's hearing returned, "no calls from bereavement professionals or medical specialists. We're hoping to learn how first contact with death has affected *ordinary* lives, people who do not deal with death every day or every week. We're still waiting for our first caller, so in the meantime, Doctor, why don't we discuss..."

She sailed off with the psychologist on an arcane analysis of Jungian death-archetypes; Webster was not really attending to the discussion. His gaze was nailed to the shimmering margin between Rita de Jesus's knees and the hemline of her green dress, and what his mind was hearing (to the extent it was hearing anything) was the seductive telepathy of the telephone handset: *No callers yet*, it whispered to him from the end table.

"Good evening, 'The Dead Channel Live,'" said a cheerful young male voice at the other end of the line. It sounded like the voice of the announcer, the deadcaster or whatever they called themselves, the one who had demonstrated the Normalized Mortality Rate for eastern Idaho. Did the deadcasters do double duty answering the phones? He wished Jack Llongo had answered the phone, he'd like to tell him how much he'd appreciated his unaffected style and delivery—

"Hello?" said the young man's voice. "Is anyone there? Do you have something for Rita? Don't be afraid, is someone there?"

"Yes," confirmed Webster, his voice sounding tinny to him, disembodied and far-off. "I, I am here. I have a story for Rita de Jesus."

"You're not a doctor, are you, sir? Or a bereavement professional?"

"No. I work in an office in The City."

The young man did not seem to care what city Webster worked in; he merely asked Webster his name, where he was calling from, and "the general nature of your story, save the details for Rita but we just need to make sure it's all right to put on the air." Sniffling and wiping at his nose, Webster told him only that it was a story about when he was a boy and encountered death for the very first time. The young man seemed satisfied with the description itself but not with the pneumatic wetness in which Webster had packaged it.

"Are you sure you'll be all right, sir?"

"Hmm? Oh, my voice, ha, don't worry, I've just caught something going around. A bug, you know. Nothing to worry about."

On the TV, Rita de Jesus was saying, "Well, Doctor, I believe we have our first caller." Suddenly without warning there was *that voice*, in his ear: "Go ahead, sir, you have a story for us?" It was followed a few seconds later by the on-screen Rita de Jesus repeating, "Go ahead, sir, you have a story for us?" Her chin was lifted, she was looking right into the camera and *into Webster's living room.*

He sat up, tossed the afghan aside, buttoned another button on his pajama top, snuffled, and said, "Uhhh..."

Rita de Jesus began explaining something to him on the phone. Something about a time-delay audio system, because of which he should turn his television's sound off — when suddenly there was his voice, horribly magnified and distorted by the television speaker ("Uhhh...," it groaned, God did he really *sound* like that?), and Rita de Jesus's voice repeating on the air, word for word, her explanation of the time delay. "So go right ahead, speak up nice and clear," she said again in public, as she had said only a moment ago in private, "just turn your TV's volume down, all right?"

Smitten, compliant, Webster pressed the mute button.

And just like that, whatever he had called to tell her stood up and bolted from his mind.

"Sir?" said Rita de Jesus's voice in his ear after a respectful but uncomfortable pause. "Are you there?"

In a panic, Webster lunged to his feet and began pacing around his living room, carrying the phone with him. Something about when he was a kid, he recalled that much. But *what* about when he was a kid?

Maybe he could jog his memory by just starting that way. "Yeah. Yes. I was, uh, I was just a kid at the time," he said. Nothing further came to him. Death, it had something to do with death, seeing death first-hand, when had he ever seen death up-close when he was a kid? His nose running, he sniffed a bit, and liked the piteous effect so much that he added a whimper.

"There, there," said the telephone-Rita de Jesus into his ear; on the screen, she and the psychologist were silent, attentive, and then the television-Rita de Jesus nodded and mouthed: *There, there.* Her voice and words, her dress and the, yes, *bereaved* expression on her face, it all suddenly put him in mind again of his ex-wife and then his ex-girlfriend and then his ex-wife and his ex-girlfriend again, phantom profiles of the two of them (and the two Rita de Jesuses, in his ear and on-screen) oscillating rapidly back and forth like two sides of a giant coin spinning on its edge...

Not sure where he was going — but certain he had to go somewhere, anywhere, if he was not to lose the two Rita de Jesuses as well as his ex-wife and -girlfriend — he stumbled on:

"Yeah, I was, uh, a kid." He paused to wipe his nose. "And my grandfather took me out to the barn first thing one morning" — his *grandfather*? both of his grandfathers had died before he was even born! — "and he, uh, he showed me..." Showed him what? A farmhand, a pig, his penis...?

"Sir?" said Rita de Jesus into his ear. "Perhaps you should call back again a bit later after you get yourself together?" On-screen, the psychologist was whispering behind her hand to Rita de Jesus, who nodded crisply and raised her chin again, her lips moving in silence: *Sir? Perhaps you should...*

"No, I'll be all right." Of all the unlikely phrases he had just shared with this stranger, that seemed the unlikeliest. Yet here he was, still lurching towards some unforeseen destination:

"... my grandfather, I called him Peppy" — *Peppy?* — "he, uh, he took me to a, a, a — what do you call it, a *stall*, that's it, Peppy took me to a stall in the barn and showed me the man" — man? what man? — "the dead man." He paused, exhausted by the imaginative effort, his nose — now that he'd been talking actively for more than a second or two — running at high tide. He blew his nose on the paper towel, which was now sopping. This old wireless phone didn't have the range to reach the kitchen, no chance to replace the paper towel by heading that way. Maybe the powder room, no, the linen closet where he kept the spare toilet paper...

"There was a dead man in your grandfather's barn," prompted an unfamiliar female voice. The psychologist, audibly antsier than Rita de Jesus. "Had he died of some disease? How did you know he was dead?"

Webster now stood in his hallway, not quite within reach of the linen closet door. Static from the crappy old handset already scratched at his ear. He couldn't reach all the way to the door, let alone the toilet paper inside, without putting the phone down — wait, no, he could lean against the wall, take the phone a little from his ear so he could inch towards the closet, *streeeetch* out the other hand and... Ha! Got it! "Hmm?

I, well, I was no expert, but I, uh...," he hemmed and hawed loudly, from the greater distance to the handset, trying to keep Rita de Jesus and the psychologist from asking questions for these critical moments. He pulled the folding door open and grabbed with his fingertips for a roll of toilet paper. Perhaps jammed too tightly among the towels and sheets, suddenly it leapt free of the shelf and rolled away from him, down the hallway floor, with Webster barely clutching the free end. He tugged carefully. About five, maybe seven yards of the stuff reeled off. That should do the trick. He didn't want to have to repeat the maneuver.

"*Anyway*," he said. "No, the man, he was a hobo, a tramp, and he, uh, didn't die of sickness." He paused to blow his nose, wadded the strip of toilet paper into a tight ball and placed it on the plate next to the soggy paper towel. So the man hadn't died of sickness, he thought: okay, then what had he died of?

Wishing for a second he could get to the kitchen, pour some more diet Coke, maybe let a Saltine dissolve in his mouth to dry him out a bit, suddenly he remembered the 7-11 where he had bought his sick-food on the way home tonight.

"He was a tramp?" said the psychologist, nearly spitting with impatience. Sniffling, Webster was gratified to see on the TV that Rita de Jesus was holding a forefinger to her lovely lips, silencing the psychologist as though to say, *Let him tell it his way*. God, he was falling in love with this woman. Maybe he'd have a chance to talk to her privately at the end of this story, however it turned out, when they broke for a commercial or something...

"Yes," he went on, inspired by his memory of the 7-11 and by Rita de Jesus's support, his confidence growing although he hadn't worked out all the details yet, "he was a homeless tramp. A Native American, an Indian, a, uh, an Apache. Everybody in my grandfather's town knew him. He made his living by selling handicrafts, Pap— er, *Peppy* told me." He paused once more for dramatic effect, and to watch the image on the television catch up with reality. Rita de Jesus and her guest were listening, spellbound by what Webster imagined to be his sudden eloquence. He tore off another foot or so of the ribbon of toilet paper, mopped at his nose, sniffed, and continued.

"Yeah, handicrafts. Like little knick-knacks and things, he used a soldering iron, like a, uh, you know, a wood-burning tool? He, uh, he moved there from Oklahoma and he brought this soldering iron, wood-burner, whatever, with him. And he made these plaques, like there was one hanging there in Peppy's barn, it said, uh, it said" — said what? ah, *perfect!* — "it had a quote on it, from Groucho Marx, you know? Peppy always loved the Marx Brothers and this, uh, this hobo had done up a little plaque for him and it was hanging on the wall of the, uh, the barn. The stall." Another pause to let that sink in, perhaps to give Rita de Jesus a little ripple of suspense. Goosebumps. He sniffed again.

Before Rita de Jesus could shiver — whatever *her* face registered right now it was not goosebumps — the psychologist butted in. "Sir? All this about the plaques is very nice but you were saying the tramp was *dead*, how did the tramp *die*?" Webster made a face at the receiver and waited a couple of seconds, snuffling, hoping to see the television-Rita de Jesus shush her guest again. But no, in fact she nodded her head as though in agreement.

Wounded, Webster sniffed and sniffed again. "I'm sorry," he said, "I just remembered that plaque in Peppy's barn. I, uh, I haven't thought of that in years." Ha, to say the least.

"So there was this tramp," he went on, "this homeless Apache man. He must have been working on one of his plaques up in the loft. There was" — whoa, wait, how could he operate a soldering iron in the loft of a barn? — "there was a, uh, like an extension cord running up the wall from an outlet on the ground floor." Utterly spent, rushing now to the conclusion: "... and he, well, the floor up there had collapsed, see, and the tramp fell out of the loft onto the ground right on top of his soldering iron. It went in his mouth. He looked like he swallowed it, it was poking out the back of his neck, and the, uh" — groping for a dramatic finale, something with which to sweep Rita de Jesus off her feet — "the tip was real hot, I guess, and the skin on his neck was like, uh, well, cauterized. The back of his hair was still smoking."

Silence on the phone; absolute stillness on the screen. Rita de Jesus at the moment seemed barely in control of some dark emotive force.

"... so anyhow, that's when Peppy pointed to the hobo and then he pointed to his wrist and up to the plaque hanging on the wall of the barn and he read it to me, 'Either he's dead or my watch has stopped.'"

The silence on his phone didn't tell him anything. He longed for the TV picture to catch up, so he could find out if Rita de Jesus had collapsed and started to sob inconsolably or what. He pressed the mute button, and there was his voice from the speaker: "...watch has stopped."

A split-second more of silence, and then Webster heard from the TV speaker something which he had not heard from the telephone receiver: a coarse *Haw haw haw!* from somewhere out of camera range, a sound man or gaffer or cameraman or somebody. Jack Llongo, maybe.

"I see," said a chilly voice in his ear. "I see, indeed. Thank you for calling." She waved her hand, then there was a click and a buzz.

Webster couldn't believe it. She'd cut him off! Rita de Jesus had *cut, him,* OFF without so much as a single simple question about his emotional state at the time of his first exposure to death! And the so-called psychologist had let her get away with it!

Flattened and breathless, he pushed the Off button on the handset. On the television, Rita de Jesus said again, "Thank you for calling." Here, though, it was followed not by a click and a buzz but by some kind of look which passed briefly between the two women, a look which communicated absolutely nothing to Webster.

Then Rita de Jesus said, "'The Dead Channel Live' will be back in a moment. Now this."

More of those stupid commercials: a local caterer specializing in "bereavement receptions"; a life-insurance company; a different life-insurance company, this one specializing in insurance for married military veterans with no children, a steady income, and the psychological wherewithal to PICK UP THE PHONE AND CALL **NOW!!!**

She cut me off, Webster was still thinking. And he'd been on the phone for, cripes, close to fifteen minutes. What was that — like twenty-five, thirty dollars? He blew his nose. When "The Dead Channel Live" returned, he took a final look at Rita de Jesus's uncaring lips and plunging neckline, its dark emerald recesses now suggesting an arctic grotto. Then he pointed his remote-control at her forehead, and shot her with the channel-down button.

The old-movie channel's current fare was a comic psychological suspense melodrama starring Jack Oakie. Oakie was a man who had awakened one morning with no memory of anything, including his name; on the floor next to his bed was a pistol from which a single bullet had been fired, and on the floor in the next room lay the spread-eagled body of a chimpanzee (dressed in a plaid sportcoat, vest, and four-in-hand) which had been shot dead. For the rest of the movie, presumably, Oakie would fight to clear his good name (once he'd remembered it) while mugging shamelessly, maybe crooning some inconsequential ditty, and eventually winning the reluctant love of the chimpanzee's trainer, who would be played (Webster bet) by a beautiful young actress who never appeared in another movie, not even one as bad as this.

But the moviemakers surprised him. He got the general plot line right — the ditty which Oakie sang rhymed "chimpanzee" and "I'm just a man, see" — but the chimp's trainer turned out to be Myrna Loy.

How about that, he thought, and lay down once again on the sofa, afghan pulled up to his chin. Myrna Loy, no kidding.

He dozed off and on, sneezing himself awake once or twice, his dreams getting all mixed up with the silly film: Jack Oakie as an Apache hobo, Myrna Loy as a talk-show hostess, her khaki safari clothing suddenly emerald green, her collar loose — and there on the floor in the Victorian parlor, clad in a camel-colored sportcoat and green slacks, there lay Webster himself, a dead monkey with a bullet through his heart. Myrna Loy sobbed, inconsolably.

The Card

After I'd written "The Dig" and "The Shot," I decided Webster really needed a third story. That was this one: "The Card." But I was never satisfied with the story as I wrote it back then. I tinkered with it from time to time, workshopped it, and then decided to just drop it. When I started to put the stories together for this book, I took another look at "The Card," too… and much to my surprise, discovered that I'd apparently started to rewrite it from scratch sometime in the mid-2010s. I hadn't finished the rewrite then, but I wrapped it up for this book. And then I repositioned it here, at the end of the main sequence of stories, both because it now fit best here, in Webster's personal chronology, and also because I realized that it echoes "The Dig" in some notable ways…

Over the years, Webster had watched with both sympathy and horror as people he knew broke down, imploded, fell apart, erupted, plumb wore out, crumpled, and/or folded up like brittle origami animals. They didn't do it as demonstratively as celebrities, whose failures of spirit, common sense, and decency were heralded with insiders' oily "concern" and with boldface headlines otherwise. But they did it just as recklessly and with equal abandon, oblivious — flat-out incapable of attending — to the awareness of others. Maybe they hadn't intended to dissolve. Maybe they lived in shame about it for days, years afterward. In looking back later, maybe they rationalized the irrational, blamed others, selectively remembered what didn't really matter and wholesale forgot everything else. But while they were *in* it, to all intents and purposes no one else but themselves existed.

So, then: Webster. For decades, he'd enmeshed himself in a network of worry, every *what-if* in one dimension balanced with a *then* in another and an *otherwise* in a third. If a god of mishap so much as sighed on the far side of town, the whole elaborate construction would vibrate, subtly, setting little warning bells a-jingle; alerted, Webster could bring everything back into nervous stasis (if not exactly harmony) by tugging slightly on this wire, or that one, or the other wire over here.

Or so he'd thought. But it wasn't a network of wires, a sculptor's armature. It was a garment of yarn. The whole structure didn't suddenly spring apart, and it didn't collapse in a discordant avalanche of *bing*s and *sprong*s, like the sounding board of a piano hitting the sidewalk. No: instead, one tiny filament of attention, stretched one too many times, finally and simply wore out — slackened just a bit. Elsewhere, a loose strand caught on something sharp and immovable...

It was just enough to tip the balance. And so Webster would *unravel*.

§

Technology had always made Webster uneasy, at best. In the old days, it comprised just a genus of particularly cold inanimate objects; nobody even called it "technology" back then — it was just *things with electricity*. But at least back then the things still made some pretense at extending human senses rather than developing their own.

But now, sheesh. Without technology, you couldn't even lock yourself in your car in a dangerous neighborhood (although really, to Webster pretty much *all* neighborhoods were dangerous). And if technology failed at the wrong moment and you'd already locked yourself in your car, you couldn't escape when the vehicle burst into flames or plunged off a bridge. Now it was all becoming, well, *entangled*. Without some technology, you couldn't even use other technology: lost remote controls, for example, turned expensive flat-panel TVs into shiny but dead portals to a nonexistent universe. Even Webster's smartphone was not so much smart as shrewd — *knowing* and, as such, capable of reflection, decision, opinion, and ultimately judgment. He never knew when someone was calling him because he kept the thing stowed away in the information vacuum of his briefcase or glove compartment, where no accidentally installed (and certainly unremovable) app could probe his life for weaknesses.

All of this ran through Webster's head as he sat in the line of vehicles at the bank that misty-gray Saturday morning (inside a vehicle which had locked its doors for him as soon as its motion exceeded some mysterious machine-sensed velocity, which was probably expressible only in metric units at best, or in binary numbers at worst). The "line" was a stubby one — a pickup in front, Webster at the back, one other car between them — probably because, Webster thought, anyone with any common sense had peeked out the bedroom window, seen the leaden fog, and (with a shudder) gotten back under the covers.

The pickup pulled slowly ahead, away from the ATM. It paused (the driver perhaps counting his cash, or stowing a deposit slip). And then it slipped forward into the murk, taillights and turn signal fuzzing and finally swallowed up in damp gray.

The car in front of him crept up a space; as it came even with the ATM, the backup lights flashed briefly white as the transmission shifted past R, to Park. An arm came out of the car window, did some invisible things with the face of the ATM, and retreated to the interior.

Webster waited a respectful moment and then eased his own car ahead.

He had been thinking about technology, as it happened, exactly because of the car in front of him. Enormous in girth, probably thirty years old if not older, it had tail fins which flared up and angled back as though to suggest the dorsal fins of Jurassic sharks. In fog-distorted perspective, it seemed barely to fit into the lane between the bank wall and the concrete posts supporting the roof over the ATM lane. Webster could easily imagine the interior of that car: a single front seat which spanned the width of the dashboard, and could be adjusted forward and back only by applying brute force to some heavy lever hidden beneath the seat; an overhead light which did not go on automatically when the door was opened, but had to be switched on with a little ridged black plastic slider switch; a radio dial which was not just visible but legible even when turned off, its numbers ranging from 54 (the "4" displayed as a superscript, like 5^4) to 17...

Webster's mind wandered. The whole cars-as-technology thing had probably begun when the automobile manufacturers started installing FM as well as AM radios, not as an option but rather as standard equipment. He remembered his father arguing with a neighbor about it; the neighbor, a HAM radio aficionado, had tried without success to persuade Webster's father that more choices were better than fewer, and that FM signals worked better than AM over long distances and around obstacles, and that anyway you couldn't turn back the clock, and so on, but Webster's father had dug in his heels, declining to be seduced by futurism for futurism's sake. The conversation had deeply impressed Webster, so deeply that—

A car horn began to sound from somewhere, not in a beep-beep get-somebody's-attention manner but as a single prolonged *beeeeeeeeeee* which did not cut off at the end, ever, and it took Webster a moment to realize that it emanated from the car in front of him. In the fog, he couldn't see into that car from here, so he had no idea what was going on. Surely the driver had to know of the noise. Why, if it were Webster's own car he'd be releasing the hood and scrambling out the door by now — not that he'd actually *know* what to do when he looked into the engine compartment, but he assumed there'd be a *thing* somewhere in there, roughly trumpet-shaped, which could be disabled with a yank of exposed wires or, in a pinch, beaten into silence with a tire iron.

The *beeeeeeeeeee* continued unabated. Webster got out of his car, without closing the door behind him (he'd learned his lesson the hard way, having been locked out with the engine running on two occasions), and approached the driver's side of the big old Oldsmobile or DeSoto or whatever the heck it was. He rapped on the car roof, and looked in through the open window.

The driver, a short elderly man in an old-fashioned but now probably stylish porkpie hat, was leaning forward in the front seat. The hat was smashed between his forehead and the big thin chrome ring (within the larger circle of the steering wheel) which operated the horn.

Beeeeeeeeeee, went the horn as Webster stood there, frozen by indecision. Should he fetch his phone from the glove compartment, call 911? And a wrecker, a locksmith, the police, the newspapers and TV stations? The horn was driving him insane, and he reached in to turn off the ignition. Blessed silence—

Please, said a woman's voice behind him, *take your card.*

Startled, Webster whirled around, half-expecting to see, in the bank's drive-through window, a teller working overtime who somehow could not sense what was happening here. But the window was shuttered. *Please take your card*, repeated the voice, stressing the *please* just a little more heavily than the first time around. Webster bent down to look at the ATM screen. TIME EXCEEDED, it said. TRANSACTION CANCELED. A debit card protruded from the slot. *PLEASE*, repeated the woman's voice, now demanding immediate response: *take, your, CARD.*

Webster looked in panic to his left, to his right. No one else there. No one else to consult. It was him and the deceased and the latter's silent car…

If their roles were reversed, what would Webster want the old man to do right now? He didn't know. So what would the old man himself probably do, whether Webster wanted him to or not?

Webster knew the answer to that one, all right.

He bolted to his car, slammed the door, reversed out of the drive-through lane, and quickly drove away from the parking lot before realizing a moment later that the fog would not likely reward high-speed driving. He eased off the accelerator pedal and drove — carefully, fearfully — to a different bank a couple miles away. It wasn't his bank, he'd have to pay for using his own card in their ATM, but it was a small price considering the alternative.

And then he drove — carefully, fearfully, checking his rearview mirror — to a diner called Eat's Café in the next town. He took his cell phone from the glove compartment. He'd call 911 after he ordered breakfast, he decided. He meant to do just that, in fact — he really did.

But once seated inside, when his hand went to his shirt pocket for the glasses which would enable him to read the menu, he found not just the glasses but a debit card.

The name on the front of the card was not Webster's. At first, he did not think he had ever in his life seen vowels and consonants arranged in quite this way. He forced himself to concentrate. Ah: ARNOLD DEPAUL, it said. Webster wondered if the all-caps embossing disguised a *D*-lowercase-*e*-capital-*P* spelling. And then he thought: *Holy cow. Here I am in a diner booth, holding a dead man's debit card and wondering about its font.* A waitress showed up at just that moment, with a stainless-steel pot of coffee in one hand and a mug and spoon in the other. She set the mug before Webster, removed the spoon and placed it on a napkin alongside. She looked down at the card and then looked up at Webster as though trying to put the name with his face. Uh-oh. Suppose she *knew* Arnold DePaul (however it was capitalized)? Supposed she — a quick glance at her name tag — suppose she was Debi DePaul, his granddaughter?

"Oh, it's not mine," said Webster. He could feel his ears reddening. "I'm holding it for someone else," he added, as if that cleared up the whole matter. "A friend."

"Pour you some coffee?" Debi said.

The boiling blood in his ears eased back to a simmer. "Um. No. No, I think — can you bring me a big glass of orange juice?" (*And a pint of vodka?* whispered an anarchic voice between the ears.)

Without a word, Debi nodded and then dropped the spoon back into the mug and carried it away.

Webster thought of stopping her — he was pretty sure he'd want coffee when the OJ was gone. But suddenly he felt again the weight and texture of embossed plastic and dull magnetic striping in his fingers. He looked down. From a silver and glossy-scarlet background, the spirit of cantankerous old Arnold DePaul glared back up at him, demanding that he, Webster, resolve what he would call *the goddam capitalization issue* once and for all so that he, Arnold, could move on to the next world without confusion of identities.

Capital D, Webster decided. *Capital P*.

Debi brought his orange juice, and Webster put the card back into his shirt pocket. He forgot all about it, in fact, until some forty minutes later, when he reinserted the reading glasses into that pocket and heard (and felt) a tiny double-clatter of plastic-and-glass against plastic.

§

All Saturday night the card sat on Webster's kitchen table alongside his laptop, propped against the glass canister of artificial-sweetener packets, bedeviling him with its rainbow rebuke. It was there Sunday morning as Webster drank his coffee; it tugged insistently at his awareness as he scanned online comics and the *Parade Magazine* Web site; and when he moved on to the local newspaper's dull black-and-white news and feature sections, none of the words on the screen made any sense at all. Too distracting, the card was. He relocated to the living room, where he promptly overturned a mugful of coffee on the rug. When he returned to the kitchen, first for cleaning supplies and paper towels and then for a carefully balanced coffee refill, the bright colors of Arnold DePaul's ATM card seemed to hoot at him from the table.

The story as it appeared on the local news site was dull and mostly uninformative. Arnold DePaul's body had been discovered by another ATM customer about ten minutes after Webster had driven off into the grayness. (About the same time, now that he thought about it, that he himself had been fumbling with his own card at the bank which was not his own.) The woman who'd found the body was not named in the article and was not interviewed for it; "She's pretty distraught," said a police source.

A bank spokesman quoted in the story seemed to dispense information as freely as a properly functioning ATM dispensed cash. Yes, he said, Mr. DePaul had withdrawn two hundred twenty dollars from his savings account; yes, the cash had all been recovered, Mr. DePaul apparently having had the presence of mind to secure it beneath his sun visor just before keeling over; no, the unnamed woman had not gotten around to conducting her own transaction. As a token of gratitude for her honesty, the bank had deposited ten dollars into the woman's checking account.

A police detective — a Sgt. Wilcox — alluded darkly to "some strange things about the case." For one thing, he said, Arnold DePaul's car was not running when his body was found. The ignition had been shut off. Between episodes of hysteria, the woman who had found the body denied having touched the ignition key, and the engine's lukewarm temperature seemed to confirm her story: it was already off when she arrived. Who knew, suggested Sgt. Wilcox, maybe Mr. DePaul had simply shut it off himself; but the suggestion sounded vague and prosaic, and, Webster was certain, convinced no one, least of all Sgt. Wilcox himself. Yes, there were a couple other "irregularities," but Sgt. Wilcox was not at liberty to discuss them at this time; the investigation was continuing.

Oh boy. *Irregularities*. Webster knew about one of them, all right: it was sitting at this instant on his kitchen table, irregular as hell. Quite possibly, the magnetic stripe on the back of the card was even now imprinting upon the grains of his artificial sweetener a characteristic molecular pattern that would enable Sgt. Wilcox (backed by a team of forensic chemists) to charge Webster with criminal irregularity (surely no more than a misdemeanor but still a blot on his life; it sounded like a sex crime). At the very least, he imagined, Sgt. Wilcox would subject him to a ruthless interrogation. Webster imagined the detective as a strong, blunt-fingered man whose crewcut and lined forehead bespoke the shrewdness of his questions. He would be wearing a gun, in a shoulder holster, and he would remove the gun and place it between them on the interrogation room's table.

In his mind's eye, Webster could see the gun, lovingly cleaned and lovingly oiled, on whose sleek black surface the pinpoints of the police station's reflected fluorescent lighting would echo the glint in Sgt. Wilcox's eyes as he meticulously poked about in every little oddball nook and inconsistent cranny in the suspect's replies.

The slow, torturous minutes of Sunday rolled by. Webster finally closed his laptop; he took a shower. Standing in the center of his living room, still damp, his hair air-drying, he debated calling Monica and Bob. He knew his story about Arnold DePaul's ATM card would entertain Monica hugely, so completely incapacitating her with laughter that Bob would have to take the phone from her. "Webster?" Bob would say in his querulous voice. "Okay, what is it this time?" (Bob would make a rotten interrogator; Wilcox would laugh him off the force.) As for Monica, yes, Webster loved to make her laugh — she laughed with what could truly be described as "gales of laughter," great whooping cries. But he also knew that when she returned to the phone, still chuckling and probably wiping tears from her eyes, she nonetheless would belabor him with a litany of incredulous, multi-dimensional practicality. "Well why don't you just—?" she would begin, as though really outlining a useful option, and Webster would cringe. He cringed now, just thinking about it.

No. He didn't think he would call Monica and Bob; not today. Not while still haunted by that — by that *irregularity* on the kitchen table.

Routine. He needed routine... Outdoors he went. Yard work, that's the ticket. *(The ticket; the card.)* It was still early in the season; the lawn did not yet need mowing, and anyhow the ground was still damp from yesterday's slow steady soaking. He would pick up all the dead branches, that was it, all the tree limbs that had fallen down over the winter. Get them out of the way. *(Dead; bank branches.)* Rooting around in the sheet-metal shed in the back yard, hunting for the wheelbarrow... Got it, buried beneath a tangle of lumber and a stepladder. The wheelbarrow's steel handles were crusted with a deposit of oxidation. He withdrew it from beneath all the other junk, and returned to the front yard. *(Deposit; withdrew.)*

Much nicer day today than yesterday. Perfect for yard work. Sun's out; deep blue sky. Birds are singing. A squirrel repeatedly dashed between the property line on the other side of the lawn and a whatever-tree in the center of this side: frenzied, neurotically indecisive the way squirrels usually are, the tail twitching a semaphore of alarm, the paws alternately scrabbling in the dirt or held before the tiny thudding chest. *(The paws; DePaul's — no, this was insane....!)*

After a couple of hours of bending and stooping, bending and straightening, tugging on loose but not quite detached tree limbs, and transporting them in the wheelbarrow to the far corner of the back yard in the vicinity of the rusting steel barrel in which he would burn them, Webster thought he'd need at least one more shower, maybe even two. He returned the wheelbarrow to the shed, wiped with the back of a forearm at his sweating brow. Technically, burning brush and leaves was illegal out here but everyone did it anyhow; Sgt. Wilcox and his comrades on the force had more disturbing irregularities to investigate than the burning of yard rubbish.

But the ground was still damp — would he even be able to get a fire going with these branches? Some of them were indeed too waterlogged, and some others were too green; he put them aside for now. The rest he broke or bent to fit into the barrel and then — with a nervous glance around to be sure no outdoors- and eco-savvy neighbor might be observing this — sprinkled the barrel's contents with gasoline, and lit the fire from the hole at the bottom of the drum. *Whoomp* it went, and settled down into a dull smoky crackling blaze.

He watched the flames for a few minutes to be sure no alarming developments were forthcoming. On an earlier occasion, thanks to a random gasoline splash, he'd had to contend with a savage geyser of fire erupting suddenly like a flame-thrower from the ignition hole at the bottom of the drum; it had left on the ground a spectacular four-foot black scar which had taken him hours to cover over with dirt and grass clippings to his satisfaction. But there was nothing like that this time, just the spitting and popping of water droplets bursting into steam, the blue and orange and yellow flames, the rising column of steam and smoke, and he returned to the house for a glass of water. To the kitchen, from whose window he could keep an eye on the fire.

He kept his gaze carefully trained on points in the kitchen where he really needed it: the cabinet, the glass, the refrigerator, the bottle of cold water, and then finally out the window. Sipping at the water, watching the tongues of flame...

Feeling at his back a sneer of plastic.

Still sipping at the water, leaning as though casually against the counter, he turned to regard his nemesis of the week, the ATM card of Arnold (Porkpie) DePaul. To wit: a man in a hat, veering without warning or invitation into Webster's life before ricocheting off at a crazy acute angle into oblivion. Wrecking the transactions of people behind him, as though his crummy two hundred twenty dollars had bought him access to their lives as well as exit from his own.

Webster went to the table, picked up the card, flexed it between the fingertips of both hands. Lighter than it looked. He smiled and returned, with the card, back outside to the burning barrel. Yes. He could burn—

Hesitation. In his head suddenly appeared the image of a jubilant District Attorney, brandishing over the jurors' heads a scorched whatever-tree limb coated with a magnetically imprinted blob of molten royal-blue, yellow, and orange plastic. Criminal irregularity, *ha!*; he'd show *them*...

To his garage he went then, and returned to the back yard with the ATM card again in his shirt pocket, the skin over his heart a-tingle, and a shovel in his hands. Four holes he dug, each in a different section of the back yard, and well away from the far corner where decades ago he'd buried— well, buried something else.

Slowly, methodically and with a grim smile, he bent the card back and forth, back and forth, back and forth — breaking it into four sections along the ragged perpendicular white fault lines which suddenly blossomed on its stressed plastic face. Four sections: the bank name; the bank logo; the ARNOLD; the DEPAUL. Severing the name of the card's owner, forever, from that of his (and Webster's) bank.

Each quadrant of the card went into its own little earthen tomb. He filled them back in with the shovel, tamped the soil down with the soles of his shoes, stood back to assess his handiwork. It looked perfect. Perfectly *innocent*. A secret buried in each secret spot, each beneath its own little Wilcox-foiling lid of soil.

Meanwhile the thick column of smoke continued to rise in an inverted cone from the barrel, growing broader and less dense with distance. It looked like the closing scene of "Citizen Kane," Webster thought, and he folded his arms and chuckled. *Rooosebuud*... Perfect.

§

Indeed, so perfect was it that the next evening, when he'd barely walked in the door after the characteristically mind-numbing trip home from work, when the doorbell rang and the man there introduced himself as Detective Sergeant Lloyd Wilcox — so perfect had it been that Webster was convinced at first that Wilcox had the wrong address.

"Yes...?" he asked Wilcox through the screen door.

This man did not look like a detective, not coarse and blunt-fingered at all. This man might have grilled a steak or two in his life, but surely never a suspect. He looked like the elevator operator at an art museum; he looked like a Scoutmaster. Gray and white thinning hair, slender build, verging on retirement, glasses. Gray rumpled suit, white rumpled shirt, no tie.

"May I come in?" Wilcox asked. "Just ask a few questions, that's all."

A few questions... "Sure, sure, come on in," holding the door open, waving him in, "just, *heh heh*, just got home from work—"

"That so? And what kind of work do you do?"

Ambiguity. Was that innocent small-talk or a sly question with an ulterior motive? Webster swallowed, stalling for time as he led Wilcox into the living room. The detective sat on the sofa; his gaze fastened upon the spot on the carpet where Webster had spilled the coffee, and then he looked up at Webster's face.

"Can I — can I get you a glass of iced tea or something?"

"No thanks. I'll just ask my questions and be on my way." Without pausing, he continued, "What line of work you say that was?"

Webster sat in the tan tweed armchair to Wilcox's left. Actually he preferred the recliner on the other side, but didn't want to appear too casual. Still, on the other hand it wouldn't do to appear too tense either...

"Er, well, I didn't say. It's kind of hard to describe. It's a management job, with a company in The City."

"A management job, is it?"

"That's right. A, well, a paper-pusher." Webster giggled stupidly, crazily, his mind racing. Managers. Men in hats. He giggled again.

Wilcox, however, was not even so much as smiling; he seemed to be evaluating Webster's psyche, his moral depth, the caliber of his knowledge and scope of his soul, and furthermore to be coming up empty-handed, disappointed, but not surprised. He sighed, audibly.

"You're probably wondering what I'm here for. Well, I'm investigating the death of an elderly man the other day, at the bank—"

"Heh, well, old guy, not something the police would normally—"

"You're right. This man, though, he died at the ATM machine. You know, the drive-in one?"

"Oh yeah sure, I know, I use that bank myself..." His voice trailing off. Surely Wilcox knew already that Webster banked there? "I, uh, I read about the fellow that died there. In the news, I mean." Wilcox was staring at him, waiting for him to continue. "He — his name was Arnold DePaul, wasn't it?"

"Mm-hmm, wow, yes, that's right. You must have a wonderful memory." Webster blushed at that, furious at himself, but grinned at Wilcox as though the detective had just bestowed upon him a Good Citizenship merit badge. "Well, listen," Wilcox went on, "let me tell you some strange stuff about this case..."

Wilcox droned on for a minute or two in a voice that failed to convey anything at all of the drama of crime-fighting. He spoke of anomalies; there were anomalies. (Not irregularities: *anomalies*.) One of them, of course, was the missing ATM card — that was what Wilcox was really after, he said, and Webster nodded distractedly.

But he was thinking of the blue plastic sections of the card, dispersed around his back yard. Had he buried them carefully enough? Could Wilcox maybe see them — even just a single blue corner of one —

protruding from the ground, should he get it into his mind to check? Holy cow. Webster himself should have checked on that as soon as he got home— Suppose the police brought in that whatsit, that ground-penetrating radar...

Wilcox had paused in his monologue and was now looking expectantly at Webster. He'd asked a question. What had he been saying, something about a phone call and an ATM transaction at a nearby... of course, that was it: they were guessing that someone had found Arnold DePaul, and then gone on to a different ATM.

As indeed, someone had.

Webster blushed again, and Wilcox at last grinned, broadly. He had a gold tooth, Webster saw. A what-was-it, a cuspid. A gold cuspid.

"All right," Webster said, "yes, I was there. At first. In line behind, behind the man." His large hands seemed to be pumping perspiration into his palms by the ounce. "I was, uh — I was afraid I'd be held responsible somehow."

"'Responsible'?"

Couldn't the man understand plain English? "Uh-huh, yeah, responsible. To blame. I had this picture in my head, heh, silly I know, too much television, this picture of being grilled by some hardened police detective." *Oh Webster you nitwit—*

"And the card?"

"The... uh, the card?" Fighting to stifle another blush. No way was he going to lead Wilcox out into his back yard to dig up the card's dismembered corpse—

"Mm-hmm. Mr. DePaul's ATM card."

"Well, I don't have it if that's what you're asking. I, uh... *I never had it.*"

Although he was still grinning, Wilcox's words at least sounded as though he were convinced of Webster's innocence. "Ah. You don't. Well, that's good." He stood at the sofa; as Webster also stood, the detective moved to the front door, Webster trailing behind. "That's good," Wilcox repeated. "Because wherever the card is, of course, it still belongs to the bank."

"Yes, of course—"

"And if anyone should try to use it, of course, the camera at the ATM machine would film the whole thing anyway."

The camera. Jesus, he'd forgotten all about the ATM *camera—*

His face burning now, Webster stammered, "Heh, heh, well, that is, well, that would be, would be silly for someone to try, try to use the card, wouldn't it then? So then the bank really, I mean you, the bank, they, you really don't have to worry about somebody trying to use it, do you?"

Wilcox was out on the porch now. He turned and looked at Webster one last time, his gold-highlighted grin a beacon of repressed hilarity. "You're right about that," he said. "I'm not worried about that at all! Appreciate your time; you have a nice night now, okay?"

He got into his unmarked tan sedan, still grinning, appeared to speak into his phone and then appeared to laugh out loud. He started the engine. Webster watched from the front door, unable to move, grinning and waving maniacally at the now-departing Wilcox as though he were a favorite uncle or an old college pal. The sedan disappeared to the west, around a bend in the road, silhouetted by the neon orange of the setting sun.

Webster shut the door, wiped the palms of his hands on his shirt. Grass seed; he wondered if he had any grass seed out in the garage…

The Job

"The Job" marks the definitive, unambiguous end of Webster's storyline. I wrote it in response to a call for stories to be included in a 2018 anthology, called Dark Tidings: Tales to Read by the Fire. *(You can find that book online, at Amazon; "The Job" is the fourth of five stories therein.) Each story in* Dark Tidings *was by a different writer; each was a winter- or Christmas-themed ghost story. I wasn't sure what I'd write when I began, but I quickly settled into my Webster comfort zone, despite the accumulated cobwebs.*

And I was pleased, on several levels, by the way it all turned out — and so very glad that I had the excuse, that is, the opportunity, to write it.

Webster's life had been cobblestoned with uncertainty, potholed with doubt, and fogged over with ambiguity. He'd sometimes guessed he knew what would happen when he arrived at the next crossroad, and what he should do when it did. What would happen next had proved him reliably wrong.

But on the night he died, Webster knew for 100% certain he was dead because of the opalescent neon sign he saw hanging in midair:

FIRST THINGS FIRST:
YOU ARE DEAD

It allowed for little misinterpretation. And a moment after he absorbed the sign's message, it winked out and dissolved.

A while passed.

§

He was now being greeted at the doorway to the afterlife by a spirit — a slender male spirit, distinguished in bearing, graying at the temples, but possessing a face beneath which seemed to lurk a youthful mischief. The spirit was dressed in a two-piece, dark gray, pinstriped Huntsman suit and Cerulean Blue Crocs. The belt: Glasgow's House of Fraser. The tie, Windsor-knotted at the collar of his brilliant white Turnbull & Asser shirt, featured the classic Charterhouse red, white, and blue stripes—

Wait, Webster wondered. *How do I know all these clothing details? I buy — well, okay,* bought *— my clothes at J.C. Penney or Kohl's...* For confirmation, he looked down at himself; he was dressed in a manner resembling the spirit's, except that his own Crocs were Winter White: *tyro* Crocs, he assumed. And yes, sewn to a sleeve of the jacket was a J.C. Penney price tag.

The spirit first plucked away the price tag on Webster's sleeve. Then he extended his right hand. With the left, he gestured at a self-adhesive name tag on his own jacket pocket. HI, said the name tag, MY NAME IS **ARKADY**. Webster couldn't be sure but he thought the name tag was actually written in Aramaic, because it consisted entirely of consonants.

Webster must have been somehow supplying the vowels on his own. He'd never even glimpsed Aramaic script in his lifetime — and until now, never so much as thought the word "Aramaic" on his own, unbidden by prose.

"And you are...?" said Arkady. "Ah, yes..." He waved a hand at the pocket of Webster's jacket, where a similar name tag had materialized. CALL ME **WEBSTER**, it said: vowel-lessly. *Aramaicly.* "Pleasure to meet you, Webster."

"Where am I? I mean, is this—"

"Yes," said Arkady. "Please excuse the clutter. This is indeed my office."

It was true: without actually passing through a door, and without, well, *sitting*, they had somehow come to be seated in a small, windowless office with whitewashed walls and a substantial desk. Or rather a desk *top*; it was fastened somehow at a point in midair, without legs, modesty panel, or other means of support. Arkady occupied the chair on the far side — the business side — of the floating desk, and Webster, a comfortably cushioned armchair on the guest side. Scattered across the desk were eighty-three unlabeled 11x17 manila folders stuffed with paper (an average of forty-three pages apiece) and, buried in the middle of the pile, one 9x12 manila folder containing seven pages, all written upon in an exquisite copperplate hand.

Not that Webster could actually see the pages. Indeed, he began thinking, *How do I even know—*

Arkady interrupted.

"Not important." He waved a hand again; something like a tiny white dove seemed to flutter from it, and evaporate. "It's how things work here. Part of the necessary process of forgetting and eventually not caring about your past. Bit by bit, your head gets stuffed with information it didn't have room for before. Meanwhile, all the everyday details you brought here with you have already started drifting to the floor. Like dandruff."

Webster involuntarily glanced down at his feet. The Winter White Crocs were buried in a small heap of finely shredded paper.

"Fear not," Arkady said with a laugh. "It all gets recycled. But enough! Shall we get down to business? Tell me how, exactly, you WENT."

Webster considered the question. He remembered going to bed — that part was clear enough...

And then... let's see...

> *I had a sip of water from the glass on the nightstand, and I set the alarm clock...*
>
> *I checked Facebook on my phone, and then fell asleep while reading an old* People Magazine *I'd found out in the garage earlier that day...*

I dreamed about eating a fried-egg sandwich at the counter in a midtown diner; the woman sitting to my left was Helen Mirren, who asked me if I liked driving the BMW, and I said What? I don't have a BMW!, *and then the waitress had come over and said she learned to drive a stick shift from a farmer uncle who—*

"Um," he said, "I guess I don't remember exactly how I WENT."

"Mmm-hmm." With a tiny ballpoint quill he'd pulled from somewhere, the spirit made a notation on a blank sheet of paper in the small folder on his desk. (The other folders had gone, possibly to the same supernatural drawer from which he'd plucked the pen.)

"All right, now: please stand up and remove your jacket, and extend your arms over your head."

Webster did as asked. He noticed Arkady examining the cuffs of his, Webster's, shirtsleeves; twisting his wrists, Webster looked at the cuffs, too. *Barrel cuffs*, he observed, *with two vertically placed buttons apiece...* On one sleeve, both buttons were fastened; on the other, only the furthermost button.

"Yes," said Arkady. "I noticed the buttons, too. Thanks. You can put your arms down now and resume sitting." He made another notation on the sheet of paper; leaning forward a bit, Webster read the exquisite copperplate letters upside-down. INDECISION, they said. Or maybe INDECISIVE, the adjective. On the other hand, without vowels they shouldn't have said *anyth—*

"So you're probably wondering where you are — or, haha, all right, cruel little joke of mine, wondering where my office is. In *that* place or *that* place, eh? Well, stop wondering, and don't worry. Just know this: neither of those places exist.

"In the meantime, welcome to your job."

§

No orientation period followed. He received no training by Arkady or anyone else, on the job or in a classroom. No one issued him textbooks, Cliff's notes, or Barron's Study Guides. He had no rehearsals. No, Webster was somehow simply *bestowed with knowledge* of what he had to do.

And thanks to the garb which — magically or otherwise — had

replaced his pinstriped suit, he felt he did understand the general nature of his new position: he now wore a black hooded gown which draped him all over, down to and over the toes of the Winter White Crocs. (He noted with relief that he did not wield a scythe, especially a Winter White one.) The gown had no Penney's or other price tag, and no self-adhesive nametag; it also lacked buttons, belts, snaps, zippers, paired Velcro strips, or other fasteners, so he held it closed with his right hand. His left hand and forearm, however, had wizened, so that the bones all but poked through the surface of the pale skin. Furthermore, the muscles of his left shoulder and upper arm had shortened so that he couldn't fully lower the limb — just swivel it this way and that from the elbow, protruding through the robe.

He waited a while longer. And another while. And a third...

The whiles, you could say, mounted.

§

Hands on his knees, drumming his fingers, he now sat in a large room — windowless, doorless, its walls going up and up and up out of sight somewhere far above. Here at floor level, the walls were lined with folding chairs. No one else was present. Generic soft jazz came from somewhere unseen. On the wall opposite Webster hung a poster; it said, in heavy black letters on a plain black background, **You Have ONE Job, Webster!** Just below the printed message, some graffiti-minded wag had spray-painted, in swirly crooked text, *LOL*. Webster squirmed in his seat. LOLs had always made him nervous and squirmy because he seldom got the joke, but this one seemed plain enough – and still gave him cause to squirm...

Without meaning to, he risked a glance at his left wrist (the bony one). *Oh, right.* He didn't wear a watch anymore. Didn't need one, did he? He guessed he'd know when the time was right for, well, whatever he waited for. Or whomever.

He waited a while more...

And it was true: when the time came, somehow he just knew. He stood up, clutched his robe tightly.

Then he was at the job site.

Far off, he heard the tolling of a clock-tower bell.

§

A winter's evening: the street and sidewalk of the city in which he found himself were slushy and freezing over; gaslight flickered unenthusiastically from the streetlamps; the people out and about, swirling around and disconcertingly *through* him on the city street, all were bundled up in heavy coats, hats and scarves, mittens and boots. (It disturbed Webster no end that he recognized none of the clothiers responsible.)

Some distance away, Webster thought he saw a figure receding from him: the figure of a burly bearded giant, dressed in a deep green robe. At some remote bubbling primordial level of his subconscious, Webster thought he recognized the giant — but they didn't get a chance to speak. The giant grinned at him with perfect teeth, gave Webster a thumbs up, touched the brim of a nonexistent cap, and vanished.

Now it was just Webster and the anonymously-dressed crowd.

None of them noticed him at all, let alone cared about him, although he still wore the head-to-toe black robe. (He flexed his feet slightly, taking comfort in the feel of the Crocs.) Webster had always been awkward and jumpy, well, *anywhere*, but especially in city crowds. With these people, though: as he passed among (and yes, disconcertingly through) the throng, they seemed less substantial, less noticeable, less real even than Webster himself. He didn't have to dodge them at all. All these people were as insubstantial as smoke.

Except for *that* one. The one straight ahead, who — a bit unnervingly — stared, lower lip a-tremble, at *Webster*.

A gaunt, elderly man, he was dressed not for an evening out in these conditions but for bed: slippers; an old-fashioned woolen nightshirt; and an even more old-fashioned nightcap on his grayhaired noggin. (Webster recognized the nightclothes' maker as John Smedley, except for the slippers — those came straight from the shelf at Harrods.)

Relieved to see someone here even less comfortable than himself, Webster approached him, skeletal arm extended. This did not reassure the old man. In fact, he dropped to one knee, babbling at Webster about (as near as Webster could determine) "shadows of things yet to come" and insisting that he'd seen enough.

But I—, Webster managed to say; it emerged from his mouth, unaccustomed to speech after all those whiles, as a drawn-out, quavering groan. Misunderstanding, the old man blanched and seized Webster's, well, his *foreclaw* he supposed you could call it.

"Lead on, Spectre!" cried the old man.

Everyone else on the street and sidewalk — preoccupied with their midwinter heres and theres and nows and thens — continued to ignore both Webster and his new elderly dependent. A horse hitched to a cart and tied to a post at the curb was giving them the side-eye, though, and stamping its feet ominously. Fearing that between the old man and the horse he'd end up the center of a spectacle, even one visible only to himself, Webster took his cue from the old man: so he led on, specific destinations unknown but, well, yes, *onward*.

§

Webster had no firsthand knowledge of, well, *leading on.* (The notion seemed so vague, so open to possibility, that it all but equated to *danger.*) Yet he found that simply putting one Croc ahead of the other, snowflakes mixing with shredded paper, seemed to work just fine. But zowie, what a depressing cavalcade of settings and *dramatis personae* ensued: two businessmen discussing the death of someone they both knew, and practically exulting; a trio of disreputable houseworkers attempting to pawn goods they'd swiped from their employer, or employers; a young man and his wife, tut-tutting at each other about the passing of a relative...

Webster recognized none of these people, but the old man with him seemed to be climbing some stairway of dread, his shivers and shudders and wordless stammering woe-is-me's running non-stop. He reminded Webster a little of his old friend Jack, whom he'd seen at work every day for over a quarter-century: Jack the chronic grump, Jack the Eeyore-in-the-flesh, Jack the unsatisfiable pessimist... But that wasn't right, either: Jack had a redeeming core of good humor — non-bitter humor, humor far removed from the gallows — and Jack also had never faltered in his kindness to Webster or other people he worked with. This old guy, though: Webster wondered if this guy even knew *anyone* with a sense of humor, anyone with a genuinely human center, or, indeed, anyone at all...

And then they arrived at the apartment.

A pleasant, domestic scene, Webster thought at first: a mother and one, two... *five* children, seated in a ragged shivering semicircle before an unlit fireplace. She was working quietly with needle, thread, and small wooden hoop at some form of handicraft. (Webster didn't know the differences, if any, between cross stitch, crewel work, appliqué, and embroidery. But he thought he must have, at one time: the little heap of paper scraps at his feet had grown visibly as soon as he and the old guy passed through the wall into this room.) As for the children, they variously — depending on their ages — read, played with toys, or squabbled.

All softly.

All quietly.

All seeming to be waiting for something...

A knock at the front door made them all jump — Webster and his companion even more than those actively present. In his startlement, Webster momentarily relaxed the grip on the front of his robe; it threatened to part and reveal whatever unimaginable vista might lie behind it. *Whoops!* Webster said; it emerged as a protracted *wooo —* which in turn made the old man wince and start to draw away before remembering that he needed Webster to, well, *lead on*. He clutched more firmly at Webster's foreclaw, while Webster reclaimed control of his robe and, to a lesser extent, of himself otherwise.

The scene in the chilly room continued to play out:

A man had entered, stamping the snow from his shoes, removing hat and gloves, and unwinding a long scarf wrapped around his face. This man was nearly as gaunt as the one fastened to Webster's arm, but a bit taller and also younger, it seemed, by two or three decades. Perhaps he wasn't gaunt, Webster thought, so much as *pre*-gaunt: headed gauntward...

The man apologized for keeping them all waiting and hugged them, one by one, both starting and ending with the woman. (*My dear*, he kept calling her: husband and wife, Webster understood.) He began to explain his lateness. It had been a long day, he said, and then he placed a hand on his wife's shoulder.

"He's dead," said the man.

His wife started, stared at him in open-mouthed shock for an instant, and then fell against him, beating on his chest. "I know he's dead, you stupid brute!" she cried. "I was *in the room when he*—"

The man held her wrists, calmed her, and held her to him, sobbing. "It's all right, my dear," he said. "No. Not Tim. I didn't mean Tim. I meant *him*, Mr.—"

The old man with Webster burst anew into Webster's awareness, wailing, "Spirit! I've seen enough! Take me away from this scene — no more, I beg you!"

Cursing to himself, Webster glanced at the little family. Whatever had transpired between the couple in that missing instant had transformed the scene: the wife was giggling, gasping for air, the children cheering; even the man — struggling against some inner conflict — was smiling broadly.

The old man tugged at Webster with growing urgency. Rolling his hooded eyes at the impatience, Webster led them to their next destination:

A simple room. Or no, not simple at all, just dark — *deeply* dark, so dark that individual objects were visible only from a foot or two away. Unable to free either hand for groping purposes, Webster was reduced to shuffling the Crocs along the floor — shredded paper scattering — and peering into the gloom, the old guy clearly not crazy about this scene and trying to pull him back, but also unwilling (or unable) to release his grip on the foreclaw.

Webster bumped his knees into a piece of furniture — ah, a dresser — snagged a Croc on the edge of a rug, and stumbled forward, barking his shins (*Owoooo*) against... oh, against a wooden bed — whoops, holy cow, someone asleep—

Beside him, the old fellow emitted another of his characteristic inarticulate wails and, again characteristically, dragged Webster's attention away. Fighting the loss of his own patience (scraps of paper swirling about the hem of the robe), Webster looked along the old man's extended arm all the way to the end of the pointing index finger and beyond:

Oh. Whoops. Wowie, his mistake: not asleep at all but flat-out *inert*. How did it go again? Ah, yes: kicked the bucket, shuffled off his mortal coil, run down the curtain, joined the choir invisible. Dead, deceased, an *ex*-sleeper in point of fact… but also kind of familiar—

"*Spirit!*" the old man practically screamed at him. "*Enough!*"

Now Webster *had* had it with the guy (an entire *clot* of shredded scraps of forbearance falling to the carpet).

C'mon, you, he said (*Mnoooooooo…!*)—

§

The bedroom was gone. The furniture was gone, and the rug with it. Gone, the pitch-blackness. They were outside, snowflakes (and paper) swirling about them and stars glittering in the night sky. Before them, a multibranching, well-worn path through grass and weeds; scattered among the plots of vegetation, clusters of small concrete blocks, monuments…

Tombstones. A *cemetery*.

The old guy had removed his hand from the foreclaw and now held both of his own hands over his face. He wailed again. Overcome with impatience, Webster turned towards him, the skeletal arm swinging like a spear stuck in his torso. The old man wailed yet again, and for a panic-stricken moment Webster fancied it *was* a spear, and he'd somehow managed to impale the old guy on the other end of it.

But no. The old guy, mercifully unspeared, was staring goggle-eyed in the direction which seemed to be indicated by Webster's pointing finger. He sank to his knees. "*No!*" he moaned. "Surely that is not the grave— Before I draw near to it, tell me, Spectre, please — tell me that things must not be thus!"

Embarrassed again for them both, Webster didn't even try to answer. What could he say? What did he know about what must or must not be? He couldn't read tea leaves, blanked on the Tarot, had never even turned up a sensible answer in a Magic 8-Ball. He tried to arrange his face in consolation, then remembered the hood which obscured his features.

The old man missed all that: he saw only that Webster continued to point. With a groan, he crept toward the grave, trembling head to toe, and leaned forward to read on the neglected grave the name—

The old man's head jerked upright, and he leapt to his feet, whirling on Webster. The floppy tip of his nightcap lashed about. "Who the *hell*," he demanded, "is *that?*"

Webster moved forward a couple feet, peered down.

Marie Limehollow, said the inscription. *1840-1863*. R.I.P, it concluded, with a superfluous flourish.

Webster thought maybe the old guy just hadn't been able to make out the carved lettering; the light here in the cemetery sure wasn't exactly optimized for gravestone legibility.

He said, "Well, the name is Marie Lime—"

"*I* know *what it says!*" yelled the old guy. "*You idiot — you pointed to the wrong goddam grave!*"

§

Overcome with laughter, Arkady pounded the top of the desk with the flat of his hands. He removed the titanium-rimmed Warby Parkers which he seemed to have affected during Webster's absence, placed them to the side of the 9x12 folder (now holding twenty-one pages), wiped at tearing eyes.

"Oh my," he finally said. "This, *this* is a first…"

"I'm sorry." Webster believed he'd said that at least twenty-three times — no, twenty-*six* times, exactly — since his return from the job. He couldn't get the stupid LOL out of his mind — the spray-painted LOL staring at him across the chair-lined room, all those whiles ago.

Arkady finished wiping his eyes and put the glasses back on. Visibly suppressing a powerful mirth within, he looked at Webster finally. "Please, Webster. *I'm* sorry. Believe me when I tell you it's not a — hmph, heh! — *fatal* issue. Specifics differ, but it happens all the time, in fact."

"All the time? But that doesn't make sense. How could it *always* happen?"

"Come, come, Webster. You *know* this. You've been through it yourself, remember? *Writers are always throwing away drafts.* They drop characters, rename them, dump incidents and whole plotlines, ball up the whole blessed thing and feed it to a shredder before starting over."

"But—"

"Shush. Look — the old guy? Yeah, he was pretty miffed. Understandably, too: he'd already been through it sixteen times, and maybe fantasized that seventeen would be the charm. It wasn't, and he should've known that. *There's almost always an eighteen*, and a nineteen and a twenty and so on — as many as it takes."

Webster thought about that. He thought about his own draft of the story for which he'd just failed the audition, crumpled up in a ball at the bottom of Charles Dickens's wastebasket.

Or worse — or maybe better? — yet another draft, starring him, of some other story by some other author, balled up or more likely torn, torn, torn again, shredded beyond recovery, beyond memory and recognition, the scraps sifting down to the bottom of a recycling bin, distributed to a landfill, blowing across the horizon...

He stood up with new confidence, and held up a magically reconstructed left hand, palm outwards. "Enough. I believe you. What's next?" He laughed, and added, "Lead on, Spectre!"

At his feet, a last scrap of discarded paper drifted to the floor. It circled his Khaki Crocs for a moment, then some unseen unfelt breeze carried it away: away from the paragraph, off the margin and finally — *finally* — off the page.

Acknowledgments

I'd like to thank all those who read and offered advice on my Webster stories over the years, including especially the members of various writing workshops I took part in at the turn of the 20th to the 21st century. In alphabetical order by last name, these folks included: Andrea King Kelly, C. Lynne Knight, Donna Long, Michael (Mac) McClelland, Lizanne Minerva, Clark Perry, Paul Shepherd, and Toni Lynn (Shrewsbury) Whitfield. I'm afraid I haven't seen a lot of those folks for many years since that time; I trust their absence from my life has nothing to do with their experience with these stories (ha).

Thanks also to the editors from whom I got some sort of feedback back when I was sending them out for publication. I don't remember and no longer have records of your names, but the gratitude is real.

Finally, special thanks to Marta Pelrine-Bacon, who cooked up and edited the *Dark Tidings* anthology in 2018, thereby motivating me, via "The Job," to conclude Webster's storyline in an uncharacteristically decisive way.

Made in the USA
Columbia, SC
26 March 2024